WHAT **READER**

THE

"I LOVED IT! AFTER THE FIRST 100 ᴘᴀɢᴇꜱ ᴏʀ SO, I COULD NO LONGER PUT IT DOWN! For years I've want-ed Robin Cook or Michael Palmer to write this story, and I'm so glad that John Adams finally did…and I must say, did as good a job with it as they would have. It may be a work of fiction, but there is more truth to it than I want to think about. Vaccine injuries are certainly NOT FICTION, I know, I have cared for my vaccine injured daughter for the past nine years. **I HIGHLY RECOMMEND THIS BOOK. IF YOU LIKE MEDICAL MYSTERIES, YOU'LL LOVE THIS ONE.**"

— *Lucille P. Addington*

"**HOLD ON TIGHT AS JOHN ADAMS' BOLD AND HIGH-VOLTAGE WRITING STYLE COMPLETELY SWEEPS YOU UP** and drops you into the clandestine side of one of the countries most powerful industries. His writing will ignite your own sense of power and what you are capable of doing with it. *THE POWER* **CAN CHANGE A PERSON'S LIFE.**"

— *Vicky Thurlow,*
Producer BREATHTHIN Video

"**A PAGE-TURNER.** Written in such a way that you feel like you are watching a true-life drama. Adams does an excel-lent job of presenting this gripping story, which sheds new light on health issues most are unaware of. **KEPT MY INTEREST RIGHT UP TO THE DRAMATIC ENDING.**"

— *Nancy Carter*

THE
POWER

JOHN ADAMS, D.C.

ISBN: 0-9704893-9-0

Although this story and its characters are fictional much is based on factual events and statistics.

Resonance Publishing   August, 2000

Cover illustration and design by Debby Reigle

Text layout by Tami Russell

Acknowledgments

I thank my wife, Lori for her support and countless hours of listening, reading and editing. Thanks to my children for their patience, support, and love.

I thank my editor Harry Brown for his expertise and wonderful suggestions. Thanks to my assistant Debby Reigle for an incredible job. I also thank a small army of proof readers: Carol Crider (no relation to Stan Crider), Kathy Petrie, Cathy Aieta, Julie Weaver, Sandy Frost and anyone else whose name I unintentionally omitted. I thank Chrystal Starling for her creative input and help. Thanks to Dr. Bill Hilty for his knowledge of emergency medicine.

I thank the many doctors of chiropractic from the not-so-distant-past who were wrongly jailed for offering the public a way to increase life force and an alternative to drugs and surgery.

I humbly thank the Creator for allowing me the inspiration and opportunity to write and publish this book.

Dedicated to the memory of my father, John Quincy Adams, and the many lessons I learned from him. Also to the memory of Dave Reid, who physically forced me to sit down and write the first page of this manuscript.

Special dedication to our friend Dawna England. Thank you for your contribution to this book and our lives. You will be missed.

Every now and then a change takes place, starting with a single thought. Subtle at first, like a ripple on a mountain pond, it soon escalates to a low distant rumble. Its magnitude expands geometrically until the very earth shifts, a sleeping giant, weary of stiff posture, rolling and stretching, oblivious to the sheer enormity of its actions and never again to return to old ways.

Chapter 1

The Mercedes sped along the bridge over Boston Harbor; the city skyline blackened by the impending storm. Inside, the rich tenor voice bargained with the Dark One for knowledge and power.

Phineas Blackmore gazed at the ominous clouds, his morning Starbuck's steaming in his hand. "Do you hear the desperation, Crider? Human nature reaching for more?"

Stanley Crider shifted nervously in the passenger seat and remained silent.

"Did you know that the greatest operatic rendition of Dr. Faustus was written by a Frenchman? Drove the Germans crazy. Didn't matter. The story line was too engaging. A man going to drastic measures to fulfill his desire. Crider, you can't keep a great man from his destiny."

The cellular flashed. Phineas Blackmore set his cup in the holder and grabbed the phone.

"What is it? What? Hold on. Crider, turn that down."

Stanley Crider fumbled with the controls, turning up the volume for a second before finally muting the aria. Phineas gave him a curious look, which curled to a snarl as he looked away and listened to the caller.

"I don't give a goddamn what the SOB attorney thinks, I want this thing dragged out as long as possible. You understand?" Phineas pointed the phone at his coffee. "Crider, I asked for sugar. Did you forget?"

"Actually, I put quite a bit…"

"They'll be old and decrepit before they see one cent from Blackmore Pharmaceuticals!" He reached into his suit pocket and produced a handful of sugar packets. He attempted to balance the phone while opening the packets and then thrust them at Crider. "Yes, I am aware of our situation. Why the hell do you think I want to hold out? What? If I wanted advice on public opinion, I wouldn't take it from my goddamn accountant. Now, do your job!" He slammed the phone down and grabbed back the sugar packets. He hastily tore open and dumped three into his coffee. "Hell, it

1

wasn't like this in my grandfather's day. He would have taken care of those hillbilly bastards personally."

He punched off the mute button and the music blasted as he wheeled onto the off ramp.

The Mercedes came to an abrupt stop and a doorman snapped to attention. Overhead, Blackmore Pharmaceuticals was chiseled deep into the granite of the Boston high-rise. The two men got out and walked through the open doors. Inside, a hush fell over the sea of employees as the men made their way to the elevator. Crider knew his boss was fuming and he stared uncomfortably at the closed doors as they rode to the top. Phineas Blackmore exited first and led the way to the boardroom. A large chandelier reflected brightly off the high gloss of a long black marble table. Phineas Blackmore set his briefcase down at the head of the gathering. He took a moment to look at each member he was about to address.

"You should all be aware of why this emergency meeting was called. We have experienced a loss for the third straight quarter due to this Cocadian Three fiasco. Consumers are staying away, even with the "certified safe" labeling. Blackmore Pharmaceuticals has lost a full thirty-two percent of the overall market and the press has not helped us, gentlemen. They have escalated this unfortunate incident." His voice thundered. "Hell, they've made a play on our slogan!"

A member near the far end leaned toward the man next to him.

"What is it?"

"Instead of three times the relief, it's now three times the grief."

"Cute."

Phineas Blackmore slapped a thick report on the table before him. "We have evidence that someone tampered with the Southern Louisiana shipment. The antacid was laced with an arsenic-like substance prior to packaging."

A murmur rose from the board members.

"Pardon me, Mr. Blackmore. Are you saying this was an

inside job?"

Blackmore glared at the man. "It is a clear case of industrial sabotage. Either someone was placed in our production line or an existing employee was bought."

Another board member spoke out. "Like Temerol in eighty-four."

Phineas Blackmore growled. "Every employee with access to the antacid is being thoroughly investigated. The traitor will be found and turned over to the authorities."

"Justice needs to be sought, but what about Blackmore Pharmaceuticals?" a member in a dark blue suit asked.

Phineas Blackmore looked at the representative from the company's law firm. "The shareholders are understandably action oriented." He gazed at the faces around the table. "They want blood, gentlemen, and they'll start at the top. Only we can rescue this company and we'll use whatever means necessary. Collectively you are a well-respected and powerful group. I have heard some in the industry and on Wall Street refer to you as the Great Board. Each of you has earned your power through hard work, good politics and an uncanny habit for coming out on top. Now, I trust that you don't care to be remembered as a member of the board that let this company go down. Am I correct?"

The men nodded.

"Good. Let's move on. Surveys indicate that regardless of the cause or containment of this mishap, the average consumer does not plan to buy our antacid again. We need a hit, gentleman, and we need it now. Our newest development, CD4C, could become the next nationally accepted vaccine and a cure for the common cold. This drug potentially represents the greatest achievement in the history of Blackmore Pharmaceuticals. I have asked Mr. Stan Crider, our research and development liaison, to update us on CD4C. Mr. Crider?"

Stanley Crider stood and cleared his throat. "Ah, things are going well. Dr. Lamont Weedleman is developing CD4C at Blackmore West, our lab in Southern California. Dr.

Weedleman feels confident that CD4C could be ready within the next six months. Apparently, there are a couple of glitches with the new formulation that weren't found until the canine testing."

Phineas Blackmore rapped his pen on the legal pad in front of him. "Jesus Christ! Why the hell is he cross-species testing at this stage? Doesn't he know that Standmark Labs is trying to beat us on this one?"

The men at the long table nodded. The representative from First Bank of Boston stood up. "I was of the understanding that the CD4C project was dead in the water."

Stanley Crider's legs trembled slightly as he waited for Mr. Blackmore's nod to answer. "We originally engineered CD4C in hopes of creating a definitive anti-AIDS serum. The researchers at Blackmore West theorized that CD4C could stall the HIV by temporarily disrupting its reproductive cycle, adding years to the average AIDS patient's life span. As you know, our progress hit a wall. The government withdrew its grants when they saw the new Stanford studies that show AIDS declining. Then the shareholders voted to no longer subsidize the project, which had run dangerously over budget. Our team disagreed on which direction to take and it appeared that CD4C was finished." Stanley's voice steadied. "Dr. Lamont Weedleman, in what can only be described as a stroke of genius, altered the configuration of the toxin and applied it to the rhinovirus most responsible for the common cold. The results were remarkable. We knew that Dr. Weedleman was on to something big."

"And this Dr. Weedleman? Who is he?"

"Lamont Weedleman is a third generation biochemist. His father and grandfather were quite well known. They are responsible for multiple patents and a text on organic chemistry and applied physics. Many of their hypotheses for subatomic cellular organization have yet to be disproved."

"Yes, but what about Lamont Weedleman. What has he done?"

"Dr. Weedleman graduated from Harvard and was

4

sought by many research and development firms. We were lucky to acquire him."

"How long has he been with Blackmore Pharmaceuticals?"

Stanley looked down. "I believe Dr. Weedleman has been with us about ten years."

"Has he made any significant contributions to the company?"

Phineas Blackmore pounded the table. "Gentlemen, Dr. Crider has been with us for over twenty years and is responsible for some fine products that have produced a good deal of money for this company. I've placed him in charge because he knows his business and wouldn't lead us on a wild goose chase. Now, if he sees potential in Dr. Weedleman's discovery then I suggest we rally our support."

"Mr. Blackmore, with all due respect. I believe I speak for the board when I express my concern that we are pinning our hopes and perhaps the survival of this company on a researcher who has yet to produce anything of significance after a decade of work."

Stanley Crider eased quietly into his seat and fidgeted with the manila file before him. The discussion continued and Phineas Blackmore became increasingly agitated. "Crider!"

"Uh, yes sir?"

"In your expert opinion, what is the potential for CD4C?"

Stanley Crider felt the dryness of his tongue stick to his teeth. He took a quick sip of water, unsure if sound would come out if he tried to speak. "CD4C could become the most universally used vaccination since polio."

"There!" Blackmore hollered. "You see, gentlemen. We are on the brink of the greatest pharmaceutical victory in the last thirty years."

In the silence that followed, Phineas Blackmore stood, clearing his throat.

"Blackmore Pharmaceuticals was built on the skillful execution of aggressive marketing of state of the art pharmaceuticals. Profits have never wavered. When my grandfather started this company over fifty years ago, competition was as fierce as it has ever been. I'll be damned if any company or saboteur is going ruin what we've built. Men, this business is war, and by God, first blood has been drawn. We will fight back and we will prevail. We will profit and we will go on. Let there be no doubt, any other outcome is unacceptable." Large vessels throbbed in each of his temples, and new blood rushed into his bulging eyes as he systematically looked again into each man's face and then at Crider.

"I want the new vaccine ready in sixty days, or people will be looking for work!"

Chapter 2

He lay face down on the floor of his waiting room, nose bloodied, wrists tightly handcuffed behind his back, praying that none of his patients would be injured as a result of his ineptitude.

The black-booted men ransacked the office and knocked hundreds of files off the shelves with the butts of their rifles. They seized the cash and checks from the drawer and ripped computers out of the wall, stacking them on the counter for confiscation. One of them screamed at the patients, triggering a frenzied stampede to the exit. Having no time to change, a patient dashed out in a gown that flapped open in the back.

"I'm sorry," he mumbled from the floor as his patients scurried past.

A man kicked him in the ribs. "Shut up, you!"

They roughly handcuffed his secretary to her chair behind the reception counter.

"I don't know who you are, but you won't get away with this. I'm sure our patients are calling the police right now!"

The man gave her cuffs an extra squeeze and laughed. "The cops ain't gonna do shit, lady. Doc, here, forgot to pay his income taxes and now Uncle Sam wants his pound of flesh. Isn't that right, Doc?"

The man walked over and rocked him back and forth on the floor with the heel of his boot. He winced as each roll sent blasts of pain down his side.

The men continued laughing and knocking things from the shelves. He could hear his secretary crying softly behind the reception counter. "How could you, Dr. Truley?"

His alarm sounded. He slammed the off button and moaned, trying to chase away lingering images of the IRS agents.

He didn't mind getting up; being awake had to be more restful than the fitful night he had just spent. He shuffled into the hallway and paused for a moment at his son's door, marveling at the peaceful and deep sleep that he appeared to be enjoying. "Okay, big guy, it's time to get up. It's a school day."

Jeffrey slowly opened his eyes and stretched his 7-year-old frame and moaned.

"I wonder what kind of great stuff you're gonna learn today?"

Jeffrey blinked a couple of times as he came to and then let out a bigger moan.

"What's wrong with you?"

"It's shot day, Dad. I'm not going. I get teased bad on shot day."

"What? Oh yeah. I almost forgot. Well, you know why you get teased, don't you?"

"Uh, yeah, Dad. It's because I'm the only freak in the entire school who doesn't get shots."

John Truley grimaced. "If I didn't know better, I'd say you're hopeless. Maybe you need another lecture on why we don't use medical drugs."

"Please Dad, anything but that."

"People ridicule what they don't understand, Jeffrey. You'll see it all your life. And besides that, the other kids are just plain jealous. You don't have to get stuck with a needle and they do. Who wouldn't be jealous? Now, roll outta that sack and let's get going. If we get ready quick enough, we can stop for a bagel."

"Yeah! I want a bagel dog, that sounds good." The boy sprang from the bed and ran toward the bathroom.

"I didn't say anything about bagel dogs. What do you say we try for an egg or some fruit with our bagel instead? Doesn't that sound a little better for breakfast? There's a reason they call those things nitrate sticks, you know."

John waited, but heard only the hiss of the shower. He ambled downstairs to make his morning coffee, trying to remember if he'd ever had a hot dog for breakfast. Kids.

In a few moments he was back in the master bath listening for Jeffrey's shower to shut off. Their condo was comfortable, but it was several years old and so was the plumbing. He set his steaming cup down on the counter and took a look at himself in the mirror. He sucked in his stomach. Not enough sit-ups. No, check that — no sit-ups. Since his wife had died he had neither the time nor desire to work out. It was something they had enjoyed doing together and now going to the gym brought back painful memories. For the most part he was in excellent shape at thirty-two and fortunate to have a job that was physical enough to provide adequate exercise to keep him that way. Well proportioned at just a fraction under six-feet with long, powerful legs and an angular torso, he was genetically blessed with a good metabolism. He kept his sandy-brown hair cropped short so it would require only a quick comb after his shower. His jaw was pronounced but reasonably matched with the rest of his lean chiseled features. He was roughly good-looking, not too pretty, just enough so he didn't have to think about it either way. He remembered being at a presentation several years ago. They were discussing how physical appearance, personality and most importantly, energy, combined to make up a "type" of individual. The leader picked John out of the large crowd and had him stand up to show an example of a "Plutonian type." She said he had the distinct appearance of having great power, power that could prove cataclysmically destructive or equally benevolent, depending on which direction he was so inclined and on which side his foes and friends resided. Personally, he questioned how much looks had to do with anything. The attention was somewhat embarrassing, but John was flattered that he at least appeared to have potential.

An hour later he walked into Truley Chiropractic. In the few minutes before his first patient arrived, he thought about his IRS dream and tried to remember if he had paid his last installment. He hated to dwell on his financial problems while at the office. He was a good, if not outstanding, chiropractor, but while he had adequately learned how to care for people during his many years in school, his preparations for operating a business had been negligible. He had made a respectable chunk of money during his first few years in practice, but learned the hard way that managing the money was a skill he greatly lacked. By the time his accountant had straightened out his affairs, he was nearly fifty thousand in arrears to Uncle Sam, and now that debt, among others that continued to accrue interest, frequently dominated his thoughts.

Janine stepped into his office, smiling brightly. "Rooms One and Two are loaded and ready, doctor."

"Thanks Janine, I'm on my way."

John rose from his desk and tried to refocus. In Room One he greeted his patient, Francine, and listened to her complaint. He had her lie face down on the table where he checked her spine for the cause of the problem. With skilled fingers, he located the locked vertebra and then checked for other vertebrae that tended to go astray in the body's attempt to counterbalance the primary misalignment.

It was only now, while he worked on his patients, that he felt comfortable.

He placed Francine on her side and made the correction. Sighing with relief, she smiled. He acknowledged her improvement and moved to the next room.

It was easy for him to feel the power generated through touching, and when he had his hands on someone's spine, things made more sense to him. Everything seemed simpler, yet more grand.

The second patient's name was Joseph and he complained of a migraine, prompting John to inspect the man's upper neck.

Trivial matters such as color of skin, style of clothes, socio-economic status, and debt vanished in this special zone that John entered when removing nerve interference. It felt like he and his patient were reduced to their lowest common denominator, that of electrical energy; and it was on this level that all things were possible in the realm of healing.

John carefully corrected the alignment of the first vertebra and then watched as Joseph's face became more relaxed.

The zone John moved into when caring for patients was addictive and he noticed that the farther he went into it, the better the results. It was here that he felt an intense, yet calming feeling of love which neither he nor his patients tried to describe. It connected them in a realm that most could not acknowledge. The beauty of it was that they need not talk about or even be aware of its existence for it to be effective. They must only go there and make the exchange for it to work.

A woman in Room Three complained of leg pain radiating from her buttock to the toes on one side. John found that her pelvis was tilted down as well as being rocked back on the right. This distortion had caused her lower lumbar spine to rotate. Using his hands, Truley made a precise adjustment to the right side of her lower back and then reexamined to confirm that her pelvis was now balanced. When she got off the table she was not yet completely free of pain, but felt definite relief and was encouraged.

It was a strong sensation and one that came naturally to John. When he was totally focused, the zone transcended time, space and physical matter. It was true and straightforward, containing no lies, hidden meaning, or fine print. It was as pure as anything he had ever experienced, matched only by the love he felt for his son.

His next patient said she had no energy and complained of becoming easily winded. Until the week before, she had been able to walk on her treadmill for thirty minutes and could now do only fifteen at the same setting. Climbing the hill near her house had also become a challenge. John suspected her diaphragm was malfunctioning and used a tape measure to quantify her excursion, which was the ability to expand her chest and take a deep breath. He then checked the area of her neck where the diaphragm's nerve supply exits the spine. He found the vertebra at that level restricted in motion and turned slightly. He informed her of the problem and its solution and then gave the bone a gentle corrective adjustment with his hand. He remeasured her excursion when she took another deep breath and found that it had increased by over one-half inch. He assured her that the improvement should be immediate and asked her to call him after her next treadmill session to let him know how it went.

John had a difficult time returning from this place of healing to the world of schedules, deadlines and mortgage payments. It was a strange dichotomy. His ability to disconnect from mundane daily events made him more successful as a healer, yet the very same talent seemed to sabotage his ability to focus on the things he needed to do to ensure monetary success. His self-esteem traveled on a never-ending roller coaster where, at the top, he felt the ultimate power and connection of tapping an unlimited reservoir of energy and possibility, while on the opposite end, he felt like a miserable failure who couldn't manage his affairs properly and often didn't meet his bills. It was on this lower part that he frequently floundered when away from his practice, comparing himself to others and wondering if he was some kind of fake. Surely someone with real competence would also have the monetary trappings of success.

He walked into the next adjustment room and was greeted by Flash Robinson's enormous smile.

"Good morning, Doc. Did you see the game?"

"I did. What happened? Only a hundred-fifty yards?"

Flash continued to smile. "I'll tell you what. You go try to run through the Oakland Raiders' line and I'll crack backs here and we'll see who likes the other's job better."

John Truley laughed. "Does that mean we're trading paychecks also?"

"All right, all right. Did you see that hit I took?"

"Which one? They all looked painful."

"I felt that spot in my low back give in the third quarter. Think you can do some magic on it, Doc?"

"You bet. Let's get you on the table."

Once Flash was face down, John Truley went to work. "You might have a hard time running in a straight line with this short leg on the left side."

Flash raised his head off the table. "No shit? One side's

shorter than the other?"

"About three-quarters of an inch. Don't worry we'll have it even in a minute or two. Let's see what's causing it." John expertly checked the football player's lower back until he located the problem.

"Flash, the last vertebra in your spine went out. It's called L5. Turn on your side toward me and we'll adjust it."

Flash quickly turned his left side up and John Truley positioned the large man. He then gave a light thrust to the misaligned bone and it made a solid clunk as it returned to its correct position.

"Oh yeah, Baby! I can tell already."

John Truley smiled. "All right, good. Let's recheck your leg length."

Flash went face down again and Truley confirmed that the soles of his expensive Italian loafers were now perfectly aligned.

"You should be good for another fifty tackles or so."

Flash jumped to his feet. "You're a good man, Doc. Hey, why don't you come and speak at the Optimist's luncheon sometime?"

John looked quizzically at his patient. "You belong to the Optimists?"

"Yeah, they do some good things in the community." He smiled coyly. "And besides, it's in my contract. You know, public relations and all. Anyway, how about it?"

John Truley shook his head. "I don't know. I get a little uneasy in front of crowds."

Flash slapped him on the shoulder. "Then it's settled. This will be good therapy for you. Show you that it's a piece of cake."

The doctor shrugged and Flash laughed and held out his big ebony hand. "Seriously, Doc, I want you to know that I appreciate how you've helped me not only stay in the game, but kept me at the top. I don't forget stuff like that. If the time comes that you ever need something, you just let ol' Flash know."

John felt the sincerity in the man's handshake and saw it

in his eyes. "Thank you, Superstar. I'll be watching on Sunday."

"All right, my man. With that, I'm outta here."

John was genuinely moved by his patient's words and smiled as he watched him walk, pain free, from the adjustment room.

There were many personal rewards for the work he did and these were the things that meant the most to him. The expressions of gratitude like the one from Flash were verbal extensions of the zone, an acknowledgment that it existed, that something beyond services and money was being exchanged. They represented his practice at its best. If only it could remain that pure and simple.

He thought about the contrast between moments like the one he just shared with Flash and the never-ending attacks from insurance companies and traditional medical beliefs. He was frustrated by the struggle and his sensitivity to it made him question his commitment to his profession. Why should he let it bother him? Why was he not satisfied? He knew that he had a talent for healing, but was he really destined to carry on this way for the rest of his life? If his life was truly on the right course, shouldn't the battle he faced on a daily basis be easier? Shouldn't all the parts of his life click into place as neatly as Flash's fifth lumbar? Maybe he was naively optimistic, but he believed that everyone had an optimal destiny that was available if they could just make the right moves and decisions. If they were open and sensitive to life's subtle clues and signs, they could successfully navigate their way to that destiny. While aligned with that correct path, they would feel the ultimate power of doing what was right and what the universe deemed ideal for them. John also knew that the fortunate person on this pathway of power would have one reassuring indicator — happiness.

It was this solace that he was lacking, making him doubt. Although he certainly loved his profession, and felt fortunate to take care of people like Flash Robinson, he felt an undeniable need to fulfill his true destiny, whatever that might be. He often wondered if his financial problems were clues dealt to convince him to alter his course. How could he tell if these money woes were some cosmic sign or just a predictable outcome of his ineptitude in business? Could he be subconsciously sabotaging himself because a part of him knew that he belonged elsewhere? He understood that life would gradually increase the symptoms until the individual finally acknowledged their existence and the need for change. The person who didn't listen would attract ever-increasing catastrophes until they received a mammoth slap, like a heart attack or a house burning down. John tried his best to listen, mainly because he wanted to be on the right track, but also because he understood this law of increasing signs.

Maybe he just needed time away to think about it. He needed to step out of his life so that he could gain a better perspective as to what was going on within it. There were so many things that made him uncertain. Perhaps the only thing he was sure of was that his dissatisfaction with the way things were had created an inner turmoil that he knew, surely, must soon come to a head.

Chapter 3

"What in God's name is going on here?"

The teacher surveyed the cafeteria as the primary graders awaited their vaccinations from the city hospital volunteers. There were two lines, each with approximately seventy-five youngsters engaged in all manner of chaos. "This is supposed to be an orderly exercise. How did it get so out of hand?"

The principal walked up to the group of teachers to share his theory on childhood psychology. "These children are acting this way because they're nervous about their shots. Look, those needles aren't very big, but in a child's imagination they're monstrous."

Near the front, Billy Simmons watched nervously as classmates ahead of him received their injections. Billy was big for a 7-year-old and he took full advantage of this as he pulled Sarah McKenzie from behind him to a place between him and the needle-toting volunteers.

"Stop it, Billy, or I'll tell the teacher." Sarah beckoned her best friend, Katie Prespo, to come join her in line in front of Billy. "You're just a fraidy cat!"

He punched her shoulder, his eyes momentarily flitting from the needles. "I'm not afraid, so shut your trap!"

All too soon for Billy, a nurse was rubbing a cotton swab on his forearm and telling him that he looked like a football player. The bite of the small needle surprised him because it did hurt, but also because the pain was slight and over quickly.

"There you go, sweety. No big deal, huh?" The nurse smiled as he bolted for the door. He was getting out before someone decided he needed another dose.

In the principal's office, Jeffrey Truley sat with his new friend, Jamul Rabin, playing tic-tac-toe on a piece of lined paper in Jamul's binder. Jamul insisted they play the game, due in part to his recent discovery that by drawing just two vertical lines he could create a complete tick-tack-toe playing surface. Back in kindergarten, they never gave him lined paper, but now that he was in the big leagues, he was entitled to all the benefits. Jeffrey was quickly bored with the contest because he and Jamul were both formidable players and every game ended in a draw.

A sixth grade teacher dressed in pink and black, her favorite combination, walked in to gossip with Mrs. Carruthers, the principal's secretary. Mrs. Carruthers was in her late sixties and had been the school secretary for almost thirty years. She had long black hair which she began coloring shortly after she started her current position. She had gained and lost hundreds of pounds over the years, battling the effects of a sedentary job, but had slowly lost the struggle, adding an average of three pounds a year to her short frame.

The teacher paused at the office mirror near the front desk to inspect her appearance and smooth the rouge she had hastily applied using the rearview mirror during her commute to work that morning. In her late thirties, she often passed for a much younger woman while attending various singles' functions around the city and took care to remain desirable in her search for the right man to fill the void in her life. When necessary, she used weight loss medication, and though it had a few side effects, she felt the benefits exceeded the risks and it always made her feel more energetic than usual. She had used Phen-fen a couple of years back, but finally became frightened by all of the publicity about heart damage and other health problems associated with the drug. She had systematically reduced as well as augmented various parts of her body to achieve a shape more closely resembling those she saw in advertisements and fashion magazines. Now she gazed at her mirrored image, into the sparkling blue eyes that according to her beloved beautician, were the perfect compliment to her platinum blond hair. Although she preferred a permed bouffant, it added several inches to her already intimidating five-feet-eleven height and dramatically reduced the number of men that would venture up to her during social outings.

Satisfied that the edges of the rouge had blended properly with the #5 tint base she had generously used that morning, she began arranging the pink bow that wrapped under her hair and came to a large tie above her head.

Jamul whispered to Jeffrey that the teacher looked like Minnie Mouse and the boys had to cover their mouths as they snickered. Self-consciously, she moved from the mirror and shot them a stern look. She then turned toward the secretary, while nodding at the boys. "Troublemakers?"

She didn't have any real reason for being in the office other than boredom, and a visit here always made her feel young and vivacious in comparison to the more matronly secretary. Her hooligans were at recess, and thankfully, her watch duty wasn't until tomorrow.

"No, these boys' families don't think that they need immunizations." Carruthers frowned, deepening the lines developed during a thankless career. She would have quit years earlier had the school district's contracts not been designed to incrementally add retirement income to every year she worked after turning fifty. Like a horse after a carrot, she traded youth for what she hoped would be greater comfort during her twilight years. Each year she swore would be her last, then after another unfulfilling summer vacation, she would return, determined to add a few more dollars per month to her pension check while reluctantly adding more pounds to her burgeoning torso.

The teacher glanced suspiciously at the boys. "I thought all kids had to be inoculated."

"For God knows what reason, the state allows parents to sign a waiver objecting to the vaccines for religious or philosophical reasons. I declare, these kids nowadays have more rights than we do. I remember not too long ago, a teacher could send a child to the principal's office for a good whuppin'. And you better believe the kid would think twice about misbehaving again."

"Well, I think it's weird to know that these children are running around without proper vaccinations." The teacher, now oblivious to the boys, checked her profile and walked out of the office.

"Bye-bye, Minnie." Jamul waved in her direction. He and Jeffrey held their sides as they tried to laugh as quietly as possible. Although Jeffrey was having fun with Jamul, he was fully aware that the teacher and the secretary did not approve of him and Jamul missing their shots. He felt bad that he couldn't make everyone happy, but he'd experienced the feeling many times before. He knew that he and his father did things differently than most people and had come to expect that he would be treated differently because of it. His dad always explained to him why he didn't get shots and why he took vitamins instead of antibiotics when he was sick. After hearing him talk about it for many years, he felt he understood and was glad to skip the shots, even though he didn't have as much to talk about when the other kids described their experiences on that day. His friends would sometimes tell him about going to the hospital to get pills and pink syrup that tasted like bubble gum when they got sick, but it wasn't until he fell out of a tree in his back yard and broke his arm, that he saw a medical doctor for the first time.

He may be different than his classmates in those ways, but he felt just the same in everything else. He liked the same games, did the same schoolwork and wore the same kind of clothes. He knew that the teacher and Mrs. Carruthers were good people; they just didn't understand. Maybe it was because when they grew up, no one like his dad had been around to help them realize that it was okay to be different. Whatever the reason, his friend Jamul didn't seem to care, and was now starting to talk like Donald Duck.

Just then the boys heard heavy footsteps coming

toward them and simultaneously looked up to see Mrs. Carruthers glaring over the counter.

"You two go back to class!"

After making plans to meet at recess, the boys parted in the hallway and Jeffrey headed toward his classroom. He couldn't help but snicker as he remembered Jamul's funny Disney character voices. He doubted that the teacher in pink and black would share his sense of humor.

Class had already begun and Jeffrey slipped in quietly, taking his seat next to Sarah McKenzie. She glanced at him and then back at their teacher, Mr. Hamilton, who was talking about shapes called spheres. Although he and his friends always said girls were weird and refused to let them play dodge ball, Jeffrey was glad that he got to sit next to Sarah. He always had a good feeling when he looked at her, and once she had given him a piece of paper when he forgot his binder. He remembered that when he looked at the piece of paper, he couldn't believe his eyes. Sarah had neatly written his name in the top right corner. He never mentioned it to anyone, especially his dodge ball buddies.

Mr. Hamilton was now holding the globe in one hand and a kick ball in the other. Sarah craned her neck, looking at someone behind Jeffrey.

"Katie! Pssst! Katie!"

He looked around and saw Katie Prespo sleeping with her head down on her desk.

"Katie! Hey, Katie!" Unable to wake her, Sarah turned back around catching Jeffrey's gaze. She smiled, and the feeling inside him intensified. He found it both pleasant and yet somewhat alarming. The feeling confused him because he didn't know what it meant. It wasn't the way he felt about the friends he played ball with and it didn't quite match how he felt about his father. All he knew was that it was strong and somewhat overwhelming. Basking in the warmth and wondering what would happen next, he looked at Sarah again and watched her eyes widen.

He quickly realized she was staring at Katie.

Just then, a coughing sound came from behind him, followed by a splash. Jeffrey felt a warm rush of liquid drench the back of his shirt, and then smelled the telltale odor of vomit.

"Ah, sick!"

Jeffrey looked at his classmates, craning to get a glimpse, and then to Mr. Hamilton, just as the kickball dropped from his teacher's hand.

Chapter 4

Janine bustled into Dr. John Truley's office with her usual smile. She was not one for subtle entrances or a moody disposition and John admired her non-stop enthusiasm. She was always laughing with people and making them feel better, a valuable asset in a chiropractic office where many patients were in pain. He had seen her coax the grumpiest patients to smile while collecting the balance on their account and soften the toughest insurance adjusters, feats deemed impossible by most. She was this way day in and day out, without being forced or phony. While most people slowed down at Janine's age, she seemed to gain momentum. On weekends she played tennis and told younger players, whom she'd out hustle for the match, that they should start thinking about their health, nutrition and structural alignment. She would take a vacation every six months and return to show everyone pictures of the latest mountain she'd climbed, dreamily relating how she had slept under the stars or ridden out a storm under a five foot tarpaulin.

Janine sensed that Dr. Truley was preoccupied this morning and offered a big sympathetic smile, chiseling away at her boss's funk.

"Looks like you've had a challenging morning, Dr. Truley."

John didn't readily share his problems with others and was embarrassed that Janine could so easily detect his mood.

"I'm okay, thanks Janine. I just have a few things to work out that are unrelated to work."

"I'm sure everything will turn out all right, Doctor. It always does. Anyway, you need to go to the school and take a change of clothes for Jeffrey. They just called and said he had an accident."

"Accident? Is everything okay?"

"The school secretary didn't elaborate. She just said something about one of his classmates getting sick."

"Sounds rather unpleasant. Tough day for everybody, I

guess." He eased from his chair and gathered his things as Janine scurried out to pull the afternoon files.

On his drive home, John reviewed the morning's events. He cruised up to the six-foot wrought iron gate that surrounded his condo subdivision, punched his code, then looked at the front row of white and brown two-story units while waiting for the gate to open. All the condos were identical and fairly nondescript. He supposed they were designed to give a Mediterranean appearance. The outstanding feature of the 78 units, serving as their greatest selling point, was a spectacular view of the north county coastline of San Diego. John enjoyed seeing the ocean view from his windows. It had a nice way of making him feel successful. Although his place was modest, it was his first home and he had worked hard for it. It seemed he worked hard for everything, and he was always amazed at how some people could make it look so easy.

John knew that most of the difficulty he had experienced was caused by his own actions. Fortunately, he found this amusing as well as a great incentive to push on, determined to make things easier by learning from mistakes. John had struggled to get through nine years of college. Although his degree only required seven, he wasted two years taking unnecessary courses while deciding what he wanted to do. At first, all he knew was that he wanted to be successful. Oddly, his father had served as a reverse role model. While growing up, he had watched him try and fail many times, and John had vowed he would take up the fight and overcome the obstacles that proved too much for his dad.

At a young age, John began reading books about how to become successful and found strength in one particular tenet of success philosophy: the only way to fail was to quit. It had appeared to John that if that were true, then only stamina and perseverance were necessary to ensure success.

His father finally did quit. Not because of unsuccessful businesses, bankruptcies, or failed marriages, but because of Lou Gherig's disease. John and the medical doctors had watched helplessly as his father lost nearly a hundred

pounds of muscle tissue in six months to the mysterious illness.

After his father's deterioration, John modified the maxim
— the only way to fail is to quit or run out of time. Although
his father's disease devastated John, it did not decrease his
determination. Armed with the strange mix of philosophy
and example and a driving desire to succeed, John pressed
on and gradually began to make headway. He worked hard
and was willing to take chances. He always felt he was destined for greatness, but the older he became, the more willing he was to just be debt free and provide a reasonable
lifestyle for his family. Many people considered him a complete success now, and this surprised him. They saw a single
father, successfully raising his boy while running a moderately busy chiropractic practice. But beneath this thin
veneer were financial obligations that John likened to a huge
dark claw, squeezing him in its grasp. The claw liked to inten-
sify its stranglehold at night, when John tried to relax.
Sometimes he would sit and pay bills, writing check after
check in a futile attempt to feed the claw. He feared it would
finally squeeze him to the point of paralysis, making it impossible to generate more income to continue the cycle. To
John, failure would mean bankruptcy, humiliation and, most
likely, an aggressive and unforgiving disease like his father's,
that would painfully finish him once and for all. Out of time.
Game over.

His school debts were like an unrelenting cancer. He had
seen the television program, Dead Beat Doctors, aired local-
ly, showing those in the community who defaulted on government guaranteed student loans. He never wanted to end
up on that show and paid his obligations faithfully. But they
just didn't seem to get any smaller.

Sandwiched between school loans and the ever-present
IRS, was a substantial note he owed his father's widow for the
start-up on his practice. In perhaps his best deal ever, his
father, Benjamin Truley, had managed to acquire a second
mortgage on his house, just prior to having it repossessed.
He loaned this money to John to begin his business. Four

years later, his father's widow still received a significant monthly check from John to pay for expenses.

Although John was responsible for all of his past debts, he hated the feeling that so many people owned a piece of him. At times he fantasized about being a settler in the old west where folks staked a claim on the new frontier and grew or hunted their food, building a home out of trees they cut down. There were no banks or credit cards to become indentured to. They'd gather firewood for heat instead of filling out a credit application to a utility company.

He was a dreamer, but not a quitter, and he would play within the rules of his era. He just didn't like being enslaved to so many financial and social institutions.

He came to an abrupt stop in his garage, still deep in thought. The condo was small but well designed, with high ceilings that gave rooms the appearance of being much larger. Jeffrey's room was just to the right of the top of the stairs and his door was covered with the obligatory skate and surf stickers. Inside was a combination of baby toys and the more sophisticated electronic toys that were ever more popular with kids his age. After sorting the dirty piles from the clean, John picked out the least wrinkled pair of jeans and a matching polo shirt and returned to the car.

It took only a few minutes to get to Jeffrey's school and John eased the white Ford Explorer into the space marked Visitor, which was about a hundred yards from the school's office. He checked his watch as he hurried up the walkway. Noting that it was just after twelve-thirty, he figured he had time to take Jeffrey out for a quick lunch before getting back for his two o'clock patient.

"Dad!"

John walked through the glass double doors that read Jefferson Elementary in gold letters. The boy leapt into his arms.

"Nice clothes." He felt the dried paint on what was apparently someone's dad's shirt, donated to the art department. Jeffrey was also wearing a baggy pair of gym shorts the principal had loaned him from the workout bag he kept in his trunk.

"Oh, Dad, it was sick! A girl named Katie barfed all over my back when I wasn't looking." Jeffrey paused for a second, remembering the gaze he'd shared with Sarah a few seconds before impact.

"You're kidding! Don't you hate it when that happens?"

Jeffrey grinned. "It sucks!"

He carried Jeffrey to the front desk. "Mrs. Carruthers, I'd like to take Jeffrey out for lunch. When does he need to be back?"

The stone-faced secretary coldly looked up the boy's schedule. "Be back at 1:15 if you want him to make it to class on time."

John had to smile. Mrs. Carruthers had been the secretary when he attended Jefferson and, although she looked quite different now, her personality was indistinguishable. When he enrolled Jeffrey in school the year before, John mentioned to her that they had met when he was a student there. She had nodded stoically and finished the paperwork. In the few dealings they had had since, the subject never surfaced again.

John glanced to his right into the nurse's room as he signed Jeffrey out. On a cot lay a little girl approximately Jeffrey's age, a blanket covering her legs. He noticed her eyes were closed and she shuddered in regular intervals. Her lips had a slight cyanotic blue appearance to them.

"That's her, Dad."

Truley looked back at the secretary. "Is she going to be all right?"

"The school nurse is tending to her."

John's instincts told him to take a closer look to see if he could help in any way, but he stopped short, remembering how he was stonewalled when he volunteered last fall to do scoliosis screenings to check the children for early detection of improper curvatures of the spine. He went round and round with the administration and was left with the distinct feeling that his offer was refused due to political reasons. He knew that the same politics were in force now and this was not his turf. No matter how much empathy he felt for the child, it didn't change the fact that he was not authorized to assist while she was at the school nursing station. Just then something clicked in his mind.

"Jeffrey? I don't suppose that's one of the children who went to the office with you instead of getting vaccinated?"

"No Dad, that was Jamul."

Truley glanced back at the child on the cot, then looked hard into Mrs. Carruthers eyes. "Where's your nurse?"

The secretary glared at him. "Nurse Johnson is in the ladies' room."

"Go get her."

"Excuse me, but you have no authority . . ."

"Now!"

The conviction in his voice startled her and she looked at the little girl and then trembled as she hurried in the direction of the teachers' lounge. John ran over to the child and felt her skin. It was cool and clammy. He quickly pulled one eyelid open. The large black pupil was dilated and fixed, looking into space.

"Jeffrey, grab those blankets on that shelf."

"Dad?"

"Do it."

Jeffrey dutifully retrieved the two blankets.

Truley stacked the blankets under the girl's legs and began to gently shake her. "Hey, wake up! Wake up!"

There was no response. He sprung from the bedside and snatched a phone from the tiny desk in the nurse's room, quickly pounding out 9-1-1.

The nurse burst in with her right shirt flap untucked and looked horrified at finding her office invaded by a strange man. "Just what do you think you're doing?"

A voice on the phone suddenly answered. "This is 911. Is this a life and death situation?"

"Yes. This is Dr. John Truley at Jefferson Elementary School. Send an ambulance right now. We have a 7-year-old girl in shock."

Chapter 5

Dr. Lamont Weedleman was in uncharted water for many reasons. He could not remember a time when he was excited about his work, and now, upon wakening, he was astonished to find himself downright enthused and looking forward to the day's discoveries. Everything had changed for him since he had stood in the laboratory's refrigerator and visualized the reconfiguration of CD4C. That moment had been like a purifying fire that filled the center of his being where only a cold, black void had previously existed. He now felt younger, renewed and recharged. Although he had never admitted to himself that he longed to be like his legendary father and grandfather, he felt a new glow of admiration, a connection with them. It was as if they had thrown him a genetic lifeline from the great beyond, reassuring him that he was, in fact, a Weedleman and there was work to be done.

Now in the lab, he labored like a man possessed. He refused to come this close to his destiny and be denied. He stood, reviewing data collected from the experiment. At first the testing had gone so smoothly. When he did the initial trials on the small and large rodents, less than five percent of the animals had died, even at ridiculously high doses of CD4C. The tests with the monkeys had been equally promising with a 4.3 percent mortality rate and an impressive 8.7 percent of monkeys experiencing only moderate morbidity which included reactions such as incontinence, anaphylaxis, sterility and frank mental retardation. It was too good to be true and appeared as if CD4C would walk right out of the lab without a hitch.

It wasn't until the second round of canine testing that results dropped below an acceptable level. In Round Two, a six-month-old Labrador that was injected with only four milligrams of CD4C died within six hours. The autopsy revealed cardiac arrest and central nervous system palsy, two very unusual responses to an injection of an attenuated virus.

It had taken four long days to ready Round Three. The animal supplier, known to the lab as "The Source", worked three days to fill Blackmore West's demand for healthy canines and the in-house pretest examinations added an additional day. Each test round included fifteen dogs, ideally consisting of various ages, breeds and both genders. The laboratory performed and recorded meticulous measurements including the usual blood, urine, saliva and fecal work up, as well as tissue samples of hair, skin and mucous membranes, followed by neurologic tests for pupillary constriction, deep tendon reflexes and reaction to pin prick. Finally, each dog was fully X-rayed. All tests were performed prior to administration of the test drug to establish a baseline for each animal. It was faithfully repeated one hour after the injection of CD4C, at six, twelve, and twenty-four hours, then daily for two weeks, and weekly for one to three months depending on indicators and need.

This labor-intensive protocol was both standard and critically important. The information derived helped the researchers decide whether it was within the realm of possibility to go public with the drug. Its documentation was essential in defending a company like Blackmore against the inevitable lawsuits that would evolve from the small percentage of people, or the grist as it was called in the industry, who had catastrophic reactions to it. The grist factor was projected by extrapolating the percentages of poor reactions by certain types of test animals to the human population that would be using the medication. Highly paid accountants calculated the number as carefully as Nevada bookmakers figure point spread for the Super Bowl. Estimated lawsuit awards were compared with projected drug profits, and if the difference fell within acceptable parameters, the drug was given the "okay" by the financial department.

Initial results from Round Three indicated a complete success. Every dog survived through the first three days after injection of CD4C with a satisfyingly low number of complications.

Stanley Crider scanned the latest results. "Well, Lamont, it looks like you've done it."

Stanley was Lamont's boss and, possibly, the only Blackmore employee Lamont trusted or cared to talk to. Although not exactly friendly, Lamont knew that the man had paid his dues in research and was instrumental in developing a few moderately successful drugs that continued to make money for the company. He was not the type to shout greetings in the morning or loudly talk about himself, a trait Lamont despised. Lamont resented many of his fellow workers who seemed to go to great lengths to prove they were happy. Their daily ritual seemed to border on hysteria. Lamont was not one of them. He was not happy. There were no family or friends to talk about while he worked. He did not attend tailgate parties or play in poker games. In fact, there were only one or two people with whom he conversed when away from work and he had never met them in person. They were friends on the internet and he knew them only by their screen names. He was comfortable talking through his computer. It was a protective buffer that allowed Lamont to relax and reveal some of his feelings to another person anonymously. It felt safer to see his words isolated on a screen where he could control what was said with little or no consequence. If he wanted to end a conversation, it could be done instantly, instead of awkwardly exchanging pleasantries while dancing around the reality that the visit was over and it was time for his guest to get out.

"Stan, I'm bothered by the Labrador in Round Two."

Since the board meeting, Stanley had closely monitored Lamont's progress with CD4C. He now reviewed the biopsy of the Labrador, then ran his finger down the breed column of each of the three rounds of canines. "Lamont, this dog that died was the only Labrador of the forty-five dogs tested. I think it was a fluke, but to be thorough, I would test more of the breed."

Lamont chuckled. "Well, we know that thorough is one thing you are! I noticed that, too, and we've made arrangements to run a few Labradors through Round Four. It just takes so damn long for the Source to fill our orders and now that we need a specific breed, who knows how long I'll be twiddling my thumbs."

"I'll see what I can do to light a fire under all of our sources to get the Labradors here ASAP. The board is giving me hell to push CD4C to completion. Old Blackmore has a real candle burning up his ass ever since this Cocadian Three thing. He and the rest of the board are counting on you to pull them out of the crapper."

"Tell 'em to go to hell." Lamont smiled and then checked himself, making a mental note to tone down his emotions. He never used to smile at work and was startled by his recent transformation. He'd better get control of himself now before he turned out like his animated co-workers.

Six days passed and the Source had not produced the dogs. There was no point in manipulating the formula until the dogs in Round Four were tested with the same batch to which the Labrador reacted. Weedleman reviewed the data on Rounds One through Three so many times that he had it memorized: forty-five dogs, nine minor skin lesions, three visual disturbances, three productive coughs, two incontinent bladders, two sterilities, and only one case of brain damage. Then there was the glaring case of specimen number twenty-three, the black Lab. The autopsy was especially startling. It wasn't so much that the dog died that bothered Weedleman; an occasional mortality was expected. It was how the dog died. The suddenness and extent of internal damage did not bode well. The Labrador was likely a fluke, or appeared to be, compared to the rest of the data.

Lamont cursed the Source, blaming them for holding up a possible breakthrough in disease prevention which could very well be the crowning achievement of his life. This event could single handedly elevate him to his rightful position of lineage beside his forefathers. People would be able to speak of the great Weedlemans as three instead of two. He had no illusions that he would ever be considered his paternal predecessor's equals, but at least he might have a chance to grab a little piece of fame himself. Maybe he would put an end to the awkward silence that occurs during a discussion of the great Weedlemans, when someone asks the inevitable question: "Didn't they have a son who followed in their field?"

During the weeks that followed his discovery with CD4C, Lamont painfully realized just how much he had repressed his need to feel worthy to his namesake. It was okay, he was feeling stronger by the minute and if releasing buried emotions helped motivate him to complete his work, then so be it. And besides, his newly found vigor was making him more tolerant of pain, emotional or otherwise.

Chief lab assistant, Sally Hobbs, was personally responsible for readying all of the subjects needed for researcher Weedleman. Although it wasn't necessary, she closely followed the experimentation from start to finish, learning as much about the work as Blackmore's security policies would allow. It was more difficult to obtain full information on the hotter projects and, as a rule, the greater a new drug's potential, the more secretive were the researchers at Blackmore. No one was to be trusted and no one should have proprietary information unless it was absolutely necessary. In this harshly competitive field, with potentially billions of dollars at stake, security was foremost. Although it had never happened at Blackmore, it was common knowledge that employees with information had been richly paid by competitors to reveal trade secrets. They could sometimes get the drug patented and marketed first, dramatically reversing the fortunes of the two companies.

Sally was not interested in trade secrets. She was, however, very interested in the well being of animals, which often created an inner turmoil. She philosophically justified her position as animal handler in the lab. She knew she was not only the most qualified, minimizing injuries to animals, but also the most humane while staying within the parameters of her job description. As a student at Pomona State, she majored in animal husbandry and was applying for veterinarian school at UC Davis when her life became forever altered by some very unusual events.

Sally was an orphan, and as a young girl, was bounced back and forth between county care facilities and various foster homes. She never landed in a place she could call home or with anyone she could call family. At sixteen, she proved to the county that she was self-sufficient by holding down two part-time jobs and making passing grades in high school. She was released with surprising ease from county custody and wished well by her social worker, who made her promise to call often and let her know how she was getting along. Sally graduated from high school with a 3.5 GPA and, after qualifying for government aid and being assured that the college had the right pre-veterinary curriculum, she enrolled in Pomona State. She did well during her first three years, though challenged by a full load of classes and two jobs. As an animal lover, she found that she excelled when her studies became applicable to her chosen field. She maintained a 3.9 GPA and appeared well on her way.

It was during the spring semester of Sally's junior year that Gladys Perkins, her social worker, called with news that would change her life forever. Gladys was thrilled about Sally's achievements and was one of the few stable influences she had. Gladys had always shown genuine concern for Sally's well being and this was a comfort through the trying years of feeling otherwise unwanted. It was with mixed feelings that Gladys broke the news to Sally, telling her that she had discovered, almost by accident from another social worker, that it appeared Sally had a sibling, a sister, never revealed by the state. Gladys was as surprised as Sally and did some research to find out what had happened.

Apparently, when Sally was two years old, her parents, John and Dorothy Hobbs, left her and her younger sister with a baby sitter while attending a ballet. On the way home that evening, a drunk driver, weaving through traffic at over 60 miles an hour, struck their car head on, killing them instantly. When it was discovered that the Hobbs' had no next of kin, the state attempted, without success, to find a home for the two girls. Prospective families were unwilling to take on the responsibility of two newly adopted children, and social administrators decided that splitting up the sisters would give them a greater chance of finding permanent homes.

Sally's sister, whose name was Mara, was six-months old at the time of the accident and was adopted shortly after being presented as a lone prospect. She was selected by Paul and Ruthie Jones, who passed the rigorous state requirements for adoptive parents. Two years later, Mrs. Jones died of ovarian cancer, leaving Paul Jones a broken man. He eventually married a woman who became an alcoholic, despised children in general, and was insanely jealous of Mara. She and Mara shared an extremely rocky relationship while Paul Jones remained depressed, unable to shake the loss of Ruthie, his first wife and true love. Mara ran away from home many times, finally dropping out of high school at sixteen. She had a record of misdemeanor violations, which included drunk and disorderly conduct and shoplifting. When the police last arrested her, she was high on heroin and riding with a convicted felon in a stolen car.

When Gladys first told Sally that she had a sister, Mara was serving an eight-week sentence in a state rehabilitation facility. No visitors were allowed. On Gladys' advice, Sally decided not to contact Mara until her program ended. Then, Gladys arranged a reunion where she and the two sisters met for lunch at a Sizzler near Sally's apartment. Sally would never forget sitting inside the restaurant, watching Mara get out of the taxi that Gladys had arranged for her. She wore tattered low-cut jeans, scuffed, yellow plastic pumps, and a lime colored halter top that did little to hide her pasty, white, emaciated abdomen complete with naval ring. A transparent outer toughness could not hide the desperate, frightened creature squinting at the sun-splashed windows of the Sizzler.

Sally waited at the table while Gladys met Mara at the front door. She led the girl to the booth and introductions were made. At first, it was all quite awkward. Then, after both girls relaxed a little and recognized each other's auburn hair, green eyes, freckles, long and slender builds, similar mannerisms and basically undeniable resemblance, the ice melted and flowed as tears from all three women. It was decided quickly, over the virtually untouched meal, that Mara would immediately move in with Sally and the two would become a family.

During the months that followed, Sally found Mara to be more like a daughter than a sister, even though she was less than two years younger. She required almost constant supervision and Sally, determined to prevent her little sister from getting back on drugs, made Mara her number one priority. She withdrew from Pomona State College in order to dedicate more time to helping her sister rebuild her life. It soon became apparent that Sally needed more money than she was making from her part time jobs so she answered an ad in a scientific trade journal that was somewhat related to her field. She landed the position and was quickly promoted to chief lab assistant in charge of animal handling at Blackmore.

This morning, as Sally finalized the preparations for Round Four of the canines, she was fully aware of the significance of the four Labradors included in the fifteen-subject pool. Upon delivery of the order, she thought it odd that nearly one-third of the dogs were the same breed and reviewed the requisition to find that it was no coincidence. Weedleman had specified that Blackmore West must have no less than three Labradors and Sally saw that they had paid nearly twice the normal price for the shipment.

She knew the experiments they were performing on a substance called CD4C were "hot" and noticed a distinct shift in Dr. Weedleman's personality. He had become much more animated around the lab and at the same time considerably less patient. He was also taking a more hands-on approach than usual and was almost working side by side with her. Until now, Dr. Weedleman had wanted nothing to do with animal preparation and Sally had assumed it was beneath him to perform the menial tasks she completed on a daily basis. She was now convinced that it was due to his inability to get along with the animals. During the post-exposure, twelve-hour follow-ups on Round Three, she had to intervene when a black, 6-year-old German Shepherd escaped its tether in the X-ray area and cornered Dr. Weedleman. Sally re-entered the lab after a short visit to the ladies' room and found the dog snarling and snapping at the frightened doctor. His admonishments of "Good dog, down boy," quickly turned to "Good for nothing, goddamn mutt," after she successfully restrained the animal. Now, with him getting in her way and looking over her shoulder, she longingly realized how much better she had liked being alone with the dogs, talking to and comforting them. Weedleman's presence was making both her and her canine friends nervous.

"We're all set, Dr. Weedleman."

"Good. Get the media from the refrigerator and let's go. The time is 12:35."

Sally administered the majority of the injections with Weedleman at her elbow. A bolus of 20 cc's of the pale, urine-colored substance was delivered intramuscularly to each animal. Weedleman took special interest in every aspect of the procedures on the Labradors and even bumped her once while she inserted the syringe into a two-year-old female with exceptionally silky brown fur. The dog whimpered and looked at her nervously with sad, dark eyes.

By five o'clock that evening, all four Labradors were dead.

Chapter 6

A direct line was opened between the paramedic in the back of the ambulance and Dr. Jules Libol in the emergency room at Good Samaritan Hospital. The doctor was busy cleaning a nine-inch gash on the leg of a man who had become careless with a new power saw. He shouted at the speaker phone in order to be heard over the hospital chatter around him.

"This is Dr. Libol, what've you got?"

"We have an unconscious, 6-year-old white female who appears to be in moderate to advanced shock. Her airways are unobstructed, but breathing is rapid and shallow. BP is eighty by palp, pulse 145 and weak, pupils fixed and dilated, fingers and lips are cyanotic."

"You have her on oxygen?" Dr. Libol was debriding the remaining redwood chips from deep in the man's wound.

"Roger that."

"I.V.?"

"I started saline with five percent dextrose"

"Do you know what caused it?"

"No sign or history of trauma. A man at her school said she received a DPT vaccine this morning. It looks like anaphylaxis."

"I agree. Is her pressure coming up at all?"

"Negative."

"Give her epinephrine 0.3 milligrams subcutaneous and Benadryl 25 milligrams IV and let's see if we can bring her back. What's your ETA?"

"Heavy traffic, Doc. Looks like a good ten to fifteen."

"Let's keep this line open."

"Will do."

Dr. Libol began closing the gash while impatiently waiting for the paramedic to report back. The weekend carpenter broke the silence.

"Sounds bad, huh?"

Libol looked up over the black frames of his glasses and

nodded gravely.

The paramedic's voice crackled through the speaker. "Doctor?"

"I'm here."

"Her BP is dropping. We're losing her."

"Well, we haven't lost her yet! Give her 0.1 milligrams of epinephrine IV and start a dopamine drip at 5 micrograms per kilogram per minute, understand?"

"I'm on it."

"How's her breathing?"

"It just stopped!"

"All right, you know the drill. Get her intubated – now! How far away are you?"

"ETA is five minutes, barring any obstructions."

"Make it four minutes and I don't care if you have to drive on the sidewalk!"

The ambulance screeched to a stop at Emergency Bay 4 of Good Samaritan Hospital. This bay was reserved for Code 3 emergencies where the promptness of attention was a matter of life or death. The comatose girl was rushed into the intensive care unit where Dr. Libol was waiting. He had just finished giving instructions to an intern to finish closing the power saw gash. He had already notified Dr. Knowles, Good Sam's top pediatric cardiopulmonary specialist, who arrived at the same time as the patient. Dr. Abdule Rhohia, who specialized in toxicology, was also summoned. Dr. Libol had learned, in his twenty plus years of experience, to engage as much qualified help as possible instead of trying to be a hero when a life hung in the balance. This girl was on the edge, and he wanted every advantage.

"Doctors, let's save this child, shall we?" Libol lifted the girl's eyelid and peered at the non-reactive pupil.

Dr. Knowles snapped his second glove on and quickly checked for a brachial pulse. "Not good. CPR time, boys. Let's get on it."

Knowles pumped the little chest rhythmically with the edge of his palm and looked up at his colleague. Dr. Libol did a quick assessment of the IV bag to find how much fluid the girl had received. "She looks like about forty-five pounds wouldn't you say? She needs more fluid and I'm increasing the dopamine to 20 micrograms per kilogram per minute. Knowles, any luck?"

Dr. Knowles had sweat beading on his forehead as he rechecked Katie's pulse. "Got it!"

"Good work. Nurse, start that IV. We need a STAT blood gas. Let's find out how bad her acidosis is."

The members of the ER worked swiftly. They had all performed similar duties many times but each time they worked to save a life, it was anything but routine. Soon the blood gas values were available to Dr. Libol.

"Fellas, she's pretty far out there. Let's increase that respirator to see if she can blow off some of that carbon dioxide."

Dr. Knowles nodded. "We'd better see some results fast if this girl's gonna make it in one piece."

"Yes, her pH is extremely toxic at this point. Her tissue is degenerating swiftly. Might we consider extracorpreal membrane oxygenation?" Dr. Rhohia, thick with a middle-eastern accent, referred to a technique of circulating the patient's blood through a machine which infuses it with oxygen before bringing it back into the body. "I can insert the arterial and venous lines."

"No, Dr. Rhohia." Knowles shook his head, knowing that his colleague's specialty was toxicology and not emergency medicine. "That technique doesn't work as well with juveniles. Let's see how the respirator does. In the meantime, let's get a MAST suit on her lower extremities to try to bring her pressure up. We've got to get some blood to her brain, otherwise she's gonna be a vegetable even if we do save her life!"

Katie Prespo's spirit looked down at the scene as the three doctors worked feverishly to keep her pale, limp body alive. Tubes and lines protruded from her mouth and arms. A nurse and one of the doctors were in the process of sliding an inflatable pair of knee-length shorts onto her small legs. She could sense the people's sincere determination and secretly thanked each for their efforts.

A familiar energy drew her into the hallway. A being she loved intensely stood outside the door where Katie's body lay. The woman was distraught, frightened, and weeping hysterically. Katie went to her mother's side and tried to comfort her.

Mrs. Prespo had been stunned to find her daughter unconscious and in an emergency room, three unknown doctors working frantically over her. She had received a page from the school while on her lunch break. When she called the number, Mrs. Carruthers answered and was uncharacteristically emotional, sending a chill down Mrs. Prespo's spine even before she heard the bad news. Nothing, however, had prepared her for this. Her daughter, who was absolutely fine that morning at breakfast, was now, less than six hours later, surrounded by doctors and fighting for her life.

Each doctor silently calculated the odds of the young patient's survival, while Dr. Libol worked intently. A child's life was on the line and he summoned all his experience, talent, and sheer will to save her. It was moments like these that gave his life meaning and made all the other bullshit worthwhile. "Nurse, I want Solu-Medrol 125 milligram IV and Tagamet 300 milligram IV ready to go. Let's get an update on blood gas."

After spending time with her mother and absorbing some of the pain she was going through, Katie's spirit was drawn away from the tantalizing brightness that beckoned her from above. She found the same three doctors leaning over her body, conversing quietly.

"Her vitals have stabilized and she is just about out of the woods." Dr. Libol sighed.

Dr. Knowles nodded. "There are indications of neurologic damage, which should be fully evaluated. I think we can all agree that the pathologic reflexes we've found represent a high probability that the cerebrum has been damaged. It's up to the neuros to find out how much. At this point, guys, I'm just thankful that she's still with us. Good job, both of you. One of us should inform the parents. I vote for Libol." He looked at the emergency room doctor.

Dr. Rhohia nodded. "A rather unpleasant responsibility."

Dr. Libol was comforted by the fact that he could tell the girl's parents that she was going to live. In all his years as a trauma doctor, he had never gotten used to the dreary task of breaking bad news to families. He had performed the somber duty hundreds of times, but it was always more difficult when the patient was a child. For a moment he toyed with the idea of letting the neurologist tell the parents about the girl's possible brain damage. The thought quickly vanished, however. He knew it would be more painful for the family to find out later and he would be skirting his responsibilities to not tell them now. This was the best time, when they weren't even sure if their daughter was going to pull through. They were more prepared for bad news and might as well have the full load at once so they could start dealing with it.

Mrs. Prespo was sitting in the waiting area, elbows propped on her lap and her face buried in her hands. Dr. Libol wasn't sure whether she was crying or praying, but imagined she was doing both. He was disappointed to see that she was by herself, with no one to comfort her. This would make it harder.

"Mrs. Prespo?

"Yes." She looked up with red glassy eyes ringed with smeared mascara.

"Your daughter is going to make it." He vaguely smiled.

The mother opened then covered her mouth, her eyes wide with renewed hope.

"Oh thank you, Doctor, thank you. I was so frightened. My husband is away on business."

"I know." He placed his hand lightly on her shoulder. "You had every reason to be petrified, but I need to tell you that your Katie may have suffered some injuries from all of this."

Mrs. Prespo was caught by surprise. She was so ecstatic over the good news that it hadn't occurred to her anything else might be wrong. Once again, she covered her mouth and peered at him with new tears welling in her eyes.

"What kind of injuries?" Her question came muffled through trembling hands.

"Katie may have suffered some brain damage."

Mrs. Prespo's hands curled and then there was an agonizing wail that reverberated through the corridors, piercing Dr. Libol's heart. He was caught off guard by the impact of her cry. A primitive cord deep inside him had been struck and his mind raced through memory to find something to compare it to. Reeling, he staggered as she buried her face in his chest, right where he hurt most. He put his arms around her, letting her sob, feeling the heat of his own tears streak his face.

Chapter 7

Dr. Libol had been summoned to hospital administration and, specifically, Chairman Frederick Von Peters's office. He'd been there a couple of times before and though curious, was not thrilled to be taken away from his busy work schedule. For the most part, he wanted nothing to do with the suits who made policy and politics for the hospital. Libol considered himself a blue-collar doctor, one who preferred hands-on work with as little interference from authority as possible. While most of his colleagues had taken advantage of their tenure, moving on to higher-paying specialties or administration, Jules had chosen to stay in the ER where he liked the action.

Von Peters's platinum-haired secretary greeted him by name when he arrived at the plush office on the top floor.

"Mr. Von Peters is expecting you, Dr. Libol. Please follow me." She opened the heavy oak door. "Dr. Libol is here."

"Thank you, Sheila. Why don't you get Jules a cup of coffee?"

"Uh, no thank you. I'm already at my ten cup limit for the day."

Von Peters's tone and use of his first name made him feel uncomfortable. He had only met the man once in passing and was not aware that they were on such familiar terms. *Damn bureaucrats.* He stopped suddenly when he saw Dr. Knowles and Dr. Rhohia already seated on the leather couch. Dr. Libol nodded at his colleagues and shook hands with a third man that he didn't know, introduced only as Mr. Deidman. Libol would later hear from a trusted source that the man was Miles Deidman, special counsel to Good Samaritan.

Von Peters cleared his throat. "First let me congratulate you three on your heroic efforts with the Prespo girl yesterday. I understand that you saved her life and she has stabilized in the ICU. I also understand that there exists some question as to the cause of her condition. Due to the sensitive nature of the issues involved, I suggest that we, as a group, stand united in our handling of this unfortunate situation. I've heard reports that speculate a connection with this girl's condition and a DPT vaccination she received at Jefferson Elementary School yesterday morning. I must remind you gentlemen, as doctors and stewards of the public trust, we have a responsibility to protect the health and well being of our community as a whole. Now, if we were to irresponsibly suggest to the public that vaccinations were dangerous, we could set the health care delivery system back fifty years." Von Peters chuckled nervously. "Can you imagine what would happen if parents stopped vaccinating their children? What happened to this child is quite unfortunate, but sometimes we are asked to do the difficult task of justifying the sacrifice of the few for the betterment of the many. The board has assured our main shareholders that this matter will be handled with complete professionalism and that they have nothing to be concerned about."

Von Peters sipped mineral water from a crystal lowball glass and looked briefly at Deidman who gave a slight nod. Deliberately, he then looked at each doctor in turn before resuming.

"Now doctors, can we agree on a diagnosis? I think that anaphylaxis of unknown origin, leaning toward food poisoning is an accurate call. What do you say?" He looked at Dr. Knowles first, who puckered his lips, shrugged and nodded.

Next he looked at Dr. Rhohia. "You are the employer, sir."

He then gazed intently at Dr. Libol for unanimous agreement.

"Well, hell, we must protect the shareholders." Libol paused, then with a smirk, stared straight into Von Peters's eyes. "Excuse me, I meant the public."

Von Peters cleared his throat once again. "Yes, well, thank you, gentlemen, for your cooperation. I know that I can count on you to properly handle this matter. Now I've taken enough of your time."

All five men rose in unison and the doctors filed out of the office.

"Public, my ass!" Dr. Knowles punched the elevator's close button.

Dr. Rhohia shook his head. "Yes, why are the shareholders involved with our diagnosis of this young patient?"

Libol chuckled. "Those damn shareholders. About ninety-five percent of those sons of bitches' portfolios are invested in drug companies."

Rhohia frowned. "I had hoped that things would be different in this country."

"They're not," the other two doctors said in unison.

Rhohia and Knowles got out on the 15th floor to grab a cup of coffee at the cafeteria, leaving Libol with his thoughts.

"Damn bureaucrats." He had felt trapped, almost claustrophobic, in Von Peters's office. It was the kind of thing that made his stomach turn. He knew the politics existed but he usually could see them coming and steer clear. Now, because he had helped to save Katie Prespo's life, he had been sucked right into the middle of the thing he detested most about medicine. The elevator opened on the first floor and he lunged through the doorway, bumping a man who was trying to get in.

"Oh, sorry." Dr. Libol took a deep breath, wanting to clear the bad vibes the meeting had left him with.

John Truley smiled. "No problem. It was my fault."

John rode the elevator to the ICU on the seventh floor. He had learned from the information clerk that the only Katie in the hospital was Katie Prespo, who was in intensive care. John doubted he would be allowed to visit her but wanted to try. He felt connected with the little girl because of the previous day's events. Besides, she was a classmate of Jeffrey's and he was concerned about her. Exiting the elevator into a carpeted corridor, John saw a nurse's station positioned about halfway down on the left. It was noticeably quiet; only a few people sat in an adjacent waiting area. John moved methodically toward the station, trying to read patient's names outside the twenty or so rooms. Not all had placards, but occasionally he could make out a name on the charts tucked inside clear plastic racks. He reached the nurses' station without finding Katie Prespo.

A stern middle-aged nurse studied him. "Can I help you?" Her voice broke the silence of the corridor.

"Yes, I'm looking for Katie Prespo."

"Are you a family member?"

"Ahh no. I just wanted to find out . . . well, you see, she's in my son's class."

"I'm sorry, sir. Only family members are allowed to visit patients on this floor."

"I see. Well, can you tell me if she's okay? We're all very concerned about her."

"I'm not allowed to give out any information. I'm sure you understand."

John looked around helplessly; he knew the nurse would give no ground. He turned and saw a woman standing a few feet away gazing at him from the waiting area. John nodded.

"I heard you say that your son is in Katie's class."

"Mrs. Prespo?"

"What's your son's name?"

"Jeffrey Truley." He walked toward her. "Is Katie going to be all right?"

"No, she's . . . she's not." She began to cry.

John approached her instinctively, putting his hands out, feeling the grief pouring from the woman. She reached for his hands but then drew back, working to control her emotions. She held one hand up to her face while the other arm crossed her midsection, holding the floodgates closed.

She looked up at John and nodded toward the elevator. "Can we walk?"

"Of course."

They walked twenty feet without saying a word. John wanted to comfort her, but he would talk only when Mrs. Prespo was ready. She stopped and turned to him.

"My . . . my baby may have . . ." She held her hand to her mouth, her eyes pinched closed. ". . . brain damage."

Her strangled words cut John to the quick, and a flurry of thoughts raced through his brain. Why did this happen?

What if something like this happened to Jeffrey? How can I comfort her? How bad is the damage? Is Katie a vegetable? He was overwhelmed with compassion for this dear mother and found himself embracing her as the words echoed inside him.

"I'm so sorry."

She nodded, sniffling and wiping her eyes. "I think I've just about run out of tears." She tried to smile, the lines in her face deepening into an agonizing grimace.

The woman was spent. She had passed the long night in a chair at Katie's side, catching a few minutes of fitful sleep when her thoughts would allow it. She had gone through most of this alone, her husband stranded in Germany due to an airline employee strike.

"Do you need some food? I could go to the cafeteria and get you something."

She took a deep breath. "Yes, I do need food and I think I need a moment away from this ICU. Let me just tell the nurse where I'll be, in case Katie wakes up."

"I'll tell her." John ran down the hallway, and soon returned with a pager from the nurses' station.

"They'll beep you if anything changes."

The cafeteria was typical. An angled metal counter covered with Plexiglas ran the length of one wall. Middle-aged women in hairnets doled out generic looking mashed potatoes and gravy, peas, chicken, roast beef and apple pie. Of the approximately fifty tables, only a few were taken. John chose one where they would have privacy and they set down with their trays.

"Mrs. Prespo?"

"Please, call me Connie."

"Certainly. Connie. I was at Jefferson Elementary with Katie at the nurse's office. In fact, I called 911 when I saw how she looked."

"You?" She gazed intently at him as she absorbed this new information. "Why you and not the nurse or someone from the school?"

"The nurse had apparently stepped out to use the restroom. I was there to bring Jeffrey . . . to take him out to lunch. I saw Katie's condition. I think it happened very quickly and it wasn't the nurse's fault."

Connie poked the grainy mashed potatoes with her fork. "I don't know what to think. I'm so confused by all of this."

"Connie, has Katie had any health problems in the past?"

"No. She's always been fairly healthy."

"Has she ever been sick after a vaccination or do you have any family history of reactions to vaccines?"

"What? Why are you asking that?"

John swallowed a bite of stale bread. "I knew the other children, including your daughter, had been vaccinated that morning. When I examined her briefly in the nurse's office, I quickly realized she was in trouble."

Connie gasped. "I forgot all about the vaccines. But that wouldn't have . . ." She suddenly pushed her chair back. "Mr. Truley, excuse me, I have to go."

He stood and offered his card. "Here is my number. Please. If I can help in any way. Maybe when the time is right you can call me and I'll bring Jeffrey and a few of Katie's friends to visit."

She paused, looked at his card and then at him. "Thank you for what you did. You may have saved my daughter's life. From what I understand, every minute counted."

He nodded and the woman turned and walked away.

John Truley returned to work to see his afternoon patients. He had difficulty focusing on his duties, running the events of the last twenty-four hours over and over in his mind. Janine appeared at the doorway while he was checking Mrs. Mulhacky's neck in Room Two. Her complaint of hand numbness was likely due to nerve interference caused by the misaligned fifth cervical vertebra that he had just identified. It was a common scenario and readily corrected in most cases.

He looked up at Janine. "Yes?"

"Mrs. Prespo is on the phone for you." His assistant smiled. She knew who the important caller was from John's account of what had happened.

"Is there a number where I can reach her in a couple of minutes?"

"Oh, she'll hold, believe me." She raised her eyebrows as she turned and left.

"Okay, let's get this straightened out, shall we?" John lightly held Mrs. Mulhacky's neck in his hands and made a gentle movement at the fifth vertebra. A quiet click was heard as the bone returned to its proper position. He let go and she moved her head and neck around.

"Wow!" She smiled. "It feels stronger and I can already feel a change in my hands!"

"The bone is back in place. All we have to do is make sure it stays there while your body heals. You will be fine. Let's check it in three days."

Back in his office, he grabbed the phone as he slid into his chair.

"Connie?"

"Dr. Truley, I'm sorry to bother you."

"No, this is perfect timing. I just finished for the day."

"I asked the doctors about the vaccine and they told me that it had nothing to do with Katie's illness. They said it was food poisoning. I have a hard time believing that because we've eaten the exact same food for the last day or two. We made yesterday's lunch together the night before and kept it in the refrigerator. We even have identical lunch boxes with cold packs in them. I need to ask you a few questions if you have time."

"Please."

"If the vaccine caused Katie's problem, then why didn't any other children get sick? Why didn't your son get sick?"

"Connie, first I want to make something clear. I don't know if the vaccine caused this problem for sure. I do know that there are documented side effects in some children when you inject vaccines such as DPT into their systems. The number of children who have problems as severe as seizures or brain damage is small, but the Center for Disease Control believes that only 10 to 15 percent of vaccine reactions are reported. Take Katie, for example. They're already saying her injury was caused by something else, so even if it was caused by the vaccine, it will go unreported."

Through the silence on the other end, John could hear hospital noise in the background. She began to sniffle and John tried to imagine the agony the woman must be going through.

"And your son? How is he?"

"Well, I don't allow Jeffrey to be vaccinated."

More silence.

"What do you mean, you don't allow it?"

John took a deep breath. It wasn't fair for her to hear this, now that it was too late.

"In many states, a parent has the right to object to the vaccinating of their children, based on religious or philosophic reasons. You must sign a waiver which the school and most of the medical profession doesn't like."

Mrs. Prespo was stunned, confused, crying.

"Why didn't . . . anyone tell me . . . about the danger . . . and that I had a right to choose?"

"I'm sorry, Connie." John leaned back in his chair, staring at the ceiling.

"Dr. Truley, I want that information." A new forcefulness was in her voice.

"About DPT?"

"All of it!"

"I'll give you everything I have. I'll bring it to the hospital." He hung up and stared at the phone. He remained motionless at his desk for a long time and then began to simmer. Finally, he went to a metal cabinet and retrieved a file containing vaccine information. There was a good deal of it, ranging from editorials written by grief stricken parents to medical journal articles citing a broad range of statistics. He even had an outdated list of the most dangerous lots of the vaccines that were in circulation at the time of the report. He reviewed some of it, especially what he thought Connie would be most interested in, and put this into a separate file. The information took on a new reality, and he quickly tucked it under his arm.

John Truley exited the elevator on the seventh floor and walked down the hallway. He didn't see Connie, and once again, began looking for the name Prespo on the placards outside the patients' rooms. When he arrived at the nurses' station, a different woman was intently filing charts with her back to the counter. John decided not to stop this time and instead made his way toward the far end of the hallway. He was still reading names, when approximately halfway down, he found what he was looking for. Someone had written "Prespo" on an index card with a black felt tip marker and clamped it to the chart holder next to the partially open door. John peered into the dimly lit room. A man in a white smock was examining a patient on one of two beds. John continued to watch the man's back as he thought of his options. Perhaps Connie had gone home to get a change of clothes. He had just decided to leave the files for her at the nurse's desk when the man moved and the patient came into better view. She was small and frail, alabaster skin contrasting sharply with jet-black hair. It was Katie. She was the same age and approximate size of Jeffrey, sending a chill down his spine.

She was strapped to the bed by belts that crossed her waist. IV tubes were taped to her forearms, where needles fed directly to the veins. They were held by tape and a harness-like apparatus that wrapped around her head. Seeing Katie made John realize that as bad as everyone else felt about what had happened, it was nothing compared to what this little 6-year-old victim was now faced with. A mixture of anger and grief lumped in his chest, as the man in the smock finished his notes and turned toward the door.

"Hello, I'm Dr. Truley. Is this the little girl who had the reaction to the vaccination?" John smiled tightly.

The doctor started to reply, then caught himself as he eyed Truley's clothes. "Dr. Truley, is it? Which department do you work in?"

"I'm a chiropractor. I practice in North County."

"Well, Dr. Truley, I don't believe you have any privileges

in this hospital." He smugly raised his eyebrows. "Now if you'll pardon me, I have rounds to finish."

The doctor brushed past John and into the hall.

"I found the girl in shock!"

The doctor stopped and turned back to John.

"In the school nurse's office just hours after she was injected with what you MD's misleadingly call an immunization. Why don't you just admit that this is a drug reaction and drop this charade about food poisoning?"

"You're the charade, sir." He pointed at John. "You and your whole damn profession." He turned and walked briskly down the hallway.

John entered the room and went to Katie's bedside. He could hear his heartbeat in his ears and took some slow, deep breaths. Soon the rhythmic hissing of the respirator was the only sound that mattered. He lightly stroked Katie's forehead with his fingertips, gently brushing back her hair.

"I'm sorry, Katie." The lump in his chest rose to his throat. He could barely whisper. "If only I could've made a difference."

Chapter 8

The answering machine had the usual assortment of disturbing messages.

"This is the Student Loan Servicing Center calling for John Truley. Please call our number; we are open twenty-four hours a day." Beep.

"Uh, yes, this is Agent McClasken of the IRS. I've been assigned your collection case. Are you aware that you missed last month's installment? Contact our office immediately to see if we can salvage your agreement." Beep.

"Hey, Johnny Boy, Jimmy here. I hope you're ready for some inspiration tonight. I'll be over to pick you up at seven o'clock sharp!" Beep.

John hit the stop button and looked at his clock. "Ah, Shit!" He grabbed the phone and pounded out Jimmy's number. It picked up on the second ring.

"Hello, everyone. You've reached the home of Dr. Jimmy McBride. If this is an emergency try my pager number at 752 . . ."

John hung up on the machine. It was too late; Jimmy was en route.

Once he arrived there would be no turning back. Jimmy was as pushy as he was outgoing, albeit in a good-natured sort of way. They had been friends since chiropractic school and occasionally went for a drink together. While John chose to spend most of his non-work time with Jeffrey and tended to shy away from the social scene, his friend Jimmy was just the opposite and lived for the interaction with others. Dr. Jimmy was a good chiropractor and had a large practice. How could he not? He networked a huge volume of people on a regular basis and passed out an extraordinary number of his business cards. One of the many social gatherings that Jimmy frequented was a monthly chiropractic philosophy meeting. He had been after John for months to attend and succeeded in wearing him down until, in a weak moment, he had consented.

John called his neighbors, the Michaels, who took care of Jeffrey after school. "Hi, Mary. It's John. I forgot about a meeting tonight that I had committed myself to. Would it be possible for Jeffrey to stay with you for a couple more hours?"

"Of course he can stay. By the way, we want you two to come over for dinner tomorrow night. How does that sound?"

"We'd love to. Thanks for everything. I don't know what I would do without you and Frank. Now, I'd better say hi to Jeffrey and let him know what's going on."

"I'll get him. We'll eat at six-thirty tomorrow, okay?"

"We'll be there."

"Good. Here's Jeffrey."

"Dad?"

"Hi, guy!"

"Hi, Dad. You home yet?"

"I am, but I have to leave right away."

"Oh, man."

"Would you like to stay over there and play with Todd or go with me to a boring meeting with a bunch of grownups?"

"Todd."

"That's what I thought. I'll see you later tonight."

"Dad?"

"Yeah."

"What happened to Katie? Is she gonna be all right?"

"Can we talk about it later?"

"Sure, Dad."

"Love you, Jeffrey. See you when I get back."

"Love ya, too, Dad."

A forceful pounding startled John as he hung up the phone. No doubt the larger-than-life Jimmy McBride. He swung open the door to reveal a tall, lean man, with bright red hair cropped to a short flat top. Jimmy sported a loud black and white plaid shirt with shiny black slacks. His shiny black loafers revealed matching black and white plaid socks. His jaws were disproportionately larger than the rest of his body, which earned him the nickname, Jimmy Megalop McBride back in school. He was showing all of his teeth now as he shouted his familiar greeting.

"Hey, Johnny!"

John came out, shutting the door behind him. Shaking his head in amusement.

"First, we'll go to the meeting; you're going love it, Big John! Then we'll head over to Flannagan's and check out some friends I want you to meet, after that..."

"Whoa, Jimmy! I said I'd go to a meeting, not all over town partying. My God, I have to work tomorrow, and besides, I haven't even seen Jeffrey yet today!"

"Come on, Johnny, you've gotta get out more often. Okay, how about this? First we go to the meeting, then we'll stop by Johnson's house. He lives right by there . . ."

The speaker was a character to behold, with a slightly balding forehead, hair long in the back and eyes that revealed an unusual intensity. His manner could be considered rough and his enthusiasm unbridled. It seemed likely that listeners in the front rows might have occasionally felt drops of spit flying from his mouth. There was something captivating about him. He had a presence that John found hard to describe. He seemed unconcerned with the formalities of social inhibition, preoccupied only with conveying the precious message deep in the recesses of his soul.

John took a couple of breaths and shifted to a more comfortable position in his chair. He felt a breeze waft through the room, gentle and fresh. Seeing the doors and windows were closed, he decided it was more in his mind than on his body. His gaze softened and he felt an unusual mixture of peace and excitement. The physical features of the speaker began to blur as his message gained clarity.

"The Power that made the body, heals the body!" The words spiked into the soft gray matter of John's awakening mind as the man leaned toward his listeners. "Innate works from above down, inside out."

A small flame flickered somewhere inside John, its light minute yet undeniable, like a flashlight appearing in the night from a distant hillside. A quiet heat radiated from the tiny beacon, gaining intensity, until a thawing sensation enveloped John's core. He shuddered, wondering how he had become so frozen. It was as if his soul had been trapped during an avalanche in some parallel universe.

"Wake up, people!" the orator commanded the crowd. "The problem is not in the laws or the media, it's in your head. Clear your head, then go clear your patients. Your mind is not limited to the space between your ears. You have all that you need to tap Universal Intelligence. Stop denying yourself and your purpose. What you are today is what you have created by your thoughts up until now. Start thinking the way God intended for you to think, without limits, without fear, without inhibition. Stop being wimps. Nobody has more power available to them than you. Wake up!

"I'd come out there and slap you if I thought it would help snap you out of your sleep." The speaker took a couple of steps toward the front row and then stopped, eliciting a few nervous laughs.

"The longer you remain in this fog, the more those who wait for you to fulfill your destiny will suffer. If your purpose is to serve, then by God, serve! Claim the power and manifest it. Your impact will be unprecedented.

"B.J. Palmer, the developer of chiropractic, once said, 'Now and then, one person who seeks to receive, does receive and makes history . . .' Well, I'm telling you to decide. Are you going to use all that you have available to you and serve your patients, and the world, with true, full-powered chiropractic, or are you not? Either way is fine, but not deciding will be your torment."

The message struck a chord with John. He had always felt down deep inside he had a lot to offer, but just couldn't access it. He had always secretly believed he was destined for greatness. His life, however, seemed to contradict these feelings, making them seem like mere fantasies. He could never quite retrieve the lofty dreams from the heavenly clouds of his mind and integrate them with the harsh texture of reality. The two existed on different planes. Planes that only united for a few blessed individuals who went on to greatness.

But here it was again. He felt it so strongly.

A beautiful understanding transcended his doubts, washing over them with a cleansing clarity. A loving feeling going beyond fame and money, beyond dream and reality. A simplified, unified theme — service to mankind on the highest level. Tap the innate love supply and fill each soul that comes near. Use brain, hands and heart as a vessel of Innate Intelligence, a conduit to the Power. The power all have at their fingertips, but for most might as well be galaxies away. And yet, with the right exposure, everyone could benefit and even embrace. Critical mass set into motion, eternal healing as physical, mental and spiritual planes coalesce, exploding the shackles of the soul, letting the power pulse through each brain wave, reverberate through bones, muscles and organs, past the cellular level, until the very atoms themselves dance in cosmic ecstasy.

John's thoughts startled him and he caught himself. What the hell is going on? He took a quick look around to see if anyone was watching him. He had been so deep in thought, he had momentarily forgotten that he was sitting in a meeting with a group of people. But it had been more than just thought. It came from his mind, but he hadn't tried to think of it. He had just let go and merged with the energy in the room. He had tapped into what he could only describe as Universal Intelligence, or Innate, as many chiropractors called it. He had hooked up a direct line to God. For a moment he had glimpsed the big picture, where everything was possible. He had felt the flow, the love, the Power.

John was oblivious to the people who were now milling around the room, shaking hands and talking.

"Johnny. Johnny. Hello, Earth to John. Hey, guy, the meeting's over. You didn't fall asleep, did you? Man, you missed some great stuff, but that's okay, we can come back next month. What do ya say?"

John looked up at Jimmy's gigantic smile.

"No, Jimmy. I don't think I missed anything."

Chapter 9

The bespectacled man meticulously emptied the entire syringe into the large black dog.

"There you go, Mildred, now show me what a good girl you are and be alive in the morning when I get back."

Lamont looked at the half-dozen patches of whitish gray skin on the dog's hindquarters. He wondered what had created the pronounced scars – a fight with another dog, a car, or some kind of abuse from the animal's owner. He wasn't worried, the dog's check-in exam looked fine. Mildred's blood chemistry, CBC, saliva, feces and structure were all negative for any disqualifying values. The Source, although irritatingly slow, had a reputation for delivering sound, healthy animals and Blackmore West hadn't had any problems so far with its subjects.

The time it took to acquire the dogs continued to be a problem, however, and research had slowed to a crawl while he waited for the Source to locate his unusual request for only Labradors. Normally, Blackmore bred the bulk of its canines, but the majority of the research was done with Beagles. Now, the need for haste with CD4C made the 9-week gestation period unacceptable, and even if newborns could be used instead of waiting the additional six weeks for the pups to mature, the demand for Labradors was so great that not even one bitch could be spared for breeding purposes. Lamont had to test each Labrador that he got his hands on, and he had to test them now.

He was so close to finishing CD4C, it was maddening. After each failure, he would refine his formula, swearing that the new conjoinment would be the one, and each time it would fail and new subjects would have to be located.

It was well known that specific breeds were vulnerable to certain diseases; however, he had not seen or read of such a breed-specific and catastrophic reaction to an attenuated virus before. It was bedeviling how the other breeds tested not only survived but had such a low occurrence of poor reactions. Neither he nor any of Blackmore's geneticists could find a reason why these dogs should not perform as well as their canine counterparts.

Mildred sat in her cage watching Weedleman take the last of his notes in a brown hardbound notebook. The dog's ears twitched as the scientist snapped on the video camera located directly in front of her. The tall skinny man turned on a light directly above the cage and then walked over and flipped off the main light just before leaving the room. Mildred whimpered quietly as the researcher shut the door to the laboratory.

The lymph nodes near Mildred's buttock muscle first detected the virus that had been weakened by Blackmore's proprietary attenuation method. Mildred's body went on full alert while it attempted to identify the strange and threatening invader. The immune system desperately searched for the correct lymphocytic clone from which it could build the proper antibody to fight the foreign virus. These clones were specific for each type of invading organism and had been developed according to the dog's gene pool during its development as an embryo. Normally, the dog's immune system would develop a sensitivity to the invader's antigen and then, through this process, use the specific clones as a place to start, developing an army of sensitized lymphocytes or antibodies to fight the disease. The problem for Mildred was that the antigens from the virus in CD4C had been slightly mutated by Blackmore's attenuation process, altering their appearance and electrical matrix. The Labrador was genetically lacking the proper clone from which to develop the appropriate antibody.

The dog's immune system panicked. Innately realizing the grave consequences of not mounting a proper defense, it began to desperately produce a similar antibody, which, unfortunately, was aggressive to the dog's own tissue. The newly sensitized antibodies were now released by the millions into the dog's circulation, moving out to fight each and every organ.

The dog lay down on her side and began panting in an

attempt to cool off. Soon, Mildred was unable to lift her head off the hard floor of her cage, while inside her the destruction raged on. As more tissue was destroyed, additional antigens were released, signaling a greater need for antibodies to be produced against them.

The antibodies were being carried by the blood stream and many found their way to the walls of the dog's heart. There the antibodies did what they were erroneously programmed to do — attack. During the next several hours, layer after layer of the cells accumulated in all regions of the heart, congesting the openings and decreasing the heart's ability to deliver vital oxygen to the rest of the body. Gradually, this lack of oxygen generated a hypovolemic shock, escalating the tissue destruction and mercifully bringing an end to the dog's suffering.

At six a.m. Lamont Weedleman was awakened by ringing. Groggily, he moved the phone to his ear, unwilling to remove his visual deprivation mask just yet.

"Yeah, this is Weedleman, and this better be good."

"Lamont? This is Stanley Crider, and I'm afraid it's not good."

"Jesus, Stan, I finally fell asleep about an hour ago and now, I suppose you're going to ruin the rest of my day."

Lamont Weedleman had always had a problem sleeping, and since the work with his latest project, it was getting worse. He already knew what the bad news was going to be.

"Mildred Six expired about twenty minutes ago. We need to talk; how long will it take for you to get down here?"

"Give me forty-five minutes. I'll come to your office."

The walls in Stanley Crider's office were lined with certificates of merit and plaques recognizing achievements in chemistry, as well as drug research and development. His attention was focused, however, on the NASDAQ stock exchange report when a rather haggard Lamont Weedleman walked in. Apparently forty-five minutes was not enough time for a shower or a shave and the clothes hanging on his gaunt frame looked like they had either been slept in or come from a pile next to the bed.

"Christ, Lamont, are you losing weight?"

"Yeah, it's from missing breakfast. So what's so important that I had to rush down here?"

"Sit down, Lamont." Crider motioned to a chair and then waited for the lanky man to get situated. "You've done some great work with the CD4C project. The thing with the Labradors is unfortunate and I'm sorry about waking you with the bad news this morning."

Weedleman shrugged his shoulders.

"This is not a perfect world, Lamont, and I think that as researchers we tend to lose touch with reality at times."

"Come on, Stan, cut the crap. You didn't drag me out of bed this morning to philosophize. What's going on? Are they pulling the plug on me?"

Crider studied him for a moment.

"On the contrary, the board has been keeping close tabs on your work and they are satisfied with CD4C."

"What the hell are you talking about?"

"I'm talking about finishing with the FDA and then going to market, Lamont."

"You're not serious."

"Everyone feels that the Labradors are a fluke and the problem is limited to one breed of canines. They feel you're chasing your tail, no pun intended, and your lab problem is unrelated to the target vaccine users. The usual monitored public application will be initiated as soon as we can get clearance."

Crider paused and watched the news sink in. "Come on, Weedleman. You tested CD4C more thoroughly than the majority of the new drugs hitting the market today. This is good news, Lamont! Maybe now you can start eating breakfast again and gain some of that weight back."

"I don't know, right now I don't feel so hungry." Weedleman stood and moved toward the door.

"Lamont, everything will be fine. You should be proud; this is a great achievement."

Weedleman stared at his friend. He suddenly felt more tired than before, as if all the stress and loss of sleep from the last few weeks had finally caught up to him. His voice was a weak whisper. "If you say so, Stan."

Sally Hobbs was in the laboratory when Lamont Weedleman walked in. She immediately noticed his dilapidated appearance and felt bad for him. He must be taking the failure with Mildred Six a little harder than the rest. She didn't blame him; she had hoped they wouldn't have to lose any more Labradors. It practically made her cry every time she found them dead or watched them die in such a painful and violent way. She was rooting for Dr. Weedleman's success with whatever drug it was that he was trying to develop just so these poor dogs wouldn't have to suffer any longer.

Dr. Weedleman stopped in front of the cage where Mildred Six lay on her side. The dog's mouth was gaping open, its long swollen tongue hanging down, resting on the floor of the cage. A white, foamy saliva had pooled and was growing in size. The man stood silent, staring at the dead animal.

"Ms. Hobbs, I won't be in today. Do the standard postmortem and then collect all records related to these experiments and place them in the red files in the cabinet in my office." He peered up from the cage with bloodshot eyes and handed her a small ring of keys. "Leave the keys on my desk and lock the door on your way out. I'll call you tomorrow."

She watched him slowly shuffle from the lab. Her concern grew as she looked at the keys in her hand. She had only been in his office once before, during her interview seven months ago. It was an unspoken rule that his office was off limits, and the casualness with which he handed her the keys was a testament to how ill he must be feeling.

She opened the cage and began the task at hand. After putting on a pair of latex gloves, she gently slid Mildred from the cage and onto an aluminum cart of approximately the same height. "Poor thing. You were a good dog and deserved better." Sally took a large sample of the dog's foamy saliva and placed it in a specimen cup. She then collected all of the standard tissue samples for immediate analysis. Next, she hefted the stiffening carcass into a large cryostorage container on wheels and after snapping down the airtight lid all the way around, she lifted one corner and burped out the excess air. There was a rope attached to the unit that she used to pull it over to the walk-in refrigerator. She placed a descriptive label on the container and then parked it inside where it would stay until the coroner was ready to do the autopsy.

It took a minute or two for Lamont's eyes to adjust to the darkness, and when it passed, he found a seat at the bar. He had been waiting on a park bench across the street for eleven o'clock when the Glass Bass opened for the day. As soon as the bartender tied his apron, Lamont ordered a double Scotch straight up. He took a big slug and felt it splash on the bottom of his empty stomach. He peered between the bottles at his reflection in the mirror behind the bar. "Hell, I'll put on some weight." He tried to think of nothing, preferring to just sit and absorb the clear brown fluid that he held before him.

"This will be my great achievement." He held up his glass and laughed. "To see how fast a 48-year-old man who skipped breakfast can load his bloodstream with ethyl alcohol." He chugged another large mouthful and thought about the controls he would need to make his experiment valid and scientifically acceptable. He knew he would need at least two other losers at the bar going shot for shot with him, one of course, with a placebo, perhaps herbal tea that tasted like scotch. He motioned for the bartender to refill his glass and thought of the roadblocks he would no doubt encounter. What if the bartender didn't pour exactly two shots in each subject's glass? What if an alcoholic at another bar was doing the same experiment and got shitfaced and published first? What if the great Weedleman the Third had to take a piss and accidentally locked himself in the bathroom? He supposed it wouldn't matter anyway; the Glass Bass would say that they were satisfied with his work as is, and cut him off.

He downed the last of his round and slammed the glass on the bar. "Himmie agin, I wanna be sure thissus a double blind study."

The bartender frowned and flipped up the scotch bottle. "I think I missed something, fella."

Lamont Weedleman peered up from his glass. "Nooo, actually it's I who missed summmething."

Sally documented the last of the tissue sample results and closed the notebook entitled: Canine Testing — Weedleman. She set it on a large stack of notebooks and dug in her pocket for Dr. Weedleman's keys. His office door had a standard doorknob lock as well as a dead bolt that required a different key. She swung the door open and gasped. The room was a complete disaster. Stacks of paper and medical texts were everywhere. A small desk in the middle of the room strained under the weight of material stacked three feet high. She spotted a large upright metal filing cabinet in one corner and weaved her way through the maze of stacks, trying not to knock anything over. She sorted through the key ring until she found a small key that fit the double-door cabinet. Inside were three horizontal drawers approximately three feet wide, and when she pulled out the top one she found it filled with hanging files. Approximately one-third were red and grouped together in the middle of the drawer. At the top of each file an index label described its contents. The subjects were alphabetical and exceptionally well organized, a significant contrast to the rest of the office. Sally read the headings to find the proper location for the data she had collected. She took the liberty to browse through each title, stopping when she reached: Purpose of Experiment.

Instinctively glancing around to be sure she was alone, she pulled out the file. She assured herself that she wasn't doing anything wrong, especially now that it appeared the experiment had been cancelled. For months she had worked on this project, handling hundreds of creatures and watching the Labradors perish. She needed to fill in the missing pieces and perhaps use these to justify her involvement in the harm that was caused to the animals. On the first page of the Purpose file was the name White Rhino, followed by a concise paragraph stating the nature of the experiment. She read carefully, suddenly doubting she would secure the peace of mind she desperately sought. The common cold? Was this the dangerous illness with which she and her heroic lab did battle? Was this really the reason Mildreds One through Six had been sacrificed? A sick feeling overwhelmed her and she felt her spirits sinking. She hurriedly finished her filing, then closed and locked the larger drawer. Stumbling to the desk, she dropped the keys in disgust. At the door she turned the lock from the inside, never looking up to see the surveillance camera mounted on the wall above it. "Those bastards," she blurted as she slammed the door closed.

Chapter 10

Dr. John Truley carefully restored the normal motion to Bud Clifford's sacrum with a gentle push that he timed perfectly with the patient's breath.

"Now, I want you to turn on your side so we can put your third lumbar back where it belongs." The doctor expertly positioned the man so that the vertebra went back into place with the slightest effort. "Did you know that the nerves that exit the spine near that vertebra are responsible for making your bladder, prostate and sexual organs function properly?"

"Thanks, Doc, maybe my wife won't show me the gate after all!"

John smiled. "Let's check it again in four weeks." He left for the next room and was surprised to find it empty. Back at the front desk he waited for Janine to finish scheduling Bud Clifford.

"Do we have a break?" he asked.

"Our new patient has car problems. She just called from her cellular. She apologized and rescheduled for later this week."

The doctor frowned. "Great. Now there's no excuse but to work on my hell pile." He walked into his office, plopped down in the chair, and pulled the large stack toward him. It was comprised of assorted professional journals he had yet to review, the latest in the never-ending requests for information from insurance companies and numerous unopened bills and junk mail. It amazed him how fast it could accumulate. Every couple of weeks, just to catch up, he placed his unopened bills in a medium-sized box and took them home. He would spend a weekend opening, sorting and hopefully paying. He figured this process alone ate up the equivalent of three or four days per month. He absolutely detested this part of his life and was readily distracted from its dreariness.

He thought of the meeting that he had attended the previous evening and his remarkable experience. How was he supposed to be so gallant and romantic about his purpose when he had to sit and open bad news mail one tenth of his life? Disgusted, he snapped on the radio and began mindlessly flipping through stations. How do people break through the morass that comes with daily life? Junk mail. Taxes. The fear of lawsuits. What was that quote by B.J. Palmer? He found a piece of paper, and wrote out what he remembered, then read it out loud.

"Now and then one person who seeks to receive, does receive, and makes history . . ."

He looked back at his stack of bills. "My receiver must be broken."

The annoying music from a radio commercial mercifully stopped and an enthusiastic voice broke in. *"Welcome back to* Health Talk, *where we talk about your health for two hours every morning during the workweek starting at 10 a.m. If you have health concerns, call us at 1-800-GET WELL. I'm your host, Dr. Bill Bordello. Now, let's talk to Mary from Cardiff. Hello, Mary, you're on the air."*

"Hello, Dr. Bill, I'm a first time caller and I just want to tell you that I love your show and listen every morning."

"Thank you, Mary. How can I help you?"

"Well, it's my husband. He snores so badly that it literally rattles our windows at night. He falls asleep so fast I don't have a chance. I've tried everything. I'd push him on his side or stomach but I can't budge him, and when I wake him up, he just falls back asleep in a minute or two and starts snoring again. I've tried sleeping in other rooms, but I can hear him from every room in the house, even if I close all the doors." The woman became increasingly upset as she described her 20-year plight with her husband's condition and sounded as if she were in tears as she finished. *"I finally got up the courage to call you, Dr. Bill. Please help me, I'm at my wit's end!"*

"Whoa! Wait a minute, Mary. Don't they have laws against spousal abuse? I mean come on; you've suffered long enough. Have you ever tried those little clamps that hold the nasal pas-

sages open? Very often that can free a person's breathing enough to stop snoring problems."

"Do you think that might work?"

"It is certainly worth a try. Now you call us back and let us know how it goes, all right, Mary from Cardiff?"

Oh thank you, Dr. Bill. Thank you. Thank you." The woman was nearly hysterical as Dr. Bill disconnected her line.

"Let's talk health. That number again, 800 GETWELL. Let's go to line 6 where we have Gina from Oceanside. Hello, Gina. You're on the air."

John Truley picked up the phone and dialed the station's number.

"AM 960, *Health Talk*."

"Hi, I'd like to speak with Dr. Bill."

"What is the nature of your health concern?"

"Actually, it's someone else's health that I'm concerned about."

"Have you ever been on radio before?"

"No, I have not."

"Okay, turn your radio down or better yet, turn it off. You can hear the show on the phone while you wait. There are a couple of callers ahead of you so it will be a few minutes."

The girl's voice was suddenly replaced by the live talk show. While John Truley listened to the next caller complaining of frequent urination, he wondered what possessed him to suddenly do this. It was not like him to rock the boat, and he wasn't sure if what he was considering had any legal implications. All he knew was that he felt he had shirked too many of his responsibilities up until now, and thankfully, he was experiencing a glimmer of what it would be like to operate from pure intent, unencumbered by inhibitions. Lethargy and inaction had gotten him to where he was and with admission of the incredible dissatisfaction he felt, he now chose to change, however futile and misguided his initial steps may be.

He was awakened from his thoughts by Dr. Bill's voice

that was now loud, clear, and directed at him.

"Hello, Line Eight, are you there?"

"Yes, hello, this is Dr. John Truley." He felt an unusual source of fortification as he listened to himself speak calmly and boldly into the phone. "I know a little girl who recently became ill and I would like to tell you about her."

"It's a pleasure to have you on the phone this morning. First tell us, doctor, what type of medicine do you practice?"

"I'm a chiropractor; however, that has little bearing on what I have to say."

"Okay, I'll bite. Go ahead, Dr. Truley."

"Two days ago a little girl in my son's class vomited on his back. When I arrived at his school with a change of clothes, I found the girl in the nurse's station in shock and I dialed 911."

Dr. Bill's eyes lit up with excitement. He shook his head and waved off the program director who was signaling at her watch for a commercial break. Flipping off his microphone he whispered to her, "This is juicy." He then flipped the microphone back on. "Oh, how awful. Please, continue."

"The paramedics came and took her to the hospital where, thankfully, the doctors were able to save her life. Her name is Katie Prespo. She is six years old and she is now lying in Good Samaritan Hospital with probable brain damage."

"Oh, that is tragic. How did this happen?"

"One hour before she threw up on my son, Katie Prespo was injected with a mandatory DPT vaccine that all children her age are expected to submit to."

"Okay, now hold on. Doctor, are you saying the vaccine caused this little girl to go into shock and then caused her brain damage?"

"It's not the first time that this has happened and it won't be the last. A number of children react tragically to vaccinations every year. The whole system is poorly monitored and only a small percentage of reactions are even reported by the medical profession."

Janine stood in his doorway signaling that the adjustment rooms were full and he was getting behind.

Dr. Truley nodded to her and continued. "Vaccines have a significant number of casualties associated with them and parents are not being told the truth regarding these risks. They are also not being informed of their constitutional rights. I spoke to the girl's mother and she was shocked to find out that there was a risk in being vaccinated. She was appalled that no one bothered to inform her of the dangers or her rights in the matter. Now, please excuse me, I must go, but let me just say one thing to any parents who are listening. Please find out the facts before you choose to have your children vaccinated and learn your rights while you are at it. Thank you very much, Dr. Bill."

"Okay, that was an interesting call from local chiropractor, John Truley. We'll take a break. Don't go away."

William Bordello, Ph.D. in health sciences, looked over in astonishment at Kim, the program director. "Did you get a load of that guy?"

"Yes, I did, and apparently our listeners did too. All of the phones lit up!"

Dr. Bill's jaw dropped. "All of them?"

"All of them."

"Whoa, baby, let's ride this for all its worth!" He snapped on his microphone when the commercial ended. "We're back. This is Dr. Bill and you are listening to *Health Talk*. If you can't get through, keep trying. Now, let's go to line four. Hello, you're on the air."

John Truley had taken a casual lunch at a healthy Chinese place after finishing his morning patients and now he sailed back into the office for the afternoon appointments. He felt somewhat liberated after his morning radio deed. He didn't know how smart it was, in terms of his own professional well-being, but at least he took action instead of letting this incident involving Katie Prespo just get swept under the rug. He was going to tell anyone who would listen, let the chips fall where they may.

When he entered Room One, he saw his patient, Gabbie Jones, sitting with a woman in her late 60's who bore a striking resemblance to her.

"Hi, Doctor Truley, I'd like you to meet my mother, Eleanor Dowdy. I finally talked her into coming to see you about her neck."

"How do you do, Mrs. Dowdy? It is a pleasure to meet you. May I compliment you on doing such a fine job of raising your daughter? I am sure it was quite a challenge."

Gabbie laughed. "She would have thought that was real funny, Doc, but she can't hear to save her life."

"Oh, I see," John said, slightly embarrassed at the missed humor. "What about hearing aids?"

"She's so stubborn, she refuses to wear them. Sometimes I think she prefers not to hear anything."

"Well, to each her own. Why don't we see if we can help with her neck problem?"

The examination took a little longer than usual because John had to first demonstrate, with the help of Gabbie, each test that he wanted the elderly woman to perform. She showed a significant loss of normal neck motion and had a distinct head tilt when at rest. John suspected that she had moderate to advanced arthritis of the spine and, with more hand signals and gestures, had her remove her earrings and necklace and put on a gown for a basic set of neck X-rays. Eleanor was quite cooperative and didn't show any other indications of being the stinker that Gabbie had warned him about.

"Your mother is a dear, sweet lady." They were waiting for the films to develop.

"Boy, she's got you fooled. Try living with her for a couple of days." She winked.

The films dropped from the processor and John retrieved them. Placing them up on the adjustment room view box, he did a quick review of the salient findings.

"Eleanor's cervical spine shows some definite degeneration, perhaps a little advanced for her age, but not too much so. She still has reasonable disc spacing between the bones." He pointed at the little pads between each vertebra on the side view. "Now, this is where I found real restriction when I palpated, or touched, her neck. This X-ray shows the very top part her spine. We took it with her mouth open so her teeth wouldn't block our view. Look at the second bone and you can see how turned it is."

"I can see it!" Gabbie shouted excitedly. She looked at her mother and pointed at the X-ray. Eleanor nodded but didn't step any closer than where she stood, six or seven feet back from the view box. Gabbie looked at John and shrugged her shoulders.

"This is what we chiropractors call a subluxation. This bone is not properly aligned with the bone next to it and therefore is, among other things, not moving properly."

"Can you fix it, Doctor Truley?" Gabbie asked matter of factly.

"I can adjust it and we can see how fast your mother's body responds. I'm sure that with the condition of her spine, her age, and the length of time this has likely been present, it will take several visits to stabilize; however, some of the benefits may be noticed much sooner. Shall we begin?"

Gabbie put her mouth up to the woman's ear and shouted, "He's going to crack your neck, Mom." The woman smiled and nodded.

John had no idea if the woman heard or understood, especially in light of the way her daughter so tactfully explained the procedure. He figured it was as close to informed consent as he was going to get. John had Mrs. Dowdy lie down on her back while he sat on a stool at the end of the table where he could lean slightly forward and easily reach her neck. He carefully slid his fingers between the table and her skull, lifting gently and taking the weight of her head into his hands. He could feel a faint pulse just under her scalp, as well as the rigidity of the muscles just below her skull. Using his fingertips, he gently massaged the taut fibers and after a minute or two, the tissue began to warm up, softening and becoming more yielding to the gentle stretch that he induced by nudging the top two vertebrae first right then left. John focused intently on the woman's spine, until the decor of the room, the patient's daughter, and the ringing phone vanished from his mind.

The words of Dr. Clarence Gonstead, one of the most famous chiropractors of all time recounted in his mind, "First become one with the patient, doctor, then become one with the bone."

Using a specific area of his right index finger, he contacted exactly the right spot on Mrs. Dowdy's second vertebra. Supporting the woman's head with his left hand, he gently lifted and turned it slightly. He expertly brought the bone to tension at the end of its limited range of motion and gave it a gentle but quick thrust, using just the right amount of force. A satisfying pop was heard as the bone set into its appropriate position.

Dr. John Truley had properly located and identified Mrs. Dowdy's misaligned second cervical vertebra. He could not, however, tell what had caused it. Based on its appearance in the X-ray, he speculated that the problem had been around for at least ten years.

Mrs. Dowdy's symptoms had gradually worsened over the last couple of years, but she hadn't given much thought to the possibility that her troubles may have started several years before that. In fact, her memory of July 4th, 1983 was quite vague indeed. It was on that day that she had enjoyed a boat ride with her family on San Diego Bay. While she was turning her head to talk to her daughter, the speeding boat hit a wake and became momentarily airborne. Eleanor's neck extended backward as the boat flew through the air. The receptors in her neck muscles alerted her brain that a dangerously sudden and extreme stretch was taking place. Sensing the potential for muscle tearing and spinal cord injury, her brain quickly ordered a contraction of all of the muscles needed to bring her chin back down toward her chest. A second or two later, when the boat landed, the flexor muscles were firing at 97% of their total capacity while the muscles that oppose flexion were completely shut off in order to aid in the body's emergency task. Once so committed to flexion of the head in order to minimize injury, the body was unable to switch gears and compensate for the sudden deceleration of the boat's impact with the water. Eleanor's head snapped forward hard, limited only by her chin striking her chest. The strain of the sudden hyperflexion and the impact of her chin on her sternum while her neck was unprotected and rotated, caused the second vertebra to wedge back, there to remain for the next seventeen years. The entire incident was over in less than three seconds.

Gabbie, who had been looking straight ahead at that moment, didn't see what happened to Eleanor, partly because her brain was preoccupied with its own management of the affair. The boat ride ended a few minutes later, after a few more bumps of lesser magnitude.

Eleanor had a stiff neck for several days for which she visited her general practitioner. After a brief inspection, the doctor ordered X-rays. Finding no indication of fracture, the patient was prescribed muscle relaxors and instructed to take her choice of over-the-counter pain relievers. Within a couple of weeks, Eleanor's neck was almost pain free and she forgot about the incident, paying little attention to the slight stiffness she now experienced when turning her head all the way to the side. She figured she was getting older after all, and decided to avoid any future boat rides.

Now, she lay on the table in this unusual doctor's office. The man had indicated that he would like her to remain resting for ten minutes. She didn't mind; she was feeling quite relaxed. There was a warm feeling at the base of her skull, as well as a pleasant sensation that her head was becoming lighter. Mucous began pooling in the back of her throat and she swallowed it, wondering if she was getting a cold. This happened repeatedly during the ten minutes that she lay there, and each time she swallowed, more fluid would collect, making her head feel lighter. Her ears began popping suddenly, as if she was coming down from a higher altitude. Amidst the gurgling and frequent popping in her head, she began to hear office sounds like Dr. Truley talking in the next room, the phone ringing at the front desk and even the bells on the front door to the office. She became very excited because for the first time in years she was hearing without the use of the hearing aids that she absolutely detested.

After finishing a routine maintenance adjustment with the patient in Room Two, John met Gabbie in the hall on her way back from the lavatory.

"Your mother's adjustment went very well. She'll need to come in twice a week for the next several weeks."

From behind the closed door of Room One an enthusiastic voice yelled, "I'll be here!"

Chapter 11

John eased into his garage and stepped from the car. He might as well have been walking on air as he clenched his fist and smiled, savoring the moment.

He looked forward to spending time with Jeffrey and walked next door to the Michaels' house. Mary and Frank Michael were a godsend for John. He had known them for a couple of years and they loved Jeffrey. They had a warm, clean house and were like a second family. Although he and Jeffrey had never talked about it, John knew his son saw Mary as a mother that he'd never had. Todd Michael, Jeffrey's best friend, was two years older and when the boys went places together they were often mistaken for brothers, much to their delight. Jeffrey stayed at the Michaels' after school until John came home from work in the evening. Occasionally, they would ask Jeffrey to join them for a weekend at their getaway home near Palm Springs.

When Mary opened the door, she greeted John and informed him that dinner was almost ready. She would neither allow him to take Jeffrey, nor decline her offer to join them for dinner. Mary was a great cook, a status that John had never quite achieved.

"Dad!" Jeffrey came running for a hug.

"Hi, guy." John gave him a big squeeze.

"We're eating spaghetti!" Jeffrey looked at Todd as they both chimed in unison, "Squash, that is!" They made faces typical of little boys talking about vegetables.

"Ah, you guys don't know what's good." Frank extended his massive hand to John. "Come in and sit down."

Frank might have been the biggest man that John knew. He stood about six feet, six inches and John guessed that he tipped the scales at a minimum of 270 pounds, which was all muscle. A knee injury had finished his short NFL career, but never stopped Frank from staying in tip-top shape with daily visits to the gym. Frank never talked about his disappointing injury – or his shortened football career, for that matter – preferring to tell John, over a beer or two, about his exploits as a bodyguard and bouncer during his younger years. John was thankful that he had never seen Frank be anything other than gentle and kind.

Mary placed half of a spaghetti squash on a plate and followed it with a green salad as Frank shoved a bowl of steaming pasta noodles in front of him.

"I can see that I'm going to have to drop by more often."

Mary smiled. "You come over anytime you want; at least that way, I won't have to worry about you."

"Yeah, you could stand some meat on your bones, guy. How you gonna have the strength to crack those backs all day." Frank wiped his face with a napkin, inadvertently flexing a huge biceps adorned with a tattoo of a menacing cobra poised to strike. "By the way, how's that sweat shop you're running down there?" Frank grinned.

John was used to the good-natured kidding. He knew Frank admired his work and had used his services on several occasions.

"Wait 'til you hear what happened today!" He told the story of Gabbie and Mrs. Dowdy.

Jeffrey beamed when his father finished. "Wow, Dad. That's cool. You made that woman hear again."

"That's wonderful!" Mary added. "We're so proud of you."

"Does this mean you're not going out of business after all?" Frank laughed, slapping John on the back.

Mary gave Frank a stern look. "Oh, will you stop!"

Frank winked at her, and they were all laughing when John's pager went off.

"Oh-oh, must be some blind guy who heard about you," Frank roared.

Mary rolled her eyes and wagged her head.

"Well, I'd better go and make this call. The dinner was great. Thank you."

"Nonsense, we still have dessert coming. Just use our phone." Mary pointed to the kitchen.

"Come on, Dad," Jeffrey begged.

John knew the pager normally meant an emergency and chances were he'd need Jeffrey to stay while he took care of it. "Okay, let me see what this is about." He excused himself and went into the kitchen where he could smell the bread pudding baking in the oven. He dialed the number, hoping that he could get off easily by offering some advice to get the person through the night. They might be able to wait until his office was open the next day. A vaguely familiar voice answered the phone.

"Hello, this is Dr. Truley. Did you page me?"

"Great, thanks for calling me back, sorry to disturb you. I called your office phone and the answering service gave me your emergency number. I just had to speak to you tonight!"

John recognized the now distinct voice and couldn't resist. "What is your health concern?"

"Very good, Dr. Truley!" Bill Bordello laughed. "That was quite a call today. I am so sorry for the little girl. Our listeners were quite moved and the phones were ringing off the hook for the rest of the day. How would you like to be on the show tomorrow so we can spend some time talking about it on the air?"

John was silent for a moment. The ball was rolling. His abrupt action today had started something that he wouldn't have dreamed of less than a week ago. He now had a chance to tell thousands of people about the dangers of vaccines and hopefully present natural health care at the same time. Maybe he could make something positive out of the tragedy that left Katie Prespo brain damaged. He felt a surge of excitement as he got ready to take another step of faith into the uncharted waters that seemed to be taking him further and further away from his comfort zone.

"I'll do it. Just tell me where and when."

"Who was it, Dad?"

"It was Dr. Bill from the radio, Jeffrey, and he wants me to be on his show tomorrow!"

"Look out world. Dr. John Truley's got a big soapbox now!" Frank rolled his eyes.

They all laughed as John took his seat. In front of him, a parfait glass was filled with warm bread pudding, its whipped cream topping just starting to melt. John Truley smiled and reached for his spoon.

Chapter 12

He arrived at the radio station just a few minutes before he was due to go on. He was nervous and slightly frazzled from seeing as many of his scheduled patients as he could before leaving his office at this usually busy time of day. He knew they would understand why Janine needed to cancel their appointments for this show, but John Truley hated to inconvenience any more patients than he had to.

The station was on the next to last floor of a tall building in downtown San Diego. When the elevator opened, John could see a gorgeous view of the harbor and the Coronado Bridge. There were many small sailboats and a few windsurfers out this morning, gliding in every direction, then giving way to an enormous battleship heading out to sea.

"Hi, I'm Dr. John Truley."

A young, casually dressed receptionist sat behind a long wooden counter. She looked up and smiled. "Good, you made it; they're expecting you. Would you like to follow me?" She got up and motioned toward a hallway beyond a set of double doors.

"Nervous?" She pushed the door open for him.

"It shows, huh?"

They stepped through the double doors and were immediately greeted by the animated sounds of morning deejays talking and laughing on the air. John had always wondered how much coffee those guys drink before doing their shows. They seemed so hyper. She led him to a door about halfway down the hall on the left. Before going in the room, he glanced toward the end of the hallway where a red lighted sign read On the Air.

John was introduced to Dr. Bill, who appeared to be in his late 20's or early 30's. He was athletic looking and wearing a shiny, yellow running suit and a new pair of

Nike cross training shoes. Dr. Bill stood up and shook his hand. His small, yet firm hand was connected to a wiry pale forearm covered with coarse black hair. John liked him right away but could tell he was full of nervous energy. He made a mental note to decline if anyone should offer him a cup of the station's coffee.

"Thanks for coming, Dr. Truley. We don't have much time. I was just going over the game plan with Kim."

John nodded at the program director and she smiled.

"I'll do my usual thing and get the show going. Then I'll introduce you. Just answer my questions and everything will be fine. How do you feel?"

"I guess I'm all right. The live factor is a little scary."

"Ahh, it's only one or two hundred thousand people." He checked his watch. "Don't think about them; it's only you and me when we go in there, okay?"

They made their way back into the hallway. A commercial was blaring as they walked toward the door below the red lighted sign. Two men came out wearing shorts and T-shirts. They were both somewhat overweight, grungy, and looked like they had just indulged in an all night fraternity party.

As they passed in the hallway one of them, carrying the remnants of a box of doughnuts, shouted, "Help me, Dr. Bill, my hemorrhoids are really burning, what should I do?"

Dr. Bill looked annoyed. "Why don't you sit on a fire hydrant and have a civil service engineer turn it on for you!"

The balding one with the thick glasses howled, "Good one, William," pointing at his partner with a smirk.

"Clowns," Dr. Bill muttered as he entered the broadcast room.

John stood aside to let Kim go in first. She looked at him, shaking her head. "They do that every day."

The room was full of compact disc players, CDs and

props like whistles, tambourines, drums and horns. Kim began clearing empty cups, soda cans and various candy wrappers from the counter near the microphones.

"Those guys get away with murder because their ratings are so high." She wadded a family size potato chip bag.

A large window stretched the entire length of the far wall and provided a breathtaking view that topped the one in the reception area.

Still nervous, John tried speaking to make sure his voice worked. "Must be easy to do the weather from this room."

Dr. Bill ignored his comment and looked at him solemnly. "Dr. Truley, you struck a nerve yesterday and it woke up the listeners. You made our show controversial and controversy is good for ratings and therefore good for the show. Can you do it again?"

John shrugged. "I can only tell you what I know."

"Well, that's enough if yesterday is any indication." Bill smiled, motioning for John to take a seat near a microphone.

The last commercial ended and Kim hit a button playing a familiar jazz melody, which Dr. Bill broke in on after a few seconds.

"Good morning, one and all, a beautiful Thursday to you, this is Dr. Bill and you are tuned to *Health Talk* where each weekday morning we talk about your health concerns. This morning we have a special guest with us whom I will introduce momentarily. Those of you who were tuned in yesterday heard this health professional call with a frightening report regarding a very sick little girl and he is here today to give us an update. I ask that you hold your calls until we first have a chance to ask him some questions here in the studio. We will open up the discussion and then you'll have a chance to talk with him also. Now, I would like to welcome Dr. John Truley, Chiropractor, from Solana Beach. Dr. Truley, welcome to

Health Talk!"

"Thank you, Dr. Bill. It's an honor to be here."

"Why don't we start with the phone call you made to *Health Talk* yesterday. Could you summarize what you told me?"

"Yes, thank you for the opportunity to share this information with your listeners. What I am about to describe happened just three days ago and it has troubled me, as I am sure it will you. On Monday, Katie Prespo was as bright and healthy as anyone else in her first grade class, including my son, Jeffrey. Monday morning, public health officials injected a DPT vaccine into her body. Within one hour she was throwing up and her body was beginning to convulse. She lost consciousness, stopped breathing and swallowed her tongue. After several hours of life-saving resuscitation, her life was spared; however, Katie now has brain damage and is in a coma. Most of this occurred before her mother could even arrive at the hospital."

There were a few seconds of silence as Dr. Bill let the story sink in for the listeners.

"Dr. Truley, you were there at the school and, in fact, personally called 911. In your mind, could there be any other reason why Katie became so ill?"

"Dr. Bill, it is difficult to be 100% sure of anything, but what happened to Katie Prespo happens to a small percentage of children every year. The medical community knows this and considers it a reasonable loss. The real crime is that parents are not properly informed of the risk, of the validity or lack thereof, in regard to the vaccines, and, lastly, of the fact that they can choose to forgo the vaccine altogether."

"Now, hold on Dr. Truley. If everyone stopped vaccinating their children, wouldn't these diseases become epidemic once again?"

"The research does not substantiate that these vaccines are actually working. In recent studies it has been shown that when an epidemic does break out with one of these diseases, the rate of infection is often similar in vaccinated and non-vaccinated children."

"Okay, let's just say that's true for a moment. Then why are we taking these risks of reaction like the one Katie experienced?"

"It's greed, Dr. Bill. The drug companies would lose over a billion dollars a year if the public became fully informed and saw vaccinations for what they really are — a 20th century superstition."

Bill glanced at the program manager who made motions at him that he translated to mean all the circuits were full; the phone lines were completely backed up.

The professionally decorated loft was located in the newly chic Gaslamp Quarter of downtown San Diego where, in recent years, the Italian restaurants and assorted nightclubs had experienced a much-appreciated boon in popularity. Station manager Larry Laguna enjoyed all the perks that living downtown had to offer — especially the night life. Although in his thirties, he was a late bloomer, only recently enjoying the spoils of bachelorhood. He was a little shorter and pudgier than he preferred at five foot six and 195 pounds, a reason for his earlier under confidence, but he was a smooth talker and appeared financially successful. A few years ago he had found that those latter attributes more than compensated for any of his physical shortcomings, both real and imagined. He had found his style of late, and was becoming increasingly comfortable with Larry Laguna, businessman, playboy.

His bushy dark eyebrows almost met in the middle of his forehead, but his eyes, his most complimented feature, were light brown and he imagined that they mesmerized his female prey. His red sports car awaited him in the parking garage and his closet was full of designer slacks and silk shirts. The air in his apartment was indelibly laden with *Polo for Men*.

On this morning, Larry took extra time away from 960

AM to entertain his newest girlfriend, Roxanne, a product of *Shanky's* discotech on 6th and B.

"Let's get some breakfast. I need fuel." Larry sat up on the edge of the bed and looked at himself in the mirrored closet doors. He never liked the way his stomach folded when he leaned forward without a shirt on. He looked up from his midsection and saw his partner's mischievous face in the reflection as she stood on the bed. Although he had seen her several times, he was still amazed at the sculpted muscles that made up her legs and abdomen. She was a fitness junky who in addition to teaching several aerobic classes daily, roller-bladed for hours on end, something he tried for all of twenty minutes before hastily retreating to his beloved car and street shoes. He was no match for her stamina and had recently wondered if she got a twisted satisfaction at pushing him to the brink of heart failure like some kind of psychotic, sexual drill sergeant. Before he could get to his feet she pounced, slapping her hard naked body on his back. With legs and arms locked around him she reared her wiry frame back, pulling him helplessly to the mattress. Deftly wriggling out from under him, she mounted him victoriously, straddling his chest while pinning his arms to the bed.

"You're going to earn your breakfast, Big Boy."

Larry surrendered, amazed at her ability to get the most out of his fatigued, yet newly aroused body. Just as she locked her mouth onto his, the phone rang.

"Don't answer it, Larry."

"Ahh, they'll just start paging me. I'll get rid of this bozo. You stay where you are. I'll be right back."

He took the call in the next room where he had set up a home fitness center, complete with a universal weight station, Soloflex machine, treadmill and ab-roller. The room represented his commitment to buying exercise equipment, just in case he ever mustered the discipline to use it. He snatched the football-shaped phone off its tee. The phone was his bonus for ordering *Sports Illustrated* in time for the swimsuit edition a few years back.

"Larry here."

"This is Travers. What the hell are you trying to do, Mr. Laguna?"

It was Clarence Travers of Apex Industries, 960 AM's largest sponsor account.

"I'm not sure what you mean." Larry watched his erection wane in the full-length mirror.

"My client doesn't see the logic in spending money to promote their products on the same station that attacks them."

"What are you talking about?"

"Perhaps you should turn on the radio and listen to your own show."

Larry heard a disapproving sternness and felt like he was ten years old when his father caught him doing the unthinkable. He knew he was in trouble but wasn't quite sure why.

"Come on, Larry!"

He covered the mouthpiece on the football and held it at arms' length. "Quiet, Roxie!"

"Pardon me?"

"Nothing, sir, I was just turning my radio on, I mean up. I was just turning it up." He switched ears. "Damn housekeeper must have turned it down."

"Well, you'd better send her down to your station!"

"Yes, sir."

"I'm hanging up now. My client has instructed me to withdraw all business with you if the program is not stopped promptly. Let's say five minutes." He hung up.

Larry looked at his watch and feverishly punched the numbers to the program manager's private line. While it was ringing, he perked his ears to the radio.

"You see, Dr. Bill, we are inoculating little children with attenuated or killed virus that can at times be devastating to their health. The drug companies won't even disclose how they measure attenuation, claiming that it's proprietary."

Larry was growing increasingly agitated when the program director finally picked up the phone.

"960 AM, Kim here."

"What the hell is going on? Who is that joker?"

"It's Dr. Truley, he's a chiropractor from..."

"Get him out of there!"

Roxanne appeared in the doorway wrapped in one of Larry's leopard print silk sheets.

"I'm leaving if you don't get off the phone."

"Good, get the hell out of here!"

"You asshole!"

"Stupid bitch!"

"Excuse me?"

"Not you, Kim. Never mind, just stop that freaking interview, and I mean now!"

"What?"

"Now!!!!"

Kim quickly laid down the phone to protect her ear, snatched a full sheet of paper, and with a fat felt marker wrote — STOP THE SHOW. She held it up to the glass so Dr. Bill could see it. John Truley's back was to her and he continued speaking. Bill saw the sign and wrinkled his forehead. "What?"

She brought the paper back down, scribbled and held it up again: STOP THE SHOW PER LARRY —— NOW!!!

"Excuse me, Dr. Truley. That's fascinating, but we have to take a station break. We'll be right back."

Ripping off the headphones, he shot from his chair and out the sound booth to Kim. "What the hell's going on?"

She held out the phone, mouthing "Larry."

He took it. "Yeah."

"Go to music, the show's over for the day!"

"You can't do that, Larry, what . . ."

"Do you like your job?"

Bill stopped short. "Yes."

"Then go to goddamn music. I'll explain later. Just stop as is. I'm coming down there!"

Larry slammed the football phone closed and spiked it hard on the plush, white Berber carpet.

Bill hung up the phone and looked at Kim. "That spineless S.O.B. stopped my show. Whoever pulls his strings apparently can't take the heat. Look at those phones!"

"Yeah, and what am I supposed to do about all those people who want to talk to you and Dr. Truley?" Kim pointed at the panel of flashing lights.

"I'll make a short announcement after the break and you take it from there with the music, at least until I find out what's going on."

Dr. Bill took his place across from John Truley and explained that they were experiencing problems. Kim began counting down with her fingers as the commercial came to an end.

"Hello, this is Dr. Bill and you've been listening to Health Talk. Unfortunately, we are presently experiencing some technical difficulties that will prevent us from completing today's program. Join me tomorrow at 10 a.m. when we will once again discuss your health concerns. We are sorry for the inconvenience." Bill pointed at Kim to start the music. He shook his head. "Son of a bitch, I'm sorry, Dr. Truley, you were doing a great job. The phone lines were completely lit up again! It's a shame we had these, uhh, technical difficulties. I certainly appreciate you coming down for the show and I hope that you were able to say most of what you wanted."

"Hey, don't worry about it. It was my pleasure. Thanks for asking me to be on and don't hesitate to call if you'd like to do it again." John stood and extended his hand to Dr. Bill. On his way out of the studio, he nodded at Kim who was furiously sifting through large stacks of compact discs. He chuckled to himself as he walked down the hallway thinking of what an exciting job these radio people had.

Fifteen minutes later, the receptionist was greeting station manager Larry Laguna as he stormed into the office.

"Send William Bordello to my office immediately! And hold all calls unless it's a sponsor."

She looked surprised. "It's funny you should mention that. We've had three of them call in the last ten minutes." She handed him a stack of messages. "They all asked for you."

Upon entering his office, Larry flung his designer satchel on the desk and fell into his red leather chair. He quickly checked the messages in his hand — all medical related sponsors – then Bill burst in. He was fuming, but one look at Larry told him to tone it down a couple of notches. Suddenly he became somehow amused.

"Talk!"

"Jesus Christ, Larry, who's got you by the balls?"

"The people who pay your salary — and mine, too, jerk-off. Now what the hell happened on your show and who is this guy?"

Bill described the phone call from John Truley the day before about Katie Prespo and her injury. "The guy was so straightforward and committed to his opinions that the callers went crazy. They ate it up. And our phones are still busy even though we cut off the show. Think what this will do for ratings, Larry!"

"Ratings aren't worth squat without sponsors, and you may have single-handedly bankrupted the whole damn station. Look at these messages — all sponsors, all pissed." Larry threw the slips of paper on the desk in front of Bill, as the phone rang.

Larry shook his head, trying to gain his composure. "What were you thinking, Guiermo?" He picked up the receiver and spoke with forced cheerfulness. "Hello, Larry Laguna here. Ah, Mr. Travers. I'm glad you called. As requested, we resolved the problem with great expediency."

Larry dragged his finger across his throat as he mouthed the words, "I'm going to kill you."

"Oh, I see. Yes. Okay. Excuse me, may I interrupt you,

Mr. Travers, for just one moment? I have *Health Talk's* host with me in the office. Perhaps he should hear this also. May I put you on speaker? I assure you my office is otherwise private. Okay, thank you, Mr. Travers."

Larry pressed the button for speaker.

"Mr. Travers, this is Dr. William Bordello. Please go ahead."

"As I was telling Mr. Laguna, my company feels that an unacceptable amount of damage has been done today. We are concerned for the well being of the public and have lost considerable confidence in your radio station."

Larry was now holding his forehead. "We're very sorry. How can we make it up to you? It was a terrible mistake. Perhaps some free air time?"

"We feel there is only one way you can correct this situation."

Larry looked like a man who'd just received a stay of execution. "What is it? We'll do anything!"

The firm voice continued. "This man, Truley, must be discredited, publicly, so that consumers, your listeners, will disregard his misinformation and the public trust can be restored."

"Ahh, okay, that sounds good. But how do we do that?" Larry was anxious to complete his penance, desperately wanting to rid his life of Mr. Traver's wrath. He shivered.

With a voice that Dr. Bill was beginning to greatly envy, Travers explained the plan. "Dr. Bordello will contact John Truley and apologize for the interruption of today's show. He will then invite him back to complete it tomorrow. I will arrange to have two specialists there at 9:45. They will introduce themselves when they arrive and will go on the show with you, Dr. Bordello, and John Truley. Under no circumstances are you to inform Truley of the fact that there will be additional guests or that there will be any change in venue. They will handle the rest."

Bill's eyes lit up. Butterflies swarmed his stomach. A

shoot out, he thought to himself, and *Health Talk* is going to be the OK Corral! He had waited his whole life for something like this, and better yet, he had made it happen. It was almost too good to be true.

"Have I made myself clear, Dr. Bordello?" asked the golden voice.

"Perfectly."

"Mr. Laguna?"

"Oh, yes sir. Crystal clear. You can count on us!"

"I'll have a courier there within the hour to pick up a tape of today's show. My men will want to review it. Good day, gentlemen."

The two looked at each other as the caller hung up.

Bill pounded on the desktop. "Can you believe it? What a stroke of luck!"

"Luck? Are you nuts? This isn't some kind of game, Guiermo. I swear if you weren't my cousin I'd shit-can you right now."

"Stop calling me that! And, no you wouldn't, Larry. You need me to do the show that's gonna save your ass. And it's going to be the best show this dump of a station has ever heard."

"It better be!" Larry watched Bill dash out the door. He slid a silk handkerchief from his front pocket and dabbed the beads of sweat that were trickling into his eyebrows.

Making an exception, John agreed to meet Jimmy McBride for a beer after work. John had told his friend to listen to the show and afterwards Jimmy called, insisting they celebrate John's new celebrity status. They met at one of Jimmy's favorite places, an Irish pub called The Field, where of course, everyone knew him. After introducing John to the waitress, Jimmy winked at him and nodded toward her while she was taking John's order.

"You need to get out, Johnny. If you'd hang around me more often you would meet a lot of great female prospects."

"If I hung around with you more often, I'd probably have my son taken away."

The waitress delivered their beer and Jimmy bought the round.

"Here's to Dr. Truley, media animal!" They clinked their glasses and took long swigs of the dark brew.

"I was real proud of you, John. You were quite passionate and surprisingly articulate."

John wiped his mouth with the back of his hand. "Well, coming from the master of communication himself, that is quite a compliment."

"Yes, Johnny boy, you had a great opportunity and you almost did it."

"Yeah, it was too bad they had to stop the show."

"No, that's not what I mean. You had enough time. You just didn't close the door," Jimmy said matter of factly.

"What!?! Jimmy, you sure this is your first beer? What the hell are you talking about — close the door? I was telling people about Katie Prespo."

"Listen up, John. I know that I joke a lot and like to have a good time, but I'm totally sincere at the moment and there's a critical lesson here if you're ready for it."

"Hi, Dr. Jimmy," a waitress, who must have just started her shift, said as she passed their table.

"Hi, there." Jimmy flashed his gargantuan trademark smile.

He looked back into John's eyes and became instantly serious.

"Katie Prespo opened the door for you through her tragedy. You had the genitalia to walk through the door. You had the passion to tell the people on the other side the truth about drugs, but damn it, John, you didn't have the knowledge to close the door after you and get the people inside to sign the contract."

John sipped his beer, letting the words sink in. "Do you know how to close the door, and if so, why haven't you done it?"

"First of all, yes, I do know how to close the door, Johnny, with facts, information, studies, and statistics. Second, I've tried many times to open the door, but I've never been positioned even half as good as you were today. That guy, Dr. Bill, gave you carte blanche, and you had the power of being present when Katie Prespo was at death's door. You were there, Johnny boy, you were at the radio station looking into the eyes of the dragon itself. You just needed a bigger sword."

They sat quietly and drank.

Then Jimmy raised his glass solemnly. "Shall we have a moment of silence for what almost was."

John's pager beeped. He grabbed it while Jimmy reached into his blue and black checked blazer and pulled out a tiny digital phone.

"Here, use this while I get us another round."

John dialed the number and was surprised to hear Dr. Bill answer after the first ring. He apologized for the interruption of the show due to the technical problems and asked if John could be there by ten the next morning to finish it properly. John heard himself agree and snapped the phone shut in amazement.

"Patient?" Jimmy asked while he continued his attempts to flag down a waitress in the increasingly crowded bar.

"Dr. Bill wants me back on the show tomorrow," he said with a boyish grin.

Jimmy's hand came down and he looked John in the eyes.

"Hell with the beer. We have work to do!"

Chapter 13

The two doctors met at their La Jolla office, which served as headquarters. It had approximately two thousand square feet divided into four separate areas, each tastefully decorated and furnished. Both doctors had a private office with the appropriate amenities, including cable television, VCR, stereo and bar. Dr. Snyder enjoyed a small putting area with a ball retriever complete with a little florescent flag, while Dr. Ridley opted for a stationary bike on which to spend idle time.

They shared a secretary who had a smaller area in front to answer calls, receive their guests and perform billing tasks. The last room of equal size to the doctors' was situated in the middle and contained a long table with ten chairs, a large dry-erase board, two separate easels for flip charts, a TV, VCR and cassette player. This was affectionately called the war room. Here an opponent's strengths and weaknesses were analyzed, strategies discussed, and battle plans drawn. Upon request, clever, hard-hitting campaigns were also formulated here, to aid in the battle against the forces of evil.

There was a noticeable absence of patient facilities or treatment rooms, but neither doctor minded. The work they did was on a grander scale, their skills too valuable and universally needed to be spent practicing common medicine with individual patients.

They were hired guns. Theirs was the sacred cause to protect the honorable practice of medicine in its present state. They were the sheriffs, and when an alternative form of medicine threatened the American Medical Association's stranglehold on health care, they were called upon to quash the rebellion — to restore order. Usually, it was chiropractic; but they had also done battle with homeopathy, acupuncture, midwifery, and even vitamin and herbal therapy.

Now they sat in the war room listening to the tape of

John Truley's radio show. Each had a yellow pad and pen, occasionally scribbling a note or raising an eyebrow. The show ended abruptly with a string of commercials, followed by music.

"What happened there?"

"One of Travers' watchdogs got wind of the show and when they heard the derogatory content, Travers was able to intervene."

"And now they want damage control," mused Dr. Snyder. "Play the tape once more."

The recorded segment was just under fifteen minutes long and the men sat silently for a few moments after hearing it again.

"This John Truley is a nobody," stated Ridley.

"An upstart maverick, emotional and working completely on his own," added Snyder.

"An easy target!"

The men looked at each other, slowly beginning to smile, then chuckling, and finally, knowing how each other's mind worked, broke into uproarious laughter.

They worked well together. They had been a team for nearly six years. It was Snyder who was the old master in his field, with experience from over thirty years of work. He was one of the original members of the Committee on Quackery, formed by the AMA back in the early sixties. The Committee's magna carta was later brought to light during testimony in an unsuccessful defense by the AMA for antitrust violations filed by five chiropractors. In the document, the goals were clearly stated — "The containment and eventual eradication of the chiropractic profession." Among its strategies, "choke off" support for chiropractic schools in an effort to cause the profession to "dry and wither on the vine," while simultaneously using inadequate chiropractic education as a platform from which to attack it. The Committee was legendary and provided important work such as drawing up and enforcing sanctions against medical doctors who referred patients to chiropractors. The heyday ended for the Committee on

Quackery as lawsuits mounted in the mid-seventies. The chiropractors, led by Chester Wilk of Chicago, waged a long and successful battle in which the AMA was found guilty of antitrust violations and forced to print the full text of the injunction in its own publication, *Journal of the American Medical Association.* Plainly put, the U.S. District Court found the AMA's conduct to be stupid, dishonest, and untrustworthy and basically described the AMA as a chronic and unrelenting lawbreaker.

But, how could common folk be expected to understand that this type of behavior was in the public's best interest? Because of the successful lawsuit by the chiropractors and the sanctions against the AMA, the pesky chiropractic profession now needed to be kept down in more clandestine ways.   New campaigns were designed to undermine public opinion and continue making chiropractic look like an unsafe, unscientific cult. The hits were carefully orchestrated to appear as if from a source other then the major medical or drug associations. Clever articles depicting chiropractors as X-ray happy, incompetent gold-diggers were frequently presented by lone, non-medical writers to popular publications, and seemed to play on public emotions without dirtying the hands of anyone who would fall under the scrutiny of the anti-trust legislation. Yes, it had become a more sophisticated game, but it was definitely the same sport, and Snyder and Ridley were major players.

Dr. Snyder was the impetus for several infamous "investigative reporting" pieces which aired on television. In one damning portrayal of chiropractic and children, he sent bogus patients, complete with hidden cameras in shopping bags, to chiropractor's offices. It was an easy feat for him to edit dialog and take phrases out of context to create a distinct appearance of incompetence on the part of the doctors. Important portions of examinations and consultations were deleted and in their place were well-rehearsed sound bites from a distinguished medical doctor and known critic of chiropractic. A well-respected and *concerned* reporter masterfully narrated the compelling expose. She neglected, however, to inform the audience that the station was turning off their fax machines to stop the barrage of complaints from chiropractic patients who objected to the show's misleading message.

Dr. Ridley brought his own talents to the team. Twenty years younger than his senior partner, he was somewhat handsome, and more important, equally competent and professional in front of a microphone or camera. He was completely committed to his job. During his years as a resident and a brief stint in practice, he had the strong realization that he did not possess a bedside manner conducive to success. He found solace in attacking beliefs that conflicted with standard medicine, finding that by being a champion of allopathy, he could save face as a medical doctor and, in fact, be revered by his colleagues. He took his crusade personally. Now in his element, he formed the perfect one-two punch with the legend that sat across the table from him.

"Are we risking public sympathy by going right for the jugular at the first bell?" Ridley asked the seasoned veteran.

"There will be a small percentage of listeners who will not appreciate our aggressiveness, but they will be far outweighed by the benefit of stopping Truley before he can start on that tired little tale about Katie Prespo."

"Of course! We'll knock out his only gun, and when he's floundering we can finish him off," Ridley reasoned, trying to contain his excitement.

Dr. Snyder chuckled. "I almost feel sorry for the poor slob; he doesn't even know it's coming."

"Well, it's coming all right!" the younger one said, tasting blood.

"What do you say we meet for breakfast before the show?"

"Steak and eggs at Maxi's?"

Dr. Snyder slapped the other man on the back. "You read my mind, partner!"

Once again, due to the short notice of his radio show appearance, John was unable to clear his schedule and saw his morning patients up until the last possible moment. He arrived at the station at ten minutes to ten, then burned up another five minutes tracking down a parking place. In a dead run, he just slipped his hand into the closing elevator, causing one busy rider to roll her eyes. The door opened to the sixteenth floor at 9:59. The receptionist just smiled and pointed toward the double doors. John burst into the hallway and ran past the morning deejays who were arguing about who played Eddie Haskel on *Leave It To Beaver*. At the studio room, Dr. Bill held the door open for John as he rushed up. For a split second their eyes met. Dr. Bill appeared very excited, likely due to his guest cutting his arrival so close, but John also detected something he couldn't put his finger on.

Kim started the jazz tune that John had heard the day before.

"We've added a couple of guests for today's show," Dr. Bill told him as they walked into the room. "Someone for you to bounce ideas off of."

John was quickly ushered into a seat at the far end of the table nearer the window. To his right were two men in suits. As the jazz refrain continued John and the mysterious men were quickly introduced.

"Dr. Truley, this is Dr. Snyder and Dr. Ridley."

John's mind raced to comprehend the situation as both men nodded. He sensed the energy in the room had assumed a near palpable anticipation. Dr. Bill was doing his introduction of Health Talk now as well as setting the stage for the show. Thoughts of foreboding, then panic, spun through John's head, the blood pounding in his ears to the point of drowning out Dr. Bill's voice.

Clarence Travers sat in his meticulously decorated office high above the city and carefully snipped the head off of his cigar. With an engraved stainless steel lighter, he toasted the cigar's foot, taking care to not let the flame touch the fine tobacco. Satisfied that both wrapper and binder were ignited 360 degrees around the edge, he pushed a gentle puff of air through the cigar to displace any residual butane vapors. After inspecting the foot one last time, he drew the rich smoke gently into his mouth, savoring all the aged Cuban blend had to offer.

The voice coming from his radio was that of Dr. Snyder. He described a list of credentials in addition to his medical degree, in a voice, clear, strong and definitely baritone.

"I believe that I speak for all the medical community when I express my concern that the public not be led to believe irresponsible statements made by questionable sources, with no scientific basis or background. I am concerned that the average, honest, hardworking individual may be duped into following the improper advice of such individuals and consequently be harmed by dangerous health practices."

Mr. Travers released a cloud of smoke, looking expressionless. "First blood," he said, nodding at the radio. "This should be over quickly."

Larry Laguna was trying to listen to the show from his loft, but forgot that his maid was scheduled that morning. When she fired up the vacuum, he stopped her abruptly.

"No cleany today, very big show, come back next week." He impatiently herded her away from the vacuum and out the front door. Once alone, he locked the deadbolt to ensure that there were no further interruptions. He had been attempting to workout when the show began and now sat listening on the couch, a towel hanging around his neck.

At John Truley's office, Janine had been calling patients since the doctor left that morning, telling them to tune into the show. She now monitored the radio for her doctor's voice while she squeezed in a last call to one of her favorite patients. She estimated that she had reached two dozen people, many of whom had in turn called others to share the exciting news that their doctor was going to be on the radio.

At the station, John sat silently, trying to fully grasp his predicament. He was frightfully disoriented by the sudden turn of events, and the lightning swiftness with which Dr. Snyder struck sent him reeling.

Dr. Ridley leaned toward his microphone, anxious to join the fray.

"Thank you for asking Dr. Snyder and me to be here this morning, Dr. Bill. It is good that we can depend on the media to act responsibly when the public safety is at risk. This fine country did not come this far and make so many advancements in the fight against disease by shirking its duties in protecting and educating the public. Now, any notion that vaccinations are anything other than a cornerstone of the average person's ability to fend off the ravages of things like polio, TB, and whooping cough is ludicrous. Billions of dollars of research, not to mention the best minds this great nation has to offer, have contributed to providing for the possibility of a safe and healthy life for you and your family."

In Dr. Jimmy McBride's chiropractic office, the patients were backing up and his frantic assistants were chatting nervously with them while their doctor remained locked in his private office. He was on one knee, yelling into his radio. "Get up, Johnny! You can do it! Engage those stiffs. Don't let them start up again. Get up! Get off the ropes!"

At the radio station, John felt the big, dark claw squeezing down on him. He figured Drs. Snyder and Ridley must have known about it and brought it to help them squash their opponent. Why had he ever thought he could change things? He had been kidding himself when he thought that by changing his mindset and his actions that he could reach his true potential. Potential, ha! His potential this morning was to get publicly humiliated. He thought about his father. No wonder he'd failed. It wasn't just that he lacked the personal discipline or desire needed to succeed; there were so many more enemies than that! There was always an ambush waiting when you finally got up the courage to try to break through and live your life the way you think, down deep, it should be. An ambush like these doctors, or his father's disease. What's the difference? Why not just give up right here and now? Yes, just quit. Forget about all of the problems. Let go of the struggle.

John relaxed and felt his body replace the tension with a pleasant numbness. He experienced a sudden peace as if he were floating and allowed it to carry him off into the grayness, weightless and free. He drifted up next to Katie Prespo's hospital bed, touching her forehead, brushing away a strand of shiny black hair. Her eyes opened and looked into his. A warm flowing love filled John's soul and just when he was sure that it would spill in great sobs from his body, he became aware of another presence at the other side of the bed. Katie slowly turned toward the figure and John followed her gaze into the angel's face. He had seen her like this before, his wife Sarah. It had been seven years since she died from complications of the Cesarean section delivery of Jeffrey. He had never forgiven himself for allowing the surgical birth to proceed ten days before Jeffrey's due date, but he had been convinced by the doctor that the breech position of their baby presented an unnecessary risk. Within forty-eight hours, a blood clot had gone to Sarah's brain, killing her. She had died with Jeffrey in her arms. Now, when John looked into her face, he saw none of the pain, none of the heartache, only love. She slowly nodded to John and then to Katie.

Dr. Snyder was talking when John interrupted, startling all three men who were beginning to doubt that he was going to say anything at all.

"I'd like to ask a couple questions, um, of the experts." He said softly, still returning to solid form.

Dr. Bill perked up. "Well! Go right ahead, Dr. Truley."

"I think what I'm hearing these two gentleman say is that the public needs to trust the medical community and to depend on those who are experts in the drug field about how and when to take drugs?"

"That is precisely correct." Dr. Snyder nodded patronizingly.

"Does that also include parents in regard to consenting for the medicating of children?"

"Absolutely!" Dr. Ridley sat up, shifting in his chair.

"Well, maybe you can help me and the listeners to understand why Kaiser Hospital in Los Angeles knowingly injected an experimental virus vaccine into over 500 infants without their parents' consent and to this day are fighting the release of documentation regarding the incident?"

The right hook came out of nowhere and connected squarely on its mark.

"Now wait just a moment, let's not lose sight of the big picture." Dr. Snyder was tapping a pen against his other hand and now slipped it forcefully into his jacket.

John continued quickly. "Maybe this one is easier. Why were multiple experimental vaccines, including anthrax, injected into one hundred and fifty thousand of our enlisted men without their knowledge or consent during Desert Storm? Don't the hard working GI's of this fine country deserve to be treated with more dignity than common guinea pigs? And now that these soldiers are afflicted with Gulf War Syndrome, the military claims that the vaccine records were "lost".

In his office, Dr. Jimmy McBride was up on his feet, marching back and forth in front of his radio chanting, "John-ny! John-ny! John-ny!" He flung the door open to his patients in the hallway and turned up the radio so all could hear. "Listen up, everyone! This is my colleague! My buddy!"

Janine, who was sitting near her radio, let out a surprised giggle. "Oh my, I didn't know that!" She rocked back and forth in the chair, trying to contain her excitement.

At the loft, Larry fumbled with his phone. "Go to a commercial! Go to a commercial!"

"Since you brought up polio, Dr. Ridley, maybe we can talk about that for a moment. Isn't it true that the incidence of polio was decreasing at a rapid rate before the vaccine was ever introduced? Then, when mass vaccination began a new epidemic was started from the vaccine itself? The only cases of polio these days are in fact due to those who contract the disease from the vaccine or from contact with a person recently vaccinated. And how about SV40, the well documented monkey virus that was being transmitted through polio vaccinations? Although the doctors were fully aware of the extreme danger, they continued administering the vaccine, choosing not to inform the public about the likelihood of contracting the virus, which is now known to cause malignant tumor growth. All this because they were afraid the public might panic if they knew the truth.

"And while you're at it, please describe to the unsuspecting public, whom you claim to protect, how the monkey virus that was knowingly injected into them, is now transmitted sexually. What can you tell us about the possible link between AIDS and the polio vaccine which is produced on monkey kidney tissue?"

Kim, the program manager, was holding up the very same sign she'd made the day before to relay Larry's instructions to stop the show. Dr. Bill had a broad grin across his face and shook his head, signaling that he had no intention of interrupting the show this time. Dr. Snyder was wiping perspiration off his brow and noticed that Dr. Bill was shaking his head. Glancing behind, he read the sign frantically waving behind the glass. He swung around furiously in his chair and glared at his host.

"Doctor?" John repeated.

Dr. Snyder could not remember being so rudely handled in his entire career. Knowing that his host was disobeying orders flabbergasted and angered him. There was silence as all waited for his reply. He looked at John Truley with squinted eyes and clenched jaw. "You think you've got it all figured out, don't you, Truley?"

"No, sir, I don't think that. None of us has it all figured out, and the sooner we can admit to that and inform the public of the facts regarding all aspects of health care, the sooner we will make this a safer world."

Kim was on the phone with Larry, who was waiting for an appropriate place to interrupt the show. He gave the word and she hit the switch disconnecting the sound booth and simultaneously starting a commercial instructing listeners who couldn't sleep to drink its mint-flavored remedy and that the junior formula came in bubble gum flavor.

Kim, red-faced, burst into the room. "Larry said the interview is over — no ifs, ands or buts!"

The doctors sat in stunned silence then began gathering their notes and filing from the room. Dr. Bill watched the door close and then looked at Kim in astonishment. "He kicked their ass! Let's go to the phones quick."

"I don't know if Larry wants any phone . . ."

"Now!"

"This is Dr. Bill with *Health Talk*. We have just a few moments left. Let's go to the phones. Line 1, you're on the air."

"My name is Gabbie Smythe. I am so happy to have gotten through. Thank you, Dr. Bill."

"Please go right ahead."

"Yes, thank you. Yesterday I took my 68-year-old mother, who had been completely deaf for fourteen years, to Dr. John Truley's office. He adjusted a bone in her neck and now she can hear everything. Even though he won't admit it, I know that it was a miracle. My mother is so excited and she got to hear your wonderful show today!"

Gabbie's voice boomed though the speakers in the hallway leading to the double doors, where the three doctors now walked. When they reached the doors, Dr. Snyder paused and looked John Truley in the eye.

"Mister, you've either got a guardian angel sitting on your shoulder or you signed a pact with the devil himself."

Chapter 14

Phineas Blackmore's swing was not pretty and the senator snickered to himself because it had been a while since he had seen it. When the drive skirted along the out of bounds, down the left of the fairway, he made his offer.

"Standard rules, say a grand each for the front and back?"

"How about two-fifty a hole, winter rules?" countered Blackmore, mentioning something about the shoddy grounds keeping in D.C.

Remembering the pharmaceutical executive's game to be decent, but at times erratic, Senator Tomlin pushed for total score.

"One-fifty a hole and total score for a thousand."

"All right, but since we're on your home turf, I'll take four strokes." Blackmore shifted his eyes to see his opponent's reaction.

"Two strokes."

Blackmore smiled. "Let's play ball."

Golf was the only exercise he ever enjoyed and a large part of Phineas Blackmore's appreciation for the game stemmed from its conduciveness to the simultaneous conduction of business. Blackmore was a workaholic, and the older he grew, the more addicted he became to the adrenaline that only business could provide. Vacations could be tolerated only after ingesting an exceptionally large dose of successful commerce that would remain in his bloodstream long enough to allow him a week or so away from the action. Let there be no mistake, he had an agenda for this round on the links with Senator Tomlin. The betting was fun, but trivial.

The senator absolutely loved golf, but also enjoyed the game within the game. He knew men like Blackmore didn't golf with him for the camaraderie. They needed him, and he relished that. His method of operating was fairly consistent. An individual would call and say they needed to talk or, if they knew the routine, just schedule the obligatory round of golf through his secretary. The senator, an avid golfer, would try to make them squirm with an interesting wager, which he considered his consultation fee, and then he would play as if that were their only purpose for being there. He could make good money at the game he loved, while letting the suspense of the guest's need build, knowing he would profit handsomely whatever it was. Life was good.

Phineas Blackmore was an impatient man, the type that might walk off the course after nine holes if he got too antsy. By the second hole, a par five, 490-yard dogleg right, he showed his hand.

"My West Coast laboratory has a new vaccine which should perform well on the market." He retrieved his fairway metal from his bag. "It's the big one. A rhinovirus vaccine for the common cold."

The senator rested in the cart, gazing down the fairway at the little white dot that was his ball.

"No shit, Phineas? That should boost shareholder morale," Senator Tomlin said, working up the value of his hand at the first opportunity.

Phineas connected well and sent his ball just left of the outermost pine tree at the corner of the dogleg. He was feeling more focused now that he had initiated some business.

"Not bad. I believe you'll be happy with that one."

"My team has given a hundred and ten percent to develop this drug properly. The public needs it ASAP, and I need some help getting it to market quickly."

The cart stopped short of the senator's ball. Smiling at Phineas, Tomlin chose his weapon. He walked over, addressed the ball, and sent a wicked drive that landed a short iron away from the green.

Getting back into the cart, he looked at Phineas. "I suspect we're speaking about the FDA?"

"We are experiencing delays with the administration that we had not anticipated. You have the power and influence to assist the public in receiving this highly beneficial medication in a more timely fashion." Phineas eyed the senator for a moment and then pulled out the same club that he had used on his last stroke.

Tomlin chuckled. "I commend your choice of using what you know works."

Phineas felt the adrenaline coursing through his arteries. His drive was true, and the ball bounded twice before rolling perfectly onto the green.

The senator nodded his approval, thrilled with the possibility of competition from his upstart opponent. "It appears that things are going well for you, Mr. Blackmore. My connection, however, is dealing with increased regulation and scrutiny. I'll require twice the normal fee."

"And you'll get it."

Using his five iron and an easy short swing, Tomlin landed his ball a foot before the green and smiled as it hopped, then rolled, stopping within ten inches of the cup. Looking satisfied, he turned to his partner. "Let's play ball, Mr. Blackmore."

After sinking their putts, they drove the cart toward the next hole.

"You know, I heard something about vaccines just yesterday. I was talking to ole' Harvey Lawton, the retired judge from San Clemente. He had just listened to some talk show there in Southern Cal, 960 I think. Said it was the damnedest thing, a couple of medical boys pretty much got an ass whipping by this guy, some natural health enthusiast."

Phineas Blackmore frowned. "960, you say?" He reached back to remove a cell phone from his golf bag and dialed a number. "Hello, Ms. Browne? Yes, this is Mr. Blackmore. Find out if we do any advertising with a station that broadcasts out there, 960 AM. If so, cancel it effective today, understood?" Phineas turned off the unit and put it back in his bag, the senator shaking his head and chuckling.

After making a few calls, Ms. Browne was informed that Blackmore Pharmaceuticals did, in fact, have an account with 960 AM. She quickly looked up the appropriate legal representative of Blackmore on her computer, but couldn't find who she wanted and was forced to search manually through some department files. She remembered seeing the files she wanted in the bottom drawer of a cabinet in the corner of the office. The drawer was heavy, and she bent low and tried to use her legs as much as possible.

In the hallway just outside the open door, security specialist Martin Hommer was getting himself a cup of coffee from the executive refreshment station. He had damn near free range of the company's facility and knew that the gourmet coffee was only found closer to the top, in the executive suites. He was only thirty-two, but had been with Blackmore nearly ten years. He started as the lowest rank of security, and spent years driving through the parking lots, shaking door handles. He had approached his job with the utmost seriousness and often bragged about its dangers to females whom he wanted to date. He spent hours staring at himself in the mirror in full regalia, deadly baton at his side. He was never late for his watch and never missed a day, opting instead to work extra hours for other guards on holidays and weekends. He was promoted and his responsibilities increased accordingly. His beat moved inside the office buildings and he was eventually required to carry a sidearm. It was with careful consideration that he selected a Glock 22, his pride and joy. It was a 40 caliber, black polymer and steel beauty, and, thankfully, because he purchased it prior to President Clinton's crime bill, it had a 14 round capacity if he kept one in the chamber, which he always did. He was fitted for a matching black holster with a quick release thumb snap and found he could draw fastest with the holster at a 15-degree rear tilt. He had doubled the time he spent with his baton in front of the mirror and often fell asleep at night resting the pistol across his chest. His new job description was top surveillance coordinator, and he had a small army of lower security men answering to him.

Officer Hommer was pouring coffee into one of the designer paper cups provided upstairs, when he noticed movement from Mr. Blackmore's front office area. He carefully set the cup down and approached the doorway, right thumb arching, ready to hit the holster's snap release at a second's notice. When he moved to his left, he had full view of Ms. Browne struggling with the low drawer. During the few minutes of tugging, her tight skirt had hiked up her thigh. Finally getting the drawer open, she settled in to locate whatever it was that she was after. The sight acted as a magnet, drawing Officer Hommer slowly toward his subject. She looked even better in real life than she did through the security monitors. Sliding through the partially opened door, he continued to silently close the gap between them. Suddenly slamming the heavy drawer closed, Ms. Browne stood up with file in hand and turned. Shrieking, she threw the file in surprise.

"Oh, I'm sorry, Ms. Browne. I saw you struggling with the drawer and was going to see if I could help."

"My god, you almost gave me a heart attack!" She held her chest before squatting to collect the scattered papers. Martin quickly joined her on the floor.

"Oh, thanks." She noticed he was looking at her while picking up the pages and felt vulnerable. They collected the loose pieces and he handed his stack to her.

"Well, if you're sure you're okay, I've got a meeting."

"Yes, thanks. I'm fine," she replied, relieved to have him going.

Picking up his coffee on his way down the hall, the security man licked his lips as he replayed in his mind the tall secretary working with the drawer. Martin Hommer then rode the elevator down to the second floor, flipping the bird into the dark lens of the elevator's security camera.

Waiting in the security office was Stanley Crider and

Claben Debero, Chief of Security for all of Blackmore Pharmaceuticals. Martin was startled to see his idol, Mr. Debero, at Blackmore West and cursed himself for fooling around before arriving at the office. Debero was a powerful and mysterious figure. He had been the Chief when Martin was first hired as a door shaker and, although Martin had only seen him a handful of times, he had spent hours talking to other security guards about the stories that surrounded the man.

"Sorry for the delay gentlemen. I was unavoidably detained upstairs."

"Okay, fine, just show us the tape of the security breach you reported." Stanley Crider pulled at his tie.

"It's in the private suite. Please follow me." Martin led the men into an adjacent room equipped with ten video monitors, a couple of chairs and a large safe.

When Crider first heard from Officer Hommer that there had been a problem in Blackmore West, he reported it directly to Claben Debero. With the pending release of the new vaccine, the laboratory had been placed on a Code Red status. This was the most dangerous stage of the drug-making process in terms of theft. The company had already invested millions of dollars and potentially hundreds of millions were at stake from future sales. If an unscrupulous lab could obtain the formulation in its completed state, they could theoretically claim ownership and attempt a patent or sell it outright to the highest bidder. It would take years to dispute ownership and would create great financial hardship to Blackmore.

Officer Hommer opened the safe, removed a small, digitized tape, and inserted it into the computer. He typed in a number and tapped a play button.

Soon the image of Sally Hobbs was seen entering what looked like Lamont Weedleman's office. There were stacks of books and papers congesting every inch of the place and the girl had to step across them to get into a large filing cabinet.

"What's she doing in there?" Crider moved close to the monitor.

"The employee entered Dr. Weedleman's office at 8:18 a.m. yesterday morning and spent just over thirteen minutes going through those files." Hommer pointed to the drawer Sally was pulling out. The men watched as she extracted a file, opened it and began reading. She flipped a couple of pages, then returned it to the drawer, along with the materials she had carried into the office.

"Back it up and enlarge the frame to see what file she was looking at," Debero ordered.

Martin set the sequence back to the frame where Sally pulled the file and enlarged the picture. After advancing several frames, the angle of the file in relation to the camera changed so the men had a clear view of the words: "Purpose of Experiment."

"Bingo," muttered the Chief of Security, who had full knowledge of all aspects of the CD4C situation, as well as practically everything else that went on in the company.

Stanley Crider's jaw dropped. "I'll be damned."

Debero spoke matter of factly. "Apparently she wasn't aware she was being taped and likely doesn't realize it now. From what I see here, she's either innocent or an incredibly stupid thief. There are some things that must be explained, however. Mr. Crider, I want you to see if Dr. Weedleman knows how this girl acquired access to his office, then report to me immediately. Officer Hommer, you are to begin constant surveillance of Ms. Hobbs, reporting all changes in her location the minute they take place. Contact me at this number." Debero handed him a slip of paper. "No one is to notify the girl or speak to anyone else about this matter. Her actions will reveal her intentions. Meanwhile, I'll do a background check and to see if there's anything in her history that might reveal a motive. Mr. Crider?"

Stanley stopped shaking his head for a moment and nodded.

"Do you understand your assignment, Officer Hommer?"

"Yes, sir!"

Sally Hobbs' apartment was located off Beach Boulevard about ten blocks from Knott's Berry Farm. The building was situated in a strip of apartments that served as a buffer between the middle class suburban residences of La Habra and a six-block stretch of seedy government-subsidized low-income housing. The apartment that served as a haven for the sisters during their dream-like reunion also acted as a constant reminder that Mara was perched precariously between her old life as junky and criminal, and something respectable. Well-manicured lawns and basketball hoops over driveways with mini-vans and SUV's could be seen from the front window, contrasting sharply with the view out the back. Litter-strewn dirt yards were choked with weeds and rusted cars. There was usually a contingent of tattooed teens or pot-bellied men huddling on the street corners amid the sounds of breaking glass, sirens and crying babies. A spillway separated the apartment building from the projects, but Sally and Mara still insisted on keeping the shades drawn on that side.

Although challenging, things had been going fairly well for the sisters. Mara was gaining weight, which added attractive curves to her long slender figure. Her auburn, shoulder length hair was beginning to shine, helping to accentuate her green eyes that had also gained a sparkle. Her previously pasty, blemished skin was coming to life with an improved diet and the sisters' nightly ritual of cleansing and moisturizing. Like Sally, Mara had a subtle and attractive array of freckles that highlighted high cheekbones, and Sally had paid her dentist to have Mara's brown, heroin junkie teeth bleached. Sally watched with great satisfaction as her sister grew more beautiful with each passing day.

Mara's paranoia was not so easily treated, however. Although she no longer found the need to confess to Sally the frightening tales of her two years as a drug user and the various methods she had resorted to in order to feed the addiction, she still refused to leave the apartment unless accompanied by her sister. Mara liked to shop for clothes and groceries or go to the beach for sunshine and exercise. She found the beach invigorating and waited anxiously, much like an impatient puppy, for Sally to return home in hopes of a walk at Newport or Huntington.

Sally had consulted many times with Gladys Perkins, her former social worker, for advice on how fast to push Mara in her reintroduction to everyday life. Mara's progress had been superb until the week before, when she received an ominous call from a ghost from her past. Sally had returned home to find Mara hiding under her bed, shaking uncontrollably. After coaxing her out, she was unable to get her to talk for almost an hour. Just as Sally decided to drive her to the hospital to have her examined, Mara opened up.

"R-R-Rocky c-called me." At the mention of the caller's name, her eyes flitted in terror.

The next day Sally had no choice but to call in sick in order to comfort her shaken sister. Over many tears and bouts of trembling, Mara gradually revealed the story of Rocky. Mara had met him two years prior to being arrested as his accessory to auto theft. He had a long history of trouble and had served time for assault, robbery, and sale and distribution of narcotics. At first he was exciting, and she was attracted to him because he paid attention to her, making her feel wanted. As the relationship evolved, he became more domineering and soon controlled her every move, often using force to make her do what he wanted. She had resisted using heroin many times until he finally threatened to leave her if she didn't try it. Once started, she became a pathetic puppet on which he vented his aggressions and lived out his fantasies. In the earlier stages of their relationship, before he became insanely possessive, he would show off her slender, youthful body by forcing her to dance topless for his friends. If he were drunk enough, he would encourage them to grab her and slap her and spray her reddening skin with beer. Often she would be so high it didn't matter to her. Nothing did. Nothing except getting her next fix. On one particularly humiliating night, Rocky ceremoniously paraded her nude in front of a business associate who fondled her roughly while Rocky held her. The man then nodded at Rocky, who left them alone with the understanding that Mara would repay a bad debt Rocky owed him. The hour she spent stuporously withstanding the violent rape, left her with injuries that required several days in bed from which to recover. During the time she and Rocky had been together, he repeatedly threatened that if she ever tried to leave him, he would track her down and kill her.

Since her rehabilitation, she had been unwilling to confront the frightening image of Rocky, never mentioning his name to Sally. She spent the last nine months in ignorant bliss about his whereabouts, hoping he was locked up indefinitely.

Now he was free and he wanted her back.

Sally called Gladys Perkins, who instructed her to notify the police. Because Rocky had not threatened Mara during his phone call, the police said there was nothing they could do and suggested, if the calls persisted, to get an unlisted number. The problem, as far as Sally was concerned, was that Mara's name was not listed with Sally's and their last names were different. So how had Rocky obtained Mara's number in the first place?

Mara had become increasingly terrified about staying alone and would not leave Sally's side when she was home, to the point of sitting next to her on the couch when they watched television and waiting outside the door while Sally used the bathroom. Sally was forever turning around while cooking or cleaning to bump face to face with her paranoid sister.

Finally, Sally could bear it no longer, as the once-peaceful apartment had become a place for Mara to hide in fear and for Sally to come home to watch her sister's anguish. Gladys suggested they arm Mara with pepper spray and Sally agreed. Sally purchased a container she could easily carry with her and now showed her sister how to use it.

"Spray for his eyes, Mara. This stuff is supposed to shoot over ten feet. If you get it in his eyes, nose or mouth, you'll incapacitate him and you can get away."

Mara looked at the canister and shook her head. "I can't."

"Mara, listen. You can."

Mara's eyes darted from the can to Sally. "If I miss, he'll kill me."

Sally shook her head. "Listen to me, Mara. First of all, you'll probably never have to use this stuff. But if you do, you need to know how."

Mara looked doubtingly at her sister.

I know you can do it, Mara. You know why?" Sally took a breath and tried to sound confident. "Because you're my sister, and we're tough. You got it? Now, spray this asshole if you see him, you got that?"

Mara stared at the pepper spray then clung to Sally like a frightened child. "When he catches me —" Her voice cracked raspy and hoarse through her tears. "If he don't kill me, he'll fill me with junk 'til I can't move."

Sally shuddered, hugging her sister every bit as hard.

Chapter 15

The reporters slouched around the room joking and drinking coffee, with the exception of Marlene Johnson who preferred mineral water because it didn't stain her teeth. She was the head anchorwoman for Channel 20 and well liked in the community. It was common knowledge that she was a health enthusiast, who, in her early forties, exercised regularly and seemed to be holding off the career-devastating aging process quite nicely. Her skin was tight with the help of one minor face lift and her eyes were clear and intelligent. Around the room, the other anchors and beat writers were just finishing up the evening's headlines, barring, of course, any late-breaking stories which would, depending on their scale of importance, be inserted into the present material.

"You know, Marlene, I might have something that would work for your health segment," offered Ralph Manstone, Marlene's male co-anchor.

"Oh, yeah? What is it? Not another story on pets and old people, I hope." She flashed a mouthful of perfect teeth.

"No. I think it has a little more zing than that. I was listening to this lively debate on vaccinations yesterday involving two MD's and a chiropractor. It was fascinating."

"All right, hold it right there." Frans Milesden, the station's program director, held up a hand. "We're not doing any anti-medical or anti-drug pieces. We'd step on way too many toes."

"I know that, Frans. I've been around long enough to know what pays the bills around here. The part I think is usable was the lady who called at the end of the show, describing how her 68-year-old mother was adjusted by the same chiropractor the day before and was cured of deafness."

"Hmm, sounds like a story." Marlene looked at the station manager. "What do you think, Frans?"

"I suppose if the interview goes badly, we could turn it into a consumer beware piece. Okay, it's all right by me. Just stay away from the drug issue!"

"I think his name was Truley. He's in North County." Ralph was happy to get them one step closer to finishing the morning session.

Marlene stood, putting on her dark blue blazer. "Can someone get Chiropractor Truley on the phone? I can be there around three. Tell him I'd like to see him work on some of his clients." One of the assistants scrambled off in search of the yellow pages.

"Okay, do we want a follow up on the huge sewage spill off Mission Beach?"

There was a chorus of groans in the room, and a senior reporter wadded a piece of paper and threw it. "I think you're beating a dead horse on that one, Frans. People in Southern California are sick of hearing about beach closings, disappearing sand, and even cliff erosion, for that matter. Don't we have any good crime pieces?"

Marlene shook her head. "We focus too much on crime."

"You're right. Crime sells. Crime is interesting. Has anybody committed any crimes around here?" Frans hollered, amidst a few chuckles.

A beat writer was reporting to the group on the three or four biggest crimes committed since the previous night's news when the assistant approached Marlene. "Okay, it's all set up with the chiropractor. The interview is at three. Here is his name, address and telephone number." The girl handed her a slip of paper.

"John Truley, D.C.," Marlene read out loud. "We'll see what you've got."

In the West Coast regional office of Apex Industries, Mr. Clarence Travers sat on the other side of the desk from his employer and waited for him to spin his chair around.

Frederick Harding was looking out the window at the downtown Los Angeles skyline, where the mid-morning sun was trying to break through a hazy ceiling of low fog and pollution. "I am not pleased with the handling of the AM radio situation."

"I'm sorry, sir."

"Your apology is accepted, Mr. Travers. Now what do you propose that I do about the thousands of people who listened to the show all the way from here to Baja? This is a very big market for the industry. Do you understand the magnitude of just a fraction of a percent of our consumer base here in California?" Harding spoke slowly, as if educating a child.

"Yes, sir. Do you think the show, tragic as it may have been, will really have an effect on us?" Travers was anxious to start looking for solutions, instead of dwelling on the problem that he had a hand in causing.

"Clarence, I am much older than you. With age, one begins to see things that are otherwise hidden. I can tell you that seemingly trivial events can prove in retrospect to be quite significant in the grand scheme of things. One man with passion can start a fire that can quickly burn out of control, destroying years of hard work. I am to blame as much as you because I agreed to take aim at this man's reputation. We could have easily allowed him his small victory and he likely would have disappeared forever. Instead, by challenging him, we've made him more powerful and surely more dangerous than before. I fear that we have created a problem many times greater than anticipated. Because of what happened yesterday, I have no choice but to ensure containment, and minimize future damage.

"I want you to commission Ridley and Snyder to design a few general pieces to turn public opinion against the man's profession. He is not to be mentioned personally and the pieces must be disseminated in the usual manner with no paper trail to the doctors or us. Use a large respectable periodical, as well as newspapers both here and in San Diego." He paused, watching the sun's rays bounce off the air particles, igniting an array of colors out over the Los Angeles basin.

"What about John Truley?"

The man turned in his high-backed chair and gazed at Travers. "Leave that to me."

Truley Chiropractic was buzzing with excitement. The office was unusually busy with people who had been rescheduled, practice members who had not been in for a while but had heard the show, and lots of first timers. Janine started a waiting list as the phone rang constantly with well wishers asking the secretary to pass along their congratulations on the success of the show. Janine could not restrain her excitement, telling them about the scheduled interview with Marlene Johnson. Several people milled around the office just to be a part of the festivities.

The television crew arrived at 2:45 to begin planning their strategy and to check lighting. Marlene Johnson was dressed smartly in a tan and black checked Donna Karan business suit. She was fully made up with her shiny brunette hair in a perfect French twist. She was very cordial to Janine and the adoring fans who found it difficult not to mob her when she walked in the door. At 2:55, John came out of an adjustment room and met Ms. Johnson and the crew. He showed them his office and they decided to first interview him behind his desk and then continue filming while he adjusted a patient. Though nervous, John found that the radio show experience of the last two days helped him keep his cool. Soon, everyone took their positions.

John was behind the medium-sized dark walnut desk with his framed credentials in the background, while Marlene sat across from him, much like a patient during a consultation. A large camera with a light on top of it rested on a stand near the end of the desk and was operated by a man wearing a headset. "Rolling." A few feet away, another member of the crew held up a bright light.

"We're here with local chiropractor, Dr. John Truley, for tonight's segment of *Health Watch*. Let's start by getting a little background on you, doctor. What is chiropractic and how does one become a chiropractor?"

"Chiropractic is the art, science and philosophy of correcting misaligned bones, called subluxations, to help restore nerve tone and the body's innate healing power. The average chiropractor has a minimum of six years of college, focusing heavily on human anatomy, neurology and physiology. Rigorous state and national board exams must be passed to become licensed."

"Dr. Truley, why does it seem that there is an animosity between medical doctors and chiropractors?"

"That's a good question, Marlene. I just want to say that I believe the majority of medical doctors, and this goes for chiropractic doctors as well, are compassionate and sincere about their duty to help people become well. Any animosity stems from the diametrically opposed approaches in doing so. Chiropractors prefer to assist a person without invasive means such as drugs or surgery, and I believe we give more credit to the body's natural ability to heal itself. Most chiropractors agree with the creed, "The power that made the body, heals the body."

"Very interesting. Now, I understand that you had a dramatic case recently, in which a woman was cured of deafness. How did you do that?"

John chuckled, thinking of Gabbie and her mother, Eleanor.

"We had a wonderful experience and I would like to explain it so that it doesn't sound so mysterious. This woman had a bone out of alignment in the very top of her neck. The subluxation caused a certain amount of nerve interference as well as some very tight neck muscles, which were blocking the drainage of fluids from her head and inner ear. When I adjusted the bone, her hearing was restored. It was very exciting, but I want to explain that I just assisted her body so that it could heal itself." John finished the story feeling a wave of exhilaration.

"May we see you work on someone?"

"Sure, I'd love to."

The camera was turned off along with the lights, making the office suddenly seem dark.

Marlene smiled at John. "You're doing very well. You seem like a natural."

John looked at her curiously. "I suddenly seem to be getting lots of practice."

He led them into the hall, which was now a zoo. People had been crowding outside the door watching and listening to the interview, but now parted to let John, Marlene and the crew get by.

"This is quite a crowd you have here."

"They heard you were coming, Marlene."

Reaching the first adjustment room, John grabbed the chart from the box on the wall.

"Now, this is an interesting case. I was just finishing the exam when you arrived and I am ready to adjust this boy. His family speaks very little English and they've driven up from Mexico to come here."

"Okay, let's get the cameras going. We can edit as necessary." Marlene patted her hair. Soon the bright lights were on and they were ready.

John introduced Marlene to the members of the Jiminez family, who were in the room with little Miguel.

"All right, Miguel, let's have you first walk down the hallway before we do any work."

A bilingual friend of the family interpreted John's instructions.

In the hallway, there were people standing in every doorway, hanging over the front counter and filling an adjacent small open suite, as 6-year-old Miguel moved to the door. He knew this was going to be a big day because he was wearing the new clothes his family had bought him. He had a striped shirt and new denim jeans turned up over a new pair of Nike tennis shoes. He stared wide-eyed at the cameras and crowd, and began to anticipate that something very big was about to happen. He became more eager than scared, knowing down deep that he was an important person and this was one of the biggest moments of his young life. His parents had told him that they were taking him to a special doctor, but he had no idea it was going to be like this.

Miguel bravely thrust his left foot out into the hallway and then pulled his right foot up to meet it. The right foot was awkwardly angled so that the toes pointed almost directly at the left one. Taking another step with the left, he began to swing his body into a rhythm and, with another drag of the right, picked up momentum. Now he motored down the hallway rather quickly, head bobbing dramatically with each step, his new white sneakers accentuating his unusual foot movement. At the end of the hallway, he turned around and waited, looking at his new doctor. John's heart felt thick and painful. He began to forget he was being interviewed and that Marlene Johnson stood at his side. The longer he looked at Miguel standing bravely, looking to him for instructions, trusting what he was doing, the more Miguel felt like his son. He would gladly trade all that was going on around them, if he could just help this kid. John motioned for Miguel to come back to the room and noticed a few people whispering to each other as the boy walked by them.

In the adjustment room, he asked Miguel to lie down on the softly padded table and the boy dove onto it before the interpreter could get the words out. John experienced a strong sensation that he was being pulled by the destiny of the day's events. He remembered that Marlene would probably like him to explain what he was doing. He forced himself to talk even though it felt like an intrusion on the connection between him and Miguel.

"Miguel's parents have informed me that his right foot has been turned in since birth and that for the last six years he has had to sleep in a pair of orthopedic shoes with a steel rod fastening them together. Surgery was recommended, but the mother was afraid it would hurt Miguel. They were referred here by one of my patients.

"I've found in my examination that little Miguel has three distinct problems. The big bone on the right side of his pelvis called the ilium is misaligned in two directions. His right femur, or hip bone, is also severely rotated inward and a muscle which normally helps turn the hip outward is short circuiting because of the other two problems. First let's adjust his pelvis." John helped Miguel turn on his left side, facing him. The doctor placed his left hand down low on the boy's pelvis and stabilized his shoulder using his right hand.

"Are you getting this?" Marlene looked to her assistant, who was carefully moving his camera while trying to dodge Miguel's family and the light man in the small room.

John smiled at Miguel and gave a thrust with his left hand causing a resounding crack to echo through the room. Miguel's mother squealed and quickly crossed herself. Miguel's eyes lit up and he smiled, blurting a few excited words in Spanish which caused chuckling among his family members. John then turned him on his back and used a lever to cock up a section of the table under the boy's pelvis.

"Now we will also set Miguel's hip into its proper alignment." John gently rotated the little boy's knee outward. He expertly positioned his left hand on the outermost portion at the top of the femur bone and gently thrust down, making a section of the table give way and drop about an inch. Next, he had Miguel turn over onto his stomach one last time to work on a muscle in his buttock.

"What are you doing now, Dr. Truley?" Marlene made a circle in the air with her index finger reminding John to keep talking.

"I'm trying to reset the fibers in the muscle that rotates Miguel's hip outward." He used his fingers to stretch the muscle's length several times. "There, let's see how he does. You can get up, Miguel, and walk down the hallway again."

The interpreter translated and several family members began asking questions and encouraging the boy. Miguel obediently got off the table, and an excited murmur arose from the gathering outside the adjustment room as they saw the boy appear in the doorway. Miguel paused, looking at all of the people, then looked back at his mother, who nodded. The office became silent as Miguel extended his left foot out into the hallway as if testing a thin layer of ice on a lake. He planted the foot and then brought the right foot slowly forward, setting it down parallel to the left. He shook his head briefly, standing stationary and looking down at his feet. He then took a more confident step and followed with his right more quickly. Again the feet were parallel. He repeated this motion, breaking into a semi-smooth stride down the hallway, sporting a huge grin on his face. The crowd erupted into cheers and applause, while Miguel's mother began sobbing, holding her arms out toward the boy. Miguel turned around and, upon seeing his mother, rushed into her arms. The cameraman was shaking his clenched and upraised fist, while still looking though the lens, and Marlene Johnson stood with her mouth open, uncharacteristically speechless. The auxiliary light man held his free hand out to Dr. Truley, who shook it warmly. The boy broke free of his mother's hug and began walking and then trotting up and down the hallway. Mrs. Jiminez was crying loudly, waving her handkerchief. She turned around with a big smile and bear-hugged Marlene Johnson as Janine passed out a box of tissues.

"I think that's a wrap." Marlene dabbed at her eyes. "Do you have anything to add, Dr. Truley?"

John looked at her and blinked. "No, I don't."

Chapter 16

Rocky set down the twelve pack and asked for non-filter Camels. Mirrors lined the walls behind the counter that no doubt provided the proprietor a view of potential shoplifters while his back was to the merchandise. The bright lights and the full view of everything, including himself, annoyed Rocky. He preferred the shadows of pool halls, strip joints and street corners where he blended in and could move about more stealthily. He gazed into the mirror to check the razored edges of his sideburns, but saw more details than he would have liked. His skin was yellowish and pockmarked, made more evident by the sharp contrast with his dark, greasy hair. The acne on his cheeks looked grotesquely purplish in the unforgiving florescence. He had not been a man long and it was only during the last couple of years that his beard required an occasional shave. He did his best to look older, tougher. His black jeans and T-shirt fit tightly over his medium frame and his trademark black leather jacket helped him exude the tough guy persona required to conduct business on the street. He had neither lost nor gained weight during his stay at the correction facility, the empty and tasteless food apparently offsetting his withdrawal from heroin. It hadn't been all that hard for him to stop the narcotic; in fact, he could have had access to it while in the joint, but he wasn't as weak as most when it came to addictions. He was more intelligent. Destined for greater things.

He studied the Vietnamese clerk's movements, making mental notes about his register, possible gun locations and positioning of the security system. Only one camera was visible and he noted that by standing on the counter he could easily access it. The clerk turned with the cigarettes in hand and Rocky gave him a ten and a hard look to see if there was any warrior inside the slightly built foreigner. He was further irritated when the clerk took the money, extracted change from the register and counted it out without looking up. It bothered Rocky that the man was able to remain a mystery. For all he knew, the guy could be fearless, willing to defend his register with his life. As he left, Rocky filed this new information in his brain under potential cash resources. He would need quick money when it was time, but for now, he wanted to stay as clean as possible. He was unwilling to jeopardize his freedom before he achieved his goal.

Placing the groceries on the passenger seat, he climbed into the black, late-model Continental. He had considered many ways to generate income, but they all involved risk. He knew he could make fast money stealing cars for the broker in Sunset Beach, but resisted the temptation, remembering the miserable nine months he had just spent at the county correctional facility. He had been fortunate to get an early release due to overcrowding. One more felony and he might not be so lucky. No, he was going to keep his nose clean, even if it meant doing without. He yearned for the high that he used to get, and thought about how good it would be next time because he hadn't had any for so long. Now, the gratification he would delay until he got his woman back was part of the excitement. Turning onto Beach Boulevard, he made his way past Chinese restaurants and doughnut shops. He wondered who the bitch was that was trying to take Mara from him. She might have to be punished for making him wait. He knew her name. Again he had been lucky, and his recent streak of luck just confirmed that it was destiny that he and Mara be reunited. One of his friends had seen Mara near the projects off the boulevard and reported it to Rocky when he found that he was out of the joint. The loser tried to trade him this vital information for the promise of a future score when Rocky got reconnected in the heroin trade, but Rocky was quick to inform him that the price for withholding information regarding his girl could be fatal. Any favors issued would be based solely on Rocky's discretion.

After two days of surveillance, Rocky had seen Mara and the woman leave the apartment building and get into a car. He followed them to the beach and watched them walk on the sand for the better part of an hour. He was caught by surprise by her transformation. He had to admit that she looked good, which made him want her more. She acted differently. It angered him to see her laughing and frolicking on the beach, happy, even though they weren't together. It made him dwell on how she hadn't visited him. How she let him rot in jail. It took every ounce of restraint to calm himself and not go after her right then and there. But he was different now. He was the master of his destiny and could not afford to let emotions spoil his plans for the future. Plans he had spent nine long months making.

He had carefully followed them home that day and was able to get close enough to see which apartment they lived in. After catching the locked entrance gate when another person entered, he had walked up to Mara's apartment just moments after she'd entered. Placing his hands on the door, he could hear their happy voices. He could feel Mara's vibrations as he rested his forehead against it before a neighbor appeared. On the way out, he matched the apartment number with the mailboxes downstairs and found the name Hobbs.

He had looked through the phone book but couldn't find a Hobbs with a woman's first name. He wrote down all the Hobbs that didn't have a definite male first name, then used this list to systematically make calls the next day. On only the third try, he struck paydirt. He savored the phone call, remembering Mara's initially cheerful voice, which became more respectful after she realized it was him. He asked her why she had not visited him in jail and told her that he called just to see how she was doing.

Now he pulled his car to the curb in front of the apartment building and parked. He could see light and an occasional shadow through drawn curtains in the front window. He longed to be inside the apartment and started feeling sorry for himself. Soon his pity turned to anger, as it always did, helping him to feel strong. Disgusted, he got out of the car, slamming the door and walked down the sidewalk that ran along the front of the apartments. Mara lived in the middle of three adjacent and identical structures. When Rocky came to the end of her building he turned right. A tall chainlink fence topped with barbwire blocked his path. He backtracked to the street and down the sidewalk to the end of the last building, which was situated at the intersection of Beach Boulevard and a small cross street. He turned and walked to the back corner of the building. A similar twelve-foot fence effectively boxed in the back of all three apartment buildings. There were no breaks that he could see, only the outward extension of barbwire the entire length. Dense brush filled the small gap between the back of the fence and the top edge of a long spillway. He was about to turn back when he noticed a small path from the sidewalk through the brush leading away from the street. His luck remained intact. He followed the trail and it turned suddenly. Rocky was just able to catch himself as his foot slipped. He peered over the edge of the spillway to see a long drop down a steeply slanted cement wall. In the moonlight, Rocky could just make out a rope dangling from a bush to his right. He barely reached it by bending and leaning out over the spillway. After a couple of hard tugs, he was satisfied it would hold his weight and he eased himself down. At the bottom, he immediately began to walk toward the back of Mara's apartment. The loud voices of revelers came from out past the spillway to his left. Once behind Mara's building, he counted windows until he found hers. With a running start, he clawed his way up the steep grade of the wall and managed to grab the heavy brush at the top. The bushes were thorny and he cursed them. Once on his feet, he panted and looked for a point of access. When he tried to push through the bushes to get next to the fence he was driven back by their density and sharp thorns. He gazed up at Mara's window and the flickering blue glow. She's watching the tube, he thought. What a waste.

The night air was beginning to chill and he decided to retreat. The only way to make a back entry would be with heavy wire cutters for the fence and something to help him reach her second story window after getting to the building. He pondered his possibilities as he slid down the side of the spillway on the seat of his pants.

Mara lay on her bed in front of the television. Although comforted that Sally was home, she found it difficult to remain on the bed instead of standing at the bathroom door while her sister finished showering. It was all she could do to wait at home by herself until her sister got off work at five o'clock every night. They would usually do something together for an hour or two, but then Sally required time to herself, taking a bath or shower and making preparations for the next day. Since starting her rehab Mara had felt anxious, and now that Rocky had called and probably knew where she lived, she was practically going crazy.

She spent endless afternoons searching for things to keep her busy. When she wasn't mindful, terrifying memories would surface, making her heart race and skin break into a clammy sweat. If she let it go long enough, she would feel the sickening pull from somewhere deep inside that yearned for the numbing effects of heroin. She tried reading books but couldn't focus long enough to complete one page without mindlessly drifting off, staring at a blur of words. She constantly watched television and often listened to the radio at the same time to help distract herself. She knew the story line of every soap opera, and the format of each trashy talk show on television. She could sing the words of any pop song and name the hosts of all the radio shows.

Sally had helped decorate her room, letting her

make it exactly as she wanted. She hadn't argued when Mara chose dolls, knickknacks and posters that a much younger girl would be attracted to. Mara wanted nothing to do with the frightening images that often accompanied heavy metal or rap music and refused to listen to it or watch MTV. She felt it was all part of a nightmare she was now trying to forget.

Sally was the most beautiful person Mara had ever known. She was sure that Sally was her only hope of ever becoming normal like the people on television. People like the Cosbys or Friends, who were nice and loving to each other. People neither ugly, nor violent. Mara found it hard not to cling to Sally whenever she was around. When she was near, Mara could feel the soothing peacefulness that she so craved.

"Whatcha doing, cookie?" Sally said, cheerfully poking her towel-covered head into Mara's room.

"Watchin' re-runs." Mara tried to act casual, but was thrilled her sister was once again in view.

"Mind if I watch the news?"

Mara didn't like the news, finding it much too scary for her tastes, but conceded so her sister would stay in the room with her. Sally flipped the channel, putting on a San Diego station that broadcast the news an hour earlier than the others. It was already half over, which was fine with Sally. She just wanted to be a little connected with the outside world and didn't necessarily want to hear about crime either. She had been so busy between Mara and work lately, that she rarely had time to read the paper, finally canceling it to save money.

Mara went to get some popsicles from the freezer, something she insisted they buy every time they went grocery shopping. For fun, Sally decided to paint her toenails with some polish Mara had. It was like a sleepover every night since the sisters had become a family again, and Sally loved it. She put her right foot on Mara's bed with a towel under it and started on the big toe. The television broadcaster reported the day's trading on the

New York Stock Exchange then followed with a story that drew Sally's attention.

"Drug giant, Blackmore Pharmaceuticals, enjoyed a sudden 12 percent leap in share values when they announced the upcoming release of their new vaccine, Rhimanditroph. The much ballyhooed vaccine is being touted as the first-ever cure for the common cold and could prove to be the silver bullet for the company that experienced three consecutive quarters of record losses, blamed on last summer's Cocadian Three scare. Seven people in Southern Louisiana died after using the antacid from an apparently tainted batch. The drug was ultimately recalled and foul play was suspected. When we come back, Hal Lennox will have the weather for you. Stay tuned."

"What's wrong?" Mara thrust a banana popsicle at Sally.

Sally sat stunned, the polish frozen inches from her toe. "Nothing. I just saw something about my company that caught me by surprise."

Mara began chatting about what happened that day on her favorite soap opera. Sally half listened, managing an occasional nod, but couldn't stop thinking about CD4C. She remembered how strange Dr. Weedleman had acted the day he gave her the keys to his office, instructing her to file everything to do with the experiment. She thought about seeing the restricted information and realized that she probably would've never suspected the drug they worked on was the same drug she just heard was going to be released. She hadn't seen Weedleman since that day and had been concerned that his illness might be serious. Now she couldn't help but wonder if somehow his strange behavior and absence were related to the impending release of CD4C.

The weather finished and Marlene Johnson appeared on screen.

"Oh, don't ya love her?" gushed Mara.

"Miracle man or just another chiropractor? On tonight's edition of Health Watch, *we take you to the office of one*

local chiropractor for some rather remarkable footage. We'll be back after this."

"Awesome," Mara shouted. "It could be the dude I heard on the radio. He talked all about . . . oh, you know, those shots for kids."

Mara blocked the TV and was now in Sally's face, her voice growing louder in her excitement. "Then a woman called. She told how the chiropractor cracked her mom's neck and fixed her hearing. It was so bitchin'!" Mara put her hands around Sally's neck. "Can't you just see it?"

"Wait a minute, Mara." Sally eased her sister's hands from her throat. "He was talking about vaccines?"

"Yeah, that's it. Vaccines."

"Well, what'd he say?"

"It was so rad. The first day, he called Dr. Bill, you know, from *Health Talk*, and told him about this little girl in his kid's class who almost died after her shot. They 911'd her to the hospital and saved her life, but now she's retarded. The next day, Dr. Bill had him come on his show and he told everybody how bad shots were and how grown-ups should know. Then, guess what? The next day he was on again. This time, two doctors tried to make him look fake, like he didn't know what he was talkin' 'bout. But, he got 'em bad!" She finished and took a big breath, happy to be so informative.

Sally thought about Mara's description of the chiropractor and the little girl damaged by a vaccine. Pictures of the Labradors flashed through her mind. She shuddered, her uneasiness growing.

Marlene appeared and the health segment began again. Suddenly, the cameras were in a doctor's office, and John Truley was introduced.

"That's him. John Truley!"

"Wow, he's attractive, isn't he?"

Mara looked at her sister in disbelief. "God, Sally. I didn't even know you looked at guys."

Sally's cheeks reddened. "Well, don't you agree?"

"I s'pose he's a babe. Little old for me. I think he's

your type."

Sally laughed at Mara's big grin. "All right, let's just watch this."

The man sat behind a desk and explained how a bone out of alignment can cause various problems and how chiropractors help the body heal without drugs. The cameras cut to a scene of a little Hispanic boy limping awkwardly down a hallway. The girls watched quietly, completely absorbed by the story. Sally held the open bottle of nail polish in one hand and a dripping popsicle in the other. Mara's was in a bowl as she nervously chewed a fingernail.

Dr. Truley adjusted the boy's back and hip. The boy returned to the hall, where he walked without a limp, while a crowd of people in the office cheered wildly. Marlene wrapped up the story and the station went to a drug commercial.

Mara pushed up and down on the bed making it bounce wildly. "Awesome. John Truley's the man. I'm next. I wanna be fixed!"

Sally stared at the TV for a moment, then looked at her bounding sister, her mind racing.

Chapter 17

John Truley pulled into the parking lot outside his office in the upscale plaza. He could see people lining up at his front door, and stretching thirty yards down the walkway, effectively blocking three other storefronts. He saw two television cameras as he glided past to the back lot, where he would enter his office through the rear door. It had been like this for almost a week, ever since he had been on the health segment with Marlene and little Miguel. The people came without appointments. Janine would repeatedly tell the ones who called that the best she could do was to put them on a waiting list. The vast majority would just form a line and John would do the best he could to see as many as possible each day. His lunch breaks now consisted of eating a sandwich while reviewing X-rays for a few minutes in the middle of the day. Some nights the office was still full and John would just leave from the back door, determined to see Jeffrey before bedtime. Janine would then inform everyone that he was gone and do her best to usher them out so she could lock up and go home.

John loved most aspects of his new popularity. The hardest part was the extremely high expectations from many of the new people. He found himself explaining that not everyone would have a miracle, but the properly applied principles of chiropractic would likely benefit them. Many did have great things happen and occasionally something exceptional would occur. On several occasions, he had patients who had suffered from a lifetime of migraines or other serious debilitations leave his office pain free. The television reporters would gobble up any good story, but John knew they would soon disappear when they found that he was no god, just a chiropractor — and John would be relieved when that happened.

Although he had invited the dramatic changes into his life, he longed for a break. All he wanted was just a couple of days to relax, sort things out, and spend more time with his son. It was ironic that he was getting what he'd wanted, and now wanted to change it again.

Rolling her eyes, Janine handed him a large stack of messages as he set his things down on the desk. "Looks like another wild one today, and don't forget you agreed to speak at the Optimist's luncheon."

John nodded, remembering his commitment to Flash Robinson to speak to the service organization. "Mention the talk to any media that are here today. We might as well make the most of all this."

"Will do. Okay, the rooms are loaded and ready for you, miracle man." She hurried out the door.

"Not you, too!" He set the stack of messages down without looking at them. Taking a deep breath, he headed toward the adjustment rooms.

The reception room was full, and Janine finally resorted to having people sign in when they arrived and then calling their name when a room opened up. While they waited, she would look for their file, and if they didn't have one, she would ask them to fill out the new patient forms. The door was propped open and people were constantly walking in to sign the list. Outside, approximately fifty people waited, the lucky ones sitting on steps or benches. Once in a while, the more courteous would give up their seat for an elderly person or someone in extreme pain. There were also a few outdoor tables provided by a nearby coffeehouse, which were also occupied, mostly by people waiting to see Dr. Truley. The proprietor wisely sent one of his workers out to take orders from the people who were unwilling to vacate their seats long enough to come in and get coffee, as was customary in his shop.

At one table, near a fountain, a pair of well-dressed men sipped espressos and watched the spectacle with more than just casual interest. They were not on Janine's waiting list and did not expect to hear their assumed names called aloud. They were, however, here for Dr. John Truley.

The two men had no personal political agenda, only instructions to observe, note, and await further instruction.

Both were highly paid professionals who commanded a substantial compensation based solely on the reputation of their past performance.

They were remarkable men, able to maintain normal lives complete with wives and families on the East Coast. Their well-behaved children were Brownies and Little Leaguers and were provided with the best life has to offer. Their wives were model citizens who were socially active and belonged to multiple service organizations. The men traveled several times a year on "business," explaining to their families that the CIA required they speak very little about their assignments. Their boss, however, was not Uncle Sam — he was Reginald Arfarian.

Although their present assignment was slightly irregular, the two men had learned to expect the unexpected. They had been paired on assignments before and enjoyed seeing each other once or twice a year.

"How are the kids?" Brock Helton asked his partner.

"Ty made Little League All Stars and Diana is walking now. How 'bout yours?" Charles Tomine inquired.

"Phillip started middle school and the girls are doing home school. The wife is gonna be ticked if I have to stay away very long on this one. You wouldn't believe the curriculum those kids have. I'm learning from it myself."

"It's hard to say how long this one's going to take. I can't imagine that this is going to turn into a quick mark. This guy looks like a nice enough fellow. Hopefully, we can get out of here without anything extreme."

"I don't know what he did, but he pissed off somebody. Hey, do you think he could fix my sciatica?" Brock perked up as he thought of it.

"Don't even think about it. Besides, look at that line!" Charles lifted his chin toward the people.

"Hell, all we're doing is sitting here anyway."

The men waited outside the coffee house for several hours, noting the flow of people in and out of the office, and the number and type of media personnel. They would occasionally take turns strolling around the plaza, but it was

Brock who needed to get up most often. At eleven forty-five, they saw John Truley race out of the office and get in his car.

"Let's go, Brock. He's either really hungry or he's in a big hurry to get somewhere." The men moved quickly toward their rented Lexus.

They followed John as he hastily drove toward the coast then south into Del Mar. He jumped out of the white Explorer in front of L' Auberge Hotel and took a ticket from the valet before running in. Brock and Charles sped up to the door, another young man appearing with a ticket.

They lost sight of John and moved swiftly around the foyer to peer down hallways.

"Charles, over here." Brock stood in front of a big placard displaying the service organization's logo with bold letters describing John Truley as the special guest speaker and the name of the meeting room. "He shouldn't be too hard to locate."

The men quickly found a room filled with about two hundred people being instructed to take their seats for lunch. There were approximately two dozen round tables seating eight people each. A man was making announcements at a front podium, while someone from the hotel was working to stop the occasional high-pitched feedback screeching from the sound system. A hostess sporting a bright name tag with Joan on it greeted Brock and Charles.

"Are you new guests?" She smiled broadly, grabbing Charles' hand and shaking it.

"Uh, yes we are." Brock glanced at Charles.

"Well, there are some seats available at this table right here." Joan led the men to a half-empty table near the back door. They looked at each other and Charles shrugged his shoulders before sliding into one of the chairs.

Another man at the table nodded at them and introduced himself. "Do you fellas have local businesses?"

"No, but we are considering it," Brock answered politely.

"Great! You'll love the community and find there are many opportunities here. These luncheons are a great place to make contacts."

"Thank you very much." Charles smiled.

Flash Robinson was now at the podium, finishing a joke. The well-dressed group laughed politely as Flash laughed the hardest.

"As most of you know, I play a little football."

The crowd burst into boisterous applause and Flash smiled, holding his hands up to calm everyone down.

"Thank you. Thank you. Okay, I can honestly tell you that the man I am about to introduce is almost solely responsible for keeping me in peak condition and in the game. He was recently featured on 960 AM talk radio and was also interviewed by Marlene Johnson on Channel 20, which aired last week. Without further ado, allow me to introduce my Doctor of Chiropractic, John Truley!"

John got up from a table near the front of the room while the group acknowledged him with a warm round of applause.

Flash stepped back from the podium, clapping and smiling. As John approached, he leaned back to the microphone. "This guy's the best!"

Flash Robinson pumped John's hand enthusiastically and ushered him to the microphone before returning to his seat.

John Truley stood for a moment and looked out at the large crowd. "Thank you, Mr. Robinson. That was very kind. Although I would love to take all the credit for Flash Robinson's health, I can't. This is why. The Power that made the body, heals the body." He paused, again looking around the room. "That's what we must all remember. I don't heal people. The medical doctor doesn't heal people. And drugs certainly don't heal people. The real doctor is inside of you. If I can do anything here today to help each and every one of you, it is to get you to acknowledge this basic truth.

"As a chiropractor, I am just a facilitator for your body to connect with the Power that heals. To become well, our bodies must be able to access Innate Intelligence, God, in order to organize and repair tissue. Your brain is the receiver and transmitter and your nerves are the conduits through which the Intelligence travels. My job as a chiropractor is to unblock the pathways from your brain to your body.

"Your heart, your liver, and all your organs receive vital nerve impulses from your brain. Every gland, every muscle and every single cell are connected via the nervous system to this Intelligence. Anything that enhances your nervous system's ability to communicate and transmit this precious life force will help you get well, while everything that diminishes its function will increase illness.

"Chiropractors are the experts in correcting spinal misalignments, called subluxations, which interfere with the brain's ability to communicate with the body. The bones that make up our spinal column protect our delicate nervous system, which is the most highly evolved tissue known to man. Yet, at the same time, the bones are moveable, allowing us to do lots of wonderful things like play sports, dance, or if you're Flash Robinson, score touchdowns and then dance." John laughed with the crowd and Flash wagged a finger at him.

"These movable bones occasionally go out of alignment and can distort the information being transferred through the spinal cord to the various organs or body parts, leading to disease. I encourage all of you to get regular chiropractic care, and make sure that those you love do the same. You don't have to come see me. Just find someone who you like or were referred to, someone who understands these basic principals. Then go get your power turned on!"

Several hands went up and John answered questions regarding specific conditions, costs and insurance coverage, and whether it was appropriate to adjust children. One gentleman in the middle of the room had been shaking his head disapprovingly throughout the talk and when he finally raised his hand to ask a question, John braced himself for the worst. It seemed there was always one heckler in every group and things were going too smoothly.

The man stood slowly so that all might hear him.

"First of all, I'd like to tell you and everyone in this room that I don't believe in chiropractic and I think this nonsense about innate intelligence is just hogwash. Now that we have that clear, let me ask my question. Mr. Truley, isn't it true that the real reason chiropractors criticize medical drugs is because you don't get to prescribe them because your license won't let you?"

As the eyes in the room turned from the man back to John, like watching a slow motion tennis match, John smiled slightly.

"Thank you for expressing your opinion and asking your question. I purposely planned to stay off of the drug issue today unless someone brought it up. Now that you have, sir, let's talk about it. First of all, I am not against the responsible use of drugs when appropriate; unfortunately, drug companies have effectively promoted the overuse of prescription as well as over-the-counter medications. Sadly, medical doctors are almost solely dependent on drug therapy for care of their patients. It is only recently that some of them have come to embrace diet and nutritional counseling as part of their protocol, as chiropractic and other holistic professions have been practicing for 100 years.

"But, let's get back to drugs. How many people, would you guess, die in the United States from adverse reactions to medical drugs? Would you believe that over 350 people die each day because they react to drugs they are given in the hospital? We're talking about well over two thousand deaths every week. It's estimated that 770,000 people have hospital-induced adverse drug reactions each year, costing an estimated 4.2 billion dollars in additional costs during the hospital stay alone, which does not include outpatient care or disability. It is also estimated that the total annual cost of these drug misadventures in the U.S. is 79 billion dollars. Now, have you ever heard of the phrase: the rising cost of medical care? Well, a nice portion of this cost is directly related to drug reactions alone. Thirty percent of people who go to the hospital will have an adverse drug reaction and three out of a hundred of those will die from it. Medical care is now the third leading killer in the U.S. No sir, it isn't that I don't prescribe drugs because I can't. I don't prescribe them because I don't want to.

"In an adverse drug reaction, the most commonly affected organ in the body is the central nervous system. The very system that transmits the vital intelligence you term hogwash. Now, if I believe in this healing power, then why would I ever want to poison the vehicle that distributes it where it needs to go? Have I answered your question yet?"

The man was shouting now. "That all sounds like a bunch of malarkey. You expect us to believe that? Is this something you chiropractors get together and make up?"

John let the man's challenge linger in the air, until all eyes returned back to him. "Actually sir, all of the information I just gave you can be found in a recent edition of the *Journal of The American Medical Association,* the allopathic profession's largest, and most respected, trade journal."

The man took his seat and John smiled at the audience. "As you see, we can have spirited discussion regarding things that we were taught as children and accepted as gospel most of our lives. Thankfully, we live in a new era when people are accepting a greater responsibility for their health and are willing to investigate the facts and try more logical and natural approaches to keeping themselves and their loved ones well. Thank you for your time. I've enjoyed speaking to you today."

Brock and Charles stood and applauded with the rest of the enthusiastic crowd to avoid looking conspicuous. They watched as a group of people rushed toward the podium, anxious to shake the doctor's hand, comment on the content of his speech, or ask for his card.

Brock leaned over to Charles. "You know, I think this is the kind of shit that's pissing off the boss."

"Yeah, this guy thinks he's the Martin Luther King of natural health care."

Brock nodded. "Someone the industry would prefer not to have around."

Chapter 18

"You're on a roll, John, don't let up. This is a once in a lifetime chance."

"Jimmy, didn't you say the same thing about the radio show?"

"Yes, but your opportunities just keep getting bigger and better! Did you see your name in the trade papers? Three of the profession's national publications are running with your story. You're an inspiration to every chiropractor in the U.S. I personally know three guys who have started speaking publicly using your format, even mentioning the Prespo girl as a rallying cry."

"You're kidding. You know, I did get a call from *The Chiropractic Journal*. I forgot all about it."

"They must have shared the information, because you're also in the other publications. Now, I hope you won't mind, Johnny, but I've decided to donate my time to become your personal agent."

"My God, what next?"

"I knew you'd love it. Now, you know that your buddy, Jimmy here, has connections all over town and I've booked you for five talks so far, including three big rotaries, the Seniors for Wellness, and the San Diego Presbyterian Church, which, by the way, is the largest in town."

"What? Jimmy, when do you think I'm going to have time for all of that?"

"Don't worry, I've either scheduled them during your lunch hour or in the evening after work. Now get this. I have a patient who makes professional quality videos of events like these. I've contracted him to create a tape that we can distribute to every chiropractor in the country. They can show them in their waiting rooms, for all their people to see. Johnny, we can reach a lot of people that way. I've also selected five chiropractors in town, who I felt had the most potential as public speakers, to observe the talks with me. From there, we'll develop a polished presentation and rehearse it with each one before sending them out into the community to do similar events. Let me tell you, these guys are into it. We can all smell the blood of the drug industry, and you're the one that started the bleeding. Are you with me?"

"Jimmy, I'm probably crazy but, yes, I'm with you. Let's do it. Now, I gotta go. Jeffrey has been patiently waiting for me." He felt excited but extremely tired.

"Okay, it's all set. Your first talk is seven-thirty tomorrow night at the church. I'll pick you up at six-forty-five. You're an awesome dude, Johnny. Now get some rest so we can go make history."

He hung up the phone and chuckled, thinking about Jimmy McBride turned loose on the rest of the nation.

John found Jeffrey playing quietly in his room and explained to him that he needed to make one more phone call. A rush of emotion welled up in his heart as Jeffrey patiently nodded, letting him know he understood his dad had other things besides him to take care of every day. It was a tough call trying to juggle his obligations to his profession, his patients and others, with his duty as father and family member to Jeffrey. He knew Jeffrey came first in his life, but wasn't he attempting to make a better world for his son? What kind of example would he be setting by being mediocre, afraid to step out and challenge the forces that tried to keep him down? He wanted Jeffrey to have a better life than his, and he certainly hoped his motivations were noble enough to warrant being away from his son so much and so often. He occasionally worried that the things he did were either for his own personal glory, or to chase away the ghosts of self-doubt and failure from his past.

He went back downstairs and paused for a moment to clear his head before dialing the phone. After a couple of rings, Mrs. Connie Prespo answered.

John cleared his throat. "Connie? Hello, this is John Truley. I just wanted to call and see how you were doing and let you know that Jeffrey and I are thinking about you and your family."

"Oh, hi, Dr. Truley. It's very nice of you to call. My husband and I are doing as well as can be expected. Katie is out of her coma and was able to leave intensive care. They are just beginning to do testing to find out the extent of her neurologic damage. She can't speak or write, but she recognizes us and is starting to get back some of her color."

John could hear her voice tighten as she spoke. "Oh, that's good news." He tried to sound positive. "I'll be sure and tell Jeffrey. And don't forget, whenever it's appropriate, I'll bring him and any of her other friends for a visit. You just let me know."

There was a pause as Connie sniffled. She then took a couple of deep breaths. "Dr. Truley, before you go I want to tell you that I have joined an organization called the National Vaccine Information Center. They are thousands of members strong. I had no idea any of this existed until it happened to Katie. Now, I talk to parents every day, whose children have been killed, brain damaged or have become autistic from mandatory vaccinations. They tell me that this is happening more frequently with the increased number of vaccines required by law. They say that everyone is being hurt, even the children of medical doctors and congressmen." There was another pause followed by more sniffles and finally the sound of Connie blowing her nose.

"I know you're speaking publicly about this problem, and I want you to know that you officially have my permission to use our name and our story. I heard about your incident on the radio and how you handled those doctors. If I can personally do anything to help, please let me know. It helps my husband and I to deal with the pain when we know that you're out there fighting so other children might not be injured like my baby."

John said good-bye and stared at the phone for a moment. He considered calling Jimmy back to tell him to push this thing harder and faster, but stopped himself and instead went upstairs feeling fortunate to be able to play with a perfectly healthy son.

The next eight weeks were a whirlwind. John talked nearly every night, and Jimmy's team was there videotaping and taking notes. The five speakers had become nine and most were already doing their own presentations. Jimmy and his video man had effectively produced two. One was a hard-hitting piece featuring the best of John's first week on the lecture circuit, speaking on the dangers of drugs. The tape came with a list of scientifically substantiated statistics and references, and even featured an interview with Connie Prespo and other members of her organization, the National Vaccine Information Center. An eight-hundred number was provided for anyone to call and obtain a free copy of the video to share with their personal organization. The second tape was designed for professionals who wanted to join the team, begin speaking publicly and work the media. The two tapes were mailed to every chiropractor in the U.S. Donations were accepted to help offset the expense of the operation, but Jimmy, who had quickly become a man possessed, funded a large part of the program out of his own pocket. Several secretaries of the involved doctors' offices and a half-dozen students at a nearby chiropractic college had volunteered to distribute the tapes, take phone orders and field questions. Two of the students spent several hours a day researching and collecting data from all professional journals worldwide that contained studies pertaining to drugs. The information they collected was often astounding and easy to incorporate into the lectures. Numerous journals whose studies revealed drug therapy in a distinctly unfavorable light, went ahead and published the studies, indicating that most M.D.s were not only ethical, but self critical.

John found himself trying to temper the aggressive nature of the speakers in training, pointing out that it was the public's ignorance of natural methods to wellness, as well as the drug institution and all of its abuses that they were fighting, not the medical doctors themselves. He reminded them that their mission was to educate the public about the risks of using drugs to mask symptoms instead of finding the cause of the problem. It was a learning time for everyone from the chiropractors to the M.D.s, from the drug companies to the public.

The World Chiropractic Alliance, an international organization of subluxation-based doctors, picked up on the momentum that Truley and company had created and launched new efforts at making the public aware of the benefits of chiropractic. Powerfully constructed articles were placed in several large publications, including *Reader's Digest* and *Time*. Among other things, the articles informed the public that chiropractors were the third largest group of health care providers in the U.S., composed of over 60,000 doctors nationwide, annually helping nearly 20 million Americans receive the benefits of chiropractic.

The combination of the national advertising campaign and the grassroots network of well-trained public speakers created an unprecedented public awareness of the simple message that there was a better way to be healthy, and it didn't include drugs or surgery.

Although the drive to reach the public was in its infancy, early studies of its impact revealed record numbers of new people entering clinics nationwide. Individual chiropractors across the country were reporting that their previously plateaued practices were increasing steadily since the program's inception. It was an exciting time for the profession, and John, Jimmy, and the group were ecstatic about the unexpected magnitude of their efforts.

McBride Chiropractic had become the official headquarters of what Dr. Jimmy had coined *The Power That Heals Campaign*. The group, consisting of the nine local speakers, Jimmy, John, and the student and secretarial volunteers, made occasion to celebrate their good fortune. Jimmy had ordered several bottles of champagne, which he passed around the room. With his characteristic flair for the dramatic, he asked for silence before the simultaneous uncorking.

"Before we toast to what has surely been the most splendid victory of my life, please let me share the significance of the moment as I see it. Just a few decades ago, our chiropractic brothers were still being imprisoned on a regular basis for practicing what they believed in. They risked their freedom, as well as the safety and well being of their families, to provide a natural method of health care to the public — a method that worked with natural laws instead of against them. Their sacrifices have paved the way for the opportunity we have recently seized. It is my belief that destiny has kindly chosen us to lead the way into a new era of health care where the majority of citizens will soon be taking part in natural health and the removal of subluxation. I believe we've helped our profession, in this short time that we have been together, to reach critical mass with the public. I want to thank you all and encourage you to press even harder to spread the word. I propose the first toast to my good friend, Dr. John Truley, who was the spark that ignited the fire!"

With that, Jimmy popped his cork, sending a foamy stream shooting through the air. The group cheered wildly amidst the sound of bottles being uncorked.

Jimmy brought the first glass to John and, after pouring one for himself, raised his glass and looked his friend in the eye.

"Not long ago we toasted to what almost was, now let us toast to what definitely is. And may I compliment you on your new and very large sword!"

Chapter 19

Seven men collectively owned nearly all of the pharmaceutical industry in the nation. Their holdings included many subsidiary drug companies which, for all intents and purposes, appeared to be completely independent. The vast majority of the smaller firms' employees, as well as management, were virtually unaware of this connection to the men.

Although originally quite competitive with one another, these powerful individuals saw the benefit of uniting on certain causes and met whenever circumstances dictated. With their tremendous influence they were able to dictate political agenda through mammoth lobbying efforts. The organization's widely distributed funds to the U.S. Congress represented the lion's portion of money received by politicians. Their contributions alone were greater than the sum of the next ten largest political interest groups, which included the American Medical Association. Their power was astounding and they bore its stewardship with the utmost seriousness.

To carry out special tasks, the Big Seven, as they were known, enlisted the services of Reginald Arfarian, a former CIA agent turned international mercenary. Mr. Arfarian had the special talent of assembling and managing a secret corps of top professionals like himself, who would perform any task requested by their employer in exchange for a luxurious lifestyle and good hours. These twenty or so men had all the necessary skills to carry out dangerous assignments which ranged from infiltrating a Fortune 500 company to conducting an assassination in a third world country. The individuals in this elite force were used only a half-dozen times a year; however, they were on call and ready to respond at a moment's notice. Using sophisticated means, the operatives could be installed quickly, often within hours, to carry out a mission and then disappear with equal swiftness. It was from this pool that special agents Helton and Tomine had been summoned.

Mano Ferguson controlled the second largest pharmaceutical organization of the seven. He was known for his thorough and effective approach to problem solving. When Frederick Harding of Apex Industries, one of Mano's subsidiaries, contacted him regarding the potential problem of one John Truley, he had considered ignoring the situation to see if it would resolve itself. It sounded absurd, one man trying to threaten an establishment as heavily entrenched as the pharmaceutical industry.

But Mano Ferguson did not rise to his lofty position by being sloppy and his man, Frederick Harding, was neither a slouch nor an alarmist; on the contrary, he was a wise and mature man who had earned Ferguson's respect over the years. If he saw something that bothered him enough to contact Mano, then it was worth looking into.

It was also Mano's nature to be extremely cautious in all business dealings, and he quickly decided to contact Reginald Arfarian, who the group referred to as "The General." Arfarian wasted no time inserting the two field operatives, Brock Helton and Charles Tomine, to monitor the rabble-rousing chiropractor's activities. The initial reports were somewhat noteworthy, but the rate at which the condition escalated was downright alarming. It was for this reason that Mano had requested that his colleagues, whom he now addressed, meet to discuss the situation.

"Practitioners of chiropractic have always been our detractors by their philosophic nature and, although they have had many charismatic leaders, no one has been able to unite and mobilize the profession and cause a serious threat to us economically, perhaps until now. I'm not saying this Truley is the one, but the preliminary figures are worthy of our serious consideration. The most disturbing factor is the speed at which this unknown has risen within his ranks to create an unprecedented commotion. His grass roots campaign, organized by his colleague, one James McBride, has created a surprising following of upstart and rebellious individuals, and from what I understand, their numbers are increasing rapidly."

"Mano, please, you can't tell me that this man has made any significant public impact?" one of the men impatiently asked, annoyed at the thought of the unlikely crusader.

"I know you gentlemen are busy, so I took the liberty of having my team perform the usual public polling, as well as our Quick Response Task Force of MD's. I think you will find the results quite interesting. We asked five questions to a random selection of over a thousand households nation-wide. It seems that there is name recognition for the man in an astounding thirteen percent of the population. Another disturbing finding was that the number of households who would consider chiropractic as an alternative to medication has climbed to seventeen percent up from twelve where it has hovered for the past six years. It has always been that high in California and parts of Colorado, but the fact that it's risen dramatically on a national scale indicates that Truley is making an impact well beyond his own backyard.

"We have approximately two-hundred medical doctors available for the instant survey we instituted in the early nineties. Seventy-eight percent reported a significantly higher incidence of non-compliance to drug recommenda-tions during the last eight weeks and a whopping nineteen percent had been personally asked by their patients what they thought of Dr. John Truley."

"That's impossible," one of the men protested. "Who the hell is this guy? I've never heard of him."

"I have," another said.

All eyes turned to the man in silence.

"My sister lives in Rancho Santa Fe. She sees him. Says he's a damn miracle man."

Mano Furguson nodded grimly at the group. "Now gen-tlemen, a course of action is indicated here and I ask you to join me in deciding what level of intervention to take on behalf of this group."

"You say the men are in place?" asked Clemente Morantz, the man who controlled the largest percentage of the pharmaceutical market.

"He could be silenced within the hour if that be the

appropriate response."

Lazarus McKenzy had shoulder-length white hair and was by far the most eccentric of the group. "That approach would likely create a monster of a martyr out of what is likely a flash in the pan. I vote to sabotage his campaign, slowing down his momentum, and judiciously make his life a living hell."

"Does he have a family?" the man next to him asked.

"He has one son who is seven years old," Mano reported. "His wife died from complications of the boy's delivery."

"Well then, I don't think our boys will have too much difficulty dampening John Truley's enthusiasm for his work," Lazarus said, looking satisfied that a difficult situation had been so simply remedied.

"Do we all agree?" Mano asked looking around the room. Each nodded in turn and the meeting adjourned with a traditional shot of bourbon, as each man drank to the others' health.

Chapter 20

Sally went through the motions of sampling, tagging and recording the data on the sixty-six rodents that were the current focus of a team of three researchers in Blackmore West. The rats were divided into three equal groups and designated by either a square, triangle or circle clipped from their right ears. She could barely focus on her tasks and had been thinking all morning about what she should do. There was still no sign of Dr. Weedleman, and the whole situation was becoming increasingly disconcerting.

She took her usual break at noon and went to Frankie's Deli, where she always had lunch. The place was already bustling with people, but she was able to locate a small table in the back near the bathrooms, next to a table crowded with construction workers. She asked the men to watch her table and sweater while she went to place her order. Sally could not stop thinking about Dr. Weedleman and the whole CD4C issue. While waiting, she realized she was bound to go crazy unless she took some type of action and, by the time she reached the front of the line, she had an idea.

"Hi, Frankie, I'll have the usual," she said to the small, white-haired, Italian man.

"Ahh, wonderful. One usual coming up!" he said with gusto as he slapped the ticket on the counter for the sandwich maker. "And how is that equally beautiful sister of yours, I think it is Mara?"

"She's great. I'll bring her down here for lunch again soon."

"Wonderful! You know the family is the most important thing," he said, looking kindly at her, knowing the story of how she and Mara had found each other after so many years.

"You're right as usual, Frankie."

He started to go on about the merits of family relationships when Sally looked through the front window and noticed Martin Hommer, the security guy from work, leaning against one of Blackmore's cars. Martin, who was always trying to talk to her, gave her the creeps. She quickly excused herself from Frankie and ducked behind the line of people. She moved swiftly to the back of the deli and into a hallway that led to the bathrooms. There was a public phone on the wall and she grabbed the phone book and began flipping through pages. Lamont Weedleman was easy to find and his address was listed. She dug in her pocket for change and then looked up and saw Frankie's scribbled message that the phone was out of order.

"Damn!"

Sally checked Lamont's address more closely and was surprised to find that it was only a few blocks away. She memorized the street numbers and returned to the dining area, thanking the construction guys as she grabbed her sweater. She glanced up to see Martin entering the deli. Hastily she retreated back into the hallway. Her mind raced, remembering that she had never seen him at the deli before today and, although he originally appeared to be waiting for another party, he was now alone. She shuddered and quickly dismissed the thought that he may have followed her there. She reflected on the last several times she had seen him and wondered if his behavior had been more suspicious of late.

"Your just getting paranoid, girl," she said aloud.

Noticing a back door for the first time, she bolted out into an alley that led behind an adjacent liquor store, then onto a side street.

After taking a moment to get her bearings, she set off at a brisk pace.

Meanwhile, inside, Frankie tossed a lunch on the counter and yelled, "Tuna on rye, mustard only!"

Martin carefully searched the room for Sally's familiar face. He noticed an empty table near the back and wondered if she could be in the restroom.

Frankie shouted louder. "Tuna on rye with mustard. Sally. Your sandwich is ready; come and get it before it gets old!"

Martin looked around the room, waiting to see if Sally would stand up to claim her lunch. When nobody made a move toward the sandwich, he burst into the back hallway hesitating for only a moment before trying the handle on the woman's bathroom door. It was unlocked, and when he opened it, found it empty. He flung the door open, crashing it into the bathroom wall, drawing attention from the construction workers watching from their table. Ignoring them, Martin looked to his right and saw the back door ajar.

Disturbed yet intrigued by the possibility that Sally may have fled, he shoved the door open and bounded into the alley. He looked both ways but there was no sign of her. He ran down the alley past the back of the liquor store to the street. Seeing no one, he sped back into the deli for one more look. The construction workers looked up as he approached from the hallway.

"Excuse me, can you fellas tell me if you saw a girl go out this back door?"

The half dozen men peered at him, panting in his blue, heavily starched uniform, complete with club and gun hanging menacingly from his belt.

One of the more burly members laughed. "Who's asking, Rent-a-Cop?"

Martin could see the group was hostile toward authority and, although on another day he may have risen to the challenge, he decided not to engage the buffoons.

"Never mind." On his way to the front door, after he was safely out of earshot, he muttered, "Dickheads!"

Martin ran through the parking lot, flung his car door open, smacking the side panel of a shiny, red Volkswagen.

A young secretary was just getting out of the driver's side of the little car. "Hey, watch it!" She hurried around to his side and spotted the new ding. "You dented it!"

Martin jammed the gearshift into reverse and backed out. The woman spun toward him, approaching his open driver's side window.

"Who's going to fix my car?"

Still smarting from the construction workers' rude treatment, Martin flipped her the bird as he spun out of Frankie's parking lot, leaving the woman in a cloud of dust and making it difficult for her to read the phone number on his car's How Am I Driving? sticker.

Martin's heart pounded with excitement. It appeared Debero had been right, one could never be too careful. Sally Hobbs was an industrial thief. Why else would she disappear out the back of a deli without her sandwich? He punched the accelerator, just making it across the street in front of oncoming traffic. A couple of drivers angrily blared their horns. At the corner in front of the liquor store, he made another dangerous left and was honked at again. He floored the Chevrolet, making the engine roar into low gear as he sped to the first cross street where he hit the brakes hard.

Sally's adrenaline was flowing as she instinctively jumped behind a hedge in someone's yard when she heard the roar of the car followed by the screech of tires. She peered through the bushes and saw the Blackmore security car stopped at the corner from which she had just come. Martin was behind the wheel looking frantically in all directions.

"My God, he is following me." The fear in her voice startled her even more. She now had no doubt that something was terribly wrong with Blackmore and its impending release of the new CD4C vaccine. She had to know what happened to Dr. Weedleman. As soon as Martin sped out of sight, she dusted herself off and ran full speed toward the address she'd seen in the phone book. As she frantically made her way through the modest residential area, she watched carefully for the metallic gray security car and listened for the roar of its engine.

Soon she arrived at Dr. Weedleman's address and found a white and gray duplex surrounded by a three-foot white picket fence. She opened the gate and entered, unable to recall if the phone book had designated a unit number. An elderly woman was on the porch of the first unit, tending to a multitude of potted flowers surrounding a rocking chair.

The woman nodded sweetly at Sally as she walked past her to the back unit. The next porch was identical but without foliage or furniture. Sun-bleached newspapers were scattered across a welcoming mat. Sally climbed the stairs and rang the buzzer. There was no answer, but she could hear the faint sound of a television and what sounded like someone shuffling things around a kitchen.

She pounded on the door. "Dr. Weedleman, this is Sally Hobbs. I want to talk to you!"

The television noise suddenly stopped. Sally waited a few moments and then pounded again.

"Dr. Weedleman, I must speak to you, it's very important!"

Silence.

"It's about CD4C!"

She waited another minute and then heard the click of the dead bolt. The door creaked open to a haggard Lamont Weedleman, wearing a week's growth of beard. His eyes were red and sunken, and his skin hung pale and flaccid around his jaws. He held a plastic cup filled with two ice cubes floating in brown fluid. He wore a tattered robe and old brown house slippers.

"What're ya doin' here?"

"My God, Dr. Weedleman! Are you okay? What's going on? You haven't been at work."

"You came to my house just to see if I was okay?" He scratched his stubbled chin.

"I was confused when you didn't come back. I know that CD4C is a cold vaccine. I know I wasn't supposed to, but I couldn't help but look at the files when I put them all together that day. And now I hear Blackmore is going to release the vaccine." She looked at his glassy eyes and wondered what he was going through and why. "Does this have something to do with you being away from work for such a long time?"

The man looked at her for a minute, swaying slightly. "Well, you might as well come and sit down. Sounds like we've got no secrets now, doesn't it?" He led her into a den lit by diffused sunshine filtered through a slightly opened venetian blind. He motioned for her to have a chair next to the muted television, then lowered his tall frame onto a well-worn brown plaid couch.

He stared into space and then took another drink. "I was so close and the bastards took it away from me. I could have perfected it, you know. I just haven't been able to go back and start a new project." He threw back the rest of the scotch.

"Why can't you work on it now? What about the last several weeks?"

Lamont looked at her and chuckled, shaking his head slowly. "The Great Board didn't think that was a good idea. They thought the FDA would become suspicious if we continued experimentation on a supposedly finished product. They wanted nothing to stand in the way of getting the vaccine onto the market." He slumped further into the couch and closed his eyes. "I bet it wasn't like this when my father and grandfather were around."

"And it shouldn't be like this now, Dr. Weedleman. It's not right." She noticed that his eyes remained closed. "Dr. Weedleman. Dr. Weedleman!" His eyes fluttered open about halfway and then closed again. "Is CD4C safe?"

She went over to the couch and took the drink from his hand and began shaking his shoulders gently, then progressively harder until he opened his eyes once again.

"Is CD4C safe?" she demanded.

"Safe is relative."

"Relative? Relative to what? All right. Let's compare it to a cold. Is it safe compared to the risks of a child getting a cold?" She shook him again to roust him from his stupor. "For God's sake, they're going to start using it next week! I was there. I saw those Labradors! Is it safe, Dr. Weedleman?"

"If I could, I'd stop it, but I can't. Now leave me alone." His head fell back on the pillow with his mouth gaping wide, exposing gold fillings. Within sixty seconds, he was snoring hard and loud.

Sally sat next to him with her head in her hands. She

thought about what he said, and how he, the man who knew the most about CD4C, would stop the vaccine's distribution if possible. She thought about Blackmore's security cop following her, and about all the Labradors, including Mildreds One through Six. She remembered Mara excitedly telling her the story about John Truley and his account of the little girl with brain damage. It dawned on her that if any children were injured from CD4C, she would be as guilty as anyone else. She looked around the room. Dr. Weedleman's house was a mess, but it was nothing compared to his office. She had an idea. She searched quickly through the house. The man's snoring could be heard easily from every room. After a few minutes she found what she was looking for in the kitchen among dozens of dirty glasses and several empty ice trays. She returned to the den, put a blanket over Lamont's legs and then let herself out, locking the door behind her.

Back on the street she moved carefully, staying close to the yards and looking for places to hide if necessary. She wasn't quite sure why Martin was after her, but became more at ease the farther she got from Dr. Weedleman's house. She decided to walk into the deli through the back door and act as if she were just returning from the bathroom. Martin would know that wasn't the case, but what could he do about it?

Out in the parking lot, Officer Martin Hommer was sitting in the Chevrolet talking on the phone.

"Yes, Mr. Debero, the suspect has been out of my sight now for about twenty minutes. I know, sir. Yes, I remember your instructions."

Sally walked through the deli and Frankie looked at her quizzically.

"You leave too long and make your sandwich stale. Now I wrap it up for you so you can take back to work." Frankie shook his head.

"I'm sorry, Frankie. Thanks, I'm sure it will still be delicious." She took the sandwich and walked out through the front door. She saw Martin sitting in his car talking on the phone and nodding his head. She started her car and drove out of the lot.

"Wait a minute." Martin looked up in astonishment. "There she goes." He quickly fired up the security car and took off after her.

"Stay back. See where she's going," instructed Debero.

"She's turning on Wilshire now and getting over to the left lane. She's . . . She's going back to work!"

"Mr. Hommer, that doesn't sound like someone who has just committed a crime. Report to my office when you get back here!" Martin heard his boss slam the phone.

He stared at the cellular, thrusting his middle finger at it. "Yes, your assholiness, sir!"

Sally arrived at Blackmore's employee lot, parked and went inside. Back in the lab she donned her white smock and looked at the line of cages containing rats. Red cards could be found on about a dozen empty cages with notes detailing the time, date and description of the animals' deaths. Sally decided it would be best if she began performing her usual work duties to see if anything was out of the ordinary. She began cleaning the bottoms of the cages, extracting fecal samples from each. She also measured and recorded the amount of food and water consumed by each rat. The process took over two hours, during which the lab appeared to be quite normal, with no sign of Martin or other security personnel. At four-thirty, the three researchers took off their smocks and left the lab. On their way out, one of them handed her instructions to prepare twenty new cages for the following day's work. The lab was now quiet with the exception of two other assistants on the far side, chatting about which movies they had seen.

Sally walked over to Dr. Weedleman's office and put her hand on the bulge in her pocket. She knew that what she was about to do could have grave consequences. She also knew that if she balked, greater harm could possibly arise. She pulled the keys taken from Weedleman's apartment out of her pocket and nervously looked around. With a shaky hand, she began trying to unlock the door. After several tries, she found the right key, making her heart pound like a drum and drowning out the two assistants' conversation. She opened the door and slipped into the office, closing it behind her. The office appeared exactly the way it had the last time she was in it. Moving quickly toward the large filing cabinet, she inadvertently knocked over a three-foot stack of papers and cursed as they scattered across the floor. She decided not to pick them up and instead remained focused on the double doors of the cabinet. Finding the correct key was easier because there were only a few small ones on the ring.

Sally realized she was holding her breath and forced herself to take a few deep breaths. For a moment, she thought a bug was crawling down her side, inside her shirt, but realized with a shudder that it was just a bead of perspiration. Was she crazy, she wondered? What possessed her to break into Weedleman's office? She thought about turning back, considering all she was risking, all she had worked for. She thought about her success and how she was able to provide for herself and Mara. Mara, who without Sally would just be another victim. An unwanted youth with no family, willing to trust anyone who showed her attention. Even someone like Rocky. After placing her trust in him, he abused her, subjecting her to cruel and degrading behavior spawned from a sick mind. He was less concerned for her well being than the average stranger on the street.

Then she thought of the Labradors and the similarities they shared with her sister. The dogs wanted only to be taken in and loved by someone. But instead of a safe haven in which to thrive, they were offered a steel cage and an experimental injection of viruses. In place of love and kinship came a painful and lonely death, and worst of all for Sally, it had come from her own hand. And for what? So their deaths could be ignored? Disregarded? It wasn't as if they were being nobly offered as a sacrifice for the good of man; no, more likely they were just a tool for a desperate company to use in an attempt to save its ass. How could people that treated living creatures with such disregard be trusted to do what is best for children? Could the enticement of the almighty dollar, or in Blackmore's case, the threat of going belly up, be enough to put children at risk?

Sally clenched her jaw and flung the cabinet's double doors open, pulling the top drawer out without hesitation. Plunging into the red files, she thumbed quickly through the rodents and monkeys to locate the file marked Canine Subjects — Weedleman. She pulled out the file and set it on top of the drawer. She dug into the third round results, seeking the lone Labrador in the bunch. Unable to find it, she again reminded herself to breathe and calm down. She skipped ahead to the latter rounds where they had added more Labradors to each experiment. Again nothing. She then noticed something peculiar and counted the subjects listed in Round Four, one in which she distinctly remembered multiple Labradors. Although there was a glaring lack of the breed in question, there was still a full compliment of subjects listed. She looked carefully at each dog and saw four she didn't remember and was certain she hadn't collected data on.

"They falsified the freakin' records!" she muttered in amazement.

Looking back behind the rounds, where the individual Mildreds' results should be, she found none. Thoroughly shaken, she shoved the file back into the drawer and wildly thumbed through all the red files, not wanting to believe, but already knowing that she would not find any records of the Labradors. It's time to get out of here, she thought, her head reeling. She slammed the drawer closed and shut the double doors. She spun around and knocked over another stack of papers, this time from Dr. Weedleman's desk. Automatically, she stooped down to pick them up. She wondered if anyone would figure out that she had been there if she just left them. She pulled the papers toward her into a pile. She looked toward the door and then above it where, to her horror, she saw a security camera perched next to a silk plant. The room suddenly spun and felt as if all the air had been sucked out of it. She fought the imaginary vacuum and drew a small, pitiful gasp. If there had been any hope before of explaining that she was in the office on official business, it was most certainly dashed now by her dumbfounded, caught-in-the-act stare at the security camera. She knew there was only one thing left to do as she bolted from the office.

Officer Martin Hommer was just returning from a leisurely trip to the executive level bathrooms and was disappointed to find Ms. Browne's door closed. As he lifted the coffeepot to smell the quality brew, his walkie-talkie broke the silence of the plush hallway.

"Come in, Hommer," a voice crackled.

"This is Hommer, go ahead."

"We have a security breach in West; got it on tape."

"I'm on my way!" Martin slammed the pot back onto the warmer.

Sally grabbed her pack and raced out of the lab. Running down the long corridor that led to the elevators, she felt tight muscles in her legs and remembered she had been running away from Blackmore security at lunch also. This time, however, there would be no coming back. She rode the elevator down to the parking garage with five other people. She gasped for air as quietly as possible, thankful that a few of them were engaged in conversation.

"We have a fleeing suspect on her way to the parking garage," the walkie-talkie on Martin's belt announced.

Martin grabbed it as he jumped into the elevator. "Roger that, I'm in pursuit. Is the suspect Sally Hobbs, by any chance?"

"Affirmative."

Martin holstered his radio. "We'll see if I'm overreacting now, Debero."

Sally ran to her car and started it up, quickly jamming it into reverse. She must beat the other cars through the security gate.

Martin had six floors to go and pulled out his phone to dial Debero's number. The Chief of Security answered personally as he had before.

"Chief, this is Officer Hommer. Sally Hobbs has breached

security and is fleeing the building. I request permission to apprehend."

"By all means, and I mean that literally. Do whatever it takes to stop her. Have you notified the gate?"

Martin cursed under his breath. "Ah, yes, sir."

"Summon me as soon as you have her in custody. I'll deal with the legal aspects, understood?"

"Roger that, Chief. You can count on me, sir."

"Let's hope so, Mr. Hommer."

Martin hung up the phone and grabbed his radio as he ran out of the elevator on the parking level. "Come in, gate!"

Sally was trying to act cool, smiling at the security guard as she drove by the gate. She watched him nod and then reach for his radio. Looking in her rear view mirror she saw him step out of his shack and into the street looking at her car as he talked. She turned and sped off toward the light at the end of the street, knowing that she had barely escaped.

Martin squealed to a stop at the gate. "Did you see her?

"She just turned right." The guard pointed.

"Damn it!" Martin screamed, pounding his steering wheel. He floored the Chevy, causing the guard at the gate to shield his eyes against flying debris.

Sally weaved through traffic while watching in her rear-view mirror for the gray and black security vehicles from Blackmore. If she could just make it to the freeway, she might have a chance to get away. Never in her life had she experienced anything like this and she was absolutely petrified. Unlike her sister, she had never been in trouble with the law. She had never even been in a fight. Apparently, she was good at avoiding conflicts, at least until now. She thought about the missing records in Weedleman's office and the magnitude of Blackmore's crime, and she became more frightened for her own safety.

A silver and black security car appeared about two blocks behind as she punched the accelerator to make it through a yellow light. What would they do to her if they caught her? She knew what she did was illegal. Would they call the cops? She didn't see any yet. No, her actions may have been illegal, but what they did was many times worse. She wondered if she should go to the police. She veered into a right turn lane, passed a couple of cars, then cut back in before the next intersection. One more block to the freeway. It would be her word against theirs. They had her on film, breaking into a restricted area, with a stolen set of keys, and looking at protected documents. What did she have? Nothing. If she could have found the Labrador records it may have been different.

Sally made it to the Interstate 5 on-ramp where road construction, as always, was in full swing. She prayed she would not be delayed and thought of how she might defend herself if one of Blackmore's guys were able to run up to her car while she was dead-stopped in traffic. She shuddered, thinking about the possibilities, and let out her breath as she drove past the heavy equipment operating on the shoulder. She could think of only one thing to do now, and it was a long shot.

Officer Hommer drove like a madman. He could see Sally's Ford Escort less than two blocks ahead. She had taken the I-5 south on-ramp and, once on the freeway, he should be able to catch up to her with minimal difficulty. There was a large tractor with a front-end loader lifting a cement divider on the right side of the ramp. It was swinging around toward the on-ramp as he turned onto it.

"No!" he yelled as a flagman stepped out to stop traffic. Martin veered right up onto the shoulder and considered making a run down the side until he saw a small trailer being unloaded by a couple of orange-vested California Transit workers. The left shoulder was also blocked by the large concrete dividers the workers were positioning to divert traffic for future construction.

"Don't you know it's rush hour!" he screamed.

The delay had already cost him five minutes. He thought about informing Debero to what was going on, but decided he would capture Sally Hobbs, then make the call. He took the phone from his belt, turned it off and threw it on the passenger seat. His radio was useless this far from Blackmore and he tossed it next to the phone. This was his game now. He was in open field, pursuing his prey, the very same prey that had made him look bad in Mr. Debero's eyes. He swore he would make things right.

At last, the flagman yielded and the security car roared south.

Chapter 21

John called the Michaels from the pay phone outside of Denny's in Laguna Niguel. He told Jeffrey about his day and reminded him how much he loved him, and then asked to speak to Mary again.

John could never have imagined being this busy. His life was so radically different since the radio and television events.

Mary's voice was soothing. "How you holding up, John?"

"I'm all right, but I hate being away from Jeffrey this much. How's he handling it?"

"Don't worry. He's like family and he knows it. This is your time, John. Do what you're supposed to. We'll take care of Jeffrey."

"Thank you for that. I have no idea what's gonna happen with all this notoriety. It can't go on indefinitely. I should be home in a couple of hours at the most."

"It's more than just notoriety, John. And like I said, don't worry about Jeffrey. We love him and we're happy to help out. That goes for Frank, too."

John hung up the phone and returned to the coffee shop. He wondered why he was there, and although he found it slightly difficult to relax, he welcomed this, his first opportunity to sit and reflect quietly. He tried to decide when the recent change in his life started and why. Was it the night Jimmy took him to the meeting where he had the unusual experience, or was it the next morning when he called the radio station? Before that, however, he had been at Katie Prespo's side when she suffered her tragic drug reaction in the nurse's office.

There was something that he was suddenly aware of. Throughout his recent adventures, starting with the phone call to Dr. Bill's radio show, he'd been able to clearly hear what many call a still, small voice inside of him. Many chiropractors would call it Innate Intelligence, others would call it God. More importantly — he had acted on it. It was this voice that would not let him disregard the phone call he had received just over an hour ago. It was the reason he left his office filled with people and was now sitting at Denny's in Laguna Niguel.

Sally Hobbs walked into the restaurant, quickly scanning the room until her eyes found a lone figure in a booth near the back. She took a couple of strides toward him and then stopped short when a wave of familiarity and connection surged through her. She shook her head and blinked a couple times, wondering if her mind was playing tricks. There was something about him. It was if she were looking at someone whom she had already shared experiences with, but she had no time to ponder and dismissed it quickly.

"Dr. Truley?"

He looked up from his coffee, caught a bit off guard by the attractive woman. "Yes."

"I'm Sally Hobbs. I'm the one who called you. Thanks for coming."

He stood and pointed to the booth. "Please."

"I know this sounds unusual, but we need to go somewhere else, preferably in your car. I'll explain once we're out of here."

John looked curiously at her and decided to comply without asking questions. He pulled two dollars from his pocket and dropped them on the table. "Shall we?"

They got into his car, and she immediately slid down low in the seat.

"Where to?" He tried not to stare at her.

"Anywhere, but it might be best if you drive for a couple of miles first." Sally looked up at him from her position below the dash. She couldn't help but notice that he looked even better in person than he did on television.

John drove west for several blocks and, although he had no idea what was going on, he looked around for any unusual cars following them.

Sally saw him glancing in the mirror. "They're probably

driving a silver and black Chevrolet."

He saw no sign of the vehicle she described and eased into a parking spot facing the ocean, between several cars with surf racks. Loud music blared from one of the cars as boys around them waxed surfboards and slipped into wet-suits.

Sally carefully sat up, looking around suspiciously. "Sorry to be acting so peculiar, but you'll understand when I tell you my story. I saw you on television, fixing that little boy's leg, and my sister told me about the radio shows you did and how you talked about the dangers of vaccines. I did not know who else to turn to." She told him about the pro-jected release of CD4C, the gruesome reactions of the Labradors, Dr. Weedleman, how she was followed by Martin, and finally, the falsified lab results and the security camera.

John listened intently. He now knew that this was no accident. He surrendered to the unfolding of events and his particular role in them. He had no idea what course of action to take, but knew Sally Hobbs was now counting on him to do his part, whatever it might be.

"Do they know where you live?" he said, not knowing what else to ask as his mind raced ahead.

"They have all my personal information, like they do on all their employees." Sally's eyes suddenly opened wide in terror. "Oh my God, my sister is home by herself! Quickly, drive me back to my car. I've got to go!"

"What a minute. It's not safe for you to go back."

"You don't understand, Dr. Truley, this could send her over the edge. I've got to go no matter what happens to me."

"Then I'll drive you. We'll take my car."

She looked into his eyes for a moment. "Okay, but stop at a phone, I've got to warn her." Tears streamed down her cheeks.

At the apartment, Mara answered the phone. After a few seconds of silence a low, quiet voice spoke that made the hair on her neck stand.

"Do you miss me, baby?"

She stood paralyzed with fear. She could hear his breathing and the memory of alcohol and stale cigarette breath, made a rush of acrid fluid bump the base of her throat.

"It's only a matter of time, baby," Rocky said in the same monotone.

Burning tears welled up in her eyes as she stammered, "Whadaya mean?"

"Don't worry, baby, I'm coming for you. I'll save you from that bitch."

Mara slammed the phone down and started whimpering, holding her arms tightly across her chest.

The phone rang again. She stared at it, knowing that if she answered he would surely jump out of it and grab her by the throat. Tears streamed from her cheeks. Ten rings, eleven rings.

"You bastard!" she screamed, ripping the phone from the wall, the receiver flying from her hand and crashing into the refrigerator before falling dead to the floor.

Sobbing, she stumbled to the counter, slumped against the sink and retched.

Martin parked the car and got out. He couldn't stand it any longer. He'd waited several minutes for some tenant to come home and open the large metal gate that blocked his entry to the apartment complex. After the delay getting on the freeway, he'd lost sight of Sally on Interstate 5. He knew where she lived from her employee records and when he came to the Beach Boulevard exit he realized that she must have gone home. Now, he would attempt to apprehend her here then take her back to Blackmore where Debero could deal with her. He walked along the building, looking for a way to get in. Seeing nothing, he continued past the apartment structure, turning down the street at the end, looking for a side or back entrance.

Now was the time to show his mettle. He had been an

officer with Blackmore for ten years, and this situation provided him the opportunity to demonstrate his talents. He would show Debero his extreme value to the company and enhance his position in the meantime. He thought of a saying he liked. It was something like, opportunity knocks but once, and can only be heard by those who are prepared. Well, here opportunity was, and if anyone was ready, it was he.

He was disappointed to find a fence, similar to the one that protected the front, extending back from the last building and then down along the length of the structures. Undaunted, he racked his brain for a plan. Martin felt some light sprinkles and looked up to see heavy cloud cover blocking the moon. Discreetly using his flashlight so as not to attract attention, he searched the formidable barrier for a point of access. His eyes fell upon a possible solution, and he quickly decided to follow a small trail he hoped would lead to an opening somewhere along the fence line. Turning off his flashlight, he followed the trail through the dense bushes down along the back of the apartments. The rain fell heavier and Martin looked up to assess the storm's potential. The trail was leading him to the left when suddenly he slipped, falling headfirst into the darkness. He plummeted fifteen feet, taking the brunt of the hard landing with his chest, while his turned head whipped viciously down, smacking the concrete with a sickening thud.

In front of the Cambrian Apartments, a black continental eased into one of the last remaining parking places along the street. Rocky looked up and smiled when he saw the light in Mara's window. He then pulled out the crumpled wad of bills he had hastily crammed into his pocket at the convenience store and began counting.

Phineas Blackmore had been en route to his West Coast Laboratory when he was informed by Claben Debero of the security breech. His Chief of Security snapped off the recording of Sally Hobbs breaking in to Lamont Weedleman's office.

"We don't know how she got her hands on the keys, but there are more important things to consider at this point. My top officer is closing in on Ms. Hobbs as we speak. I am afraid, however, the situation has become a little more complex. I had one of my men review the movements of Ms. Hobbs throughout the day. She placed a phone call at approximately 4:30 this afternoon. I think you should listen to the conversation." Debero moved to an oversized tape player and began rewinding.

"How did you get it on tape?" asked Phineas Blackmore.

Claben Debero looked expressionless at him.

"Mr. Blackmore, it's my job to maintain the security of this company, and I use every means possible to do just that. We have every phone in this building tapped. With the exception of yours, of course."

The CEO looked at him sternly, as the taped conversation began.

"I must speak to the doctor now. Please, interrupt him; this is an emergency!"

"Okay, just a moment, I'll see if I can get him."

"The man you are about to hear is a chiropractor from North County, San Diego," Debero explained.

"Hello, this is Dr. Truley."

"Oh, thank God. Look, my name is Sally Hobbs. I need to meet with you this afternoon. Please don't ask any questions. I have vital information that must get to you. Please, trust me."

There was a pause as the man named Truley must have been digesting the mysterious request.

"I am going to drive down from Orange County. Please meet me part way. I must see you!"

"All right, I can be in Laguna Niguel at 6 p.m. There's a Denny's there. Will that do?"

"Yes, thank you."

Debero clicked off the tape and the men sat in silence.

"Is this woman selling the CD4C formula?" a confused Blackmore asked.

"She doesn't fit the profile for a trade secret thief and passing it to a practicing chiropractor would be, well, let's just say, highly irregular."

"John Truley. That name sounds familiar. I can't place it. What do you make of this, Debero?"

"We did a background check on this guy. He's a small potato. He has a solo practice in San Diego, where he's been for four years. He has no police record. No significant history of military service, travel abroad, or anything that would suggest connections with a larger organization. He has significant debt, which might possibly be a motive, including a large sum owed to the IRS. This part is interesting. Lately, he's created a stir in the media by voicing his opinion on natural health care and accentuating it with a couple of dramatic cures, one of them occurring while he was being interviewed on local television."

"That's it. John Truley. He's the guy who made those media specialists look bad on the radio station I shit-canned. Wait a minute! That whole thing was about vaccinations. Jesus, he's gotta be stopped. We can't afford to have him spewing our improprieties with CD4C to the media!" Blackmore's face grew redder.

"All right, take it easy. I have an idea. If in fact that's what's happening, Sally Hobbs doesn't have a shred of evidence to back up any claims that Blackmore acted improperly. Beyond her word, that is. We have her on tape breaking into a secured office, viewing valuable proprietary documents belonging to the company she works for. Then, we have a taped conversation that implicates John Truley as a contact who is meeting her to receive the trade secrets. All we have to do is notify the authorities and let them pick up the two. We'll press charges, and they'll never get a chance to speak to the media. The problem will be solved."

Blackmore thought for a moment. "All right, but I want your boys to stay on it. I don't want those two talking to anyone! Understand?"

The five teens waited for their turn at the top of the rope. They were taking the shortcut to the barrio they called home, on the other side of the spillway. Each proudly wore the distinctive colors identifying them with the neighborhood's long-established gang.

As the first one reached the bottom of the rope and looked down as he prepared to jump the remaining distance, he saw a dark crumpled figure. "Hey, homies, get down here quick!"

Each one then expertly slid down the rope to the spillway.

"Ese, check it out. I think it's a dead body!"

"Hey, man, it's a cop." One nudged a leg with his foot.

"It's not a cop, man. It's a rent-a-cop."

"I don't know who he is, but I gotta piss." The tallest member stood over the body and unzipped his pants.

"Yeah, me too. I gotta piss, too," another said, laughing.

The two young men streamed their urine onto the crumpled figure.

"Wait, man, first see if the dude has any money, before you piss all over him."

"Go ahead and look, Bro."

"Stop pissing then."

"You think I'm superman or something? I can't stop pissing in the middle."

"Man, you dudes are loco. When they autopsy this vato, they'll know you from your DNA, and you'll be busted for capping him. Then only O.J.'s attorneys can get you off."

"DNA? What you think, I'm jacking off?" the tall one said, spinning around to throw his stream in his detractor's direction.

The warm fluid filled Hommer's ear, bringing him back to consciousness. His thoughts were hazy for a second and then he remembered. Opening his eyes, he saw several pairs of shoes and a lightning bolt of pain arced through his head as he managed to lift it from the concrete.

"Holy shit, man, the dude's alive."

The boys lurched back and spun away in panic, half-wetting themselves.

Smelling and tasting urine, Hommer felt white-hot anger coarse through his battered body. He swiftly reached under himself to feel for his weapon. Drawing the Glock, he raised to his knees. The boys scattered in all directions as the large caliber barrel appeared. Hommer squeezed the Austrian-made piece, drawing down the full measure of the built-in trigger safety. He took a bead through the illuminated night sights and centered on the back of one of the fleeing hoodlums. His head pounded as he gritted his teeth. His barrel flashed and the spillway exploded with noise, as the 40-caliber report echoed over the startled scream of the boy as he slammed to the ground. Martin lowered the gun and squinted, eyes stinging from the urine. He spat furiously to clear his mouth of the vile taste, then thrust the gun up with one hand and fired a half-dozen rounds in the general direction of the rest.

He slowly made his way to the writhing figure lying face down. Martin roughly rolled the boy over with his foot. Terrified eyes looked up. The boy's left shoulder produced a slow, yet steady stream of glistening fluid appearing black in the dim light of the spillway. Martin reached down and squeezed the boy's jaw, prying his mouth open. He jammed his gun barrel past the white teeth, watching with twisted satisfaction as the green illumination of his front site disappeared down the boy's throat.

"You like to piss on people, punk? How'd you like it if I pull this trigger and then pissed on your brain?"

Martin's mouth wrinkled into a sneer as he noted the beads of perspiration on the forehead before him. "Think we'd be even then, Bro?"

Martin glanced around. "Where's your comrades, soldier?" He retrieved his gun from the boy's mouth then whipped it with authority across the side of his head. He wiped the saliva and blood from the barrel and leaned close to the moaning figure. "Don't bite off more than you can chew next time, Homeboy."

His laughter was cut short as pain seared through his

head. He closed his eyes and took inventory of his battered frame. Nothing seemed broken. Bracing hands on thighs, he struggled to his feet. He peered down the empty spillway and made a few awkward steps. "Ahhh. Goddam it!" The pain was excruciating. After twenty yards the stiffness eased and he wondered how long he had been out. He cursed his missteps and the difficulties he'd experienced trying to capture the Hobbs girl. She had embarrassed him in front of his mentor, Claben Debero, and now this. He cursed aloud and increased his pace down the spillway toward the back of her apartment. With all his experience and toughness, how could this woman prove so difficult? He would make things right. No wimpy, lab assistant bitch would get the best of him.

He stopped directly behind Sally's building and began counting windows. He calculated Sally's second-story apartment to be the fifth and sixth windows from the left. The security fence loomed over him from atop the steep side of the spillway. He clenched his jaw and ran. His momentum took him near the top but his shoes slipped on the rain-soaked walls. He was forced to turn and run back down the steep wall, nearly sprawling face first on the floor of the spillway once again. Hands on his knees, he panted. Backing further from the wall, he sprinted headlong to gain more speed. This time his fingers reached the top edge of the wall, but a thin layer of mud made it difficult to maintain a grip. He pumped his feet furiously, trying to propel himself up. Unwilling to give in to gravity, he finally slid backward, his knees and hands scraping the coarse cement, forcing him to tuck his body and roll half-way down. He lay still, facing the night sky, his hands and knees afire. Mind-numbing pain quickened in the left side of his forehead, urine crackling and gurgling in his right ear. He felt as if he'd been beaten with a baseball bat. He didn't deserve this. How had this happened? He thought of Sally Hobbs, Claben Debero, and the gang of juveniles. Anger gradually steeled him, connecting him with something primal. Beyond pain and reason, he had only one thought — kill. He willed himself up and to the middle of the spillway where he circled back and charged the wall. An animal scream issued from within as he dug his bloody finger-nails into the wall, fighting for every inch. Again he grabbed the top of the ledge. With cat-like agility, he perched motion-less for a split-second at the top, defying physics, knees dig-ging in, fingers unwilling to yield to the slippery mud. The bushes lay just beyond. Another scream and he lunged for-ward, the raw tissue of his knees scrabbling the wall. Arms straining, he clawed at the brush, the cement edge knocking the wind from him. Gaining a hand-hold, he pulled his knees up on the ledge and finally stood, catching his breath. He quickly zipped his jacket and jumped into the brush. His pants and jacket tore as he fought through, at last grabbing the chain link fence. He peered up at the lines of barbwire and then vomited, splattering the mud on the other side. He attacked the fence, thinking how war was hellish, just as he had imagined while drifting off so many nights, pistol in hand. At the top, he went partly through and partly over the wire and awoke face down in the soft mud on the other side. The brown ooze was soothing and cool on his hands and knees.

He used the remnants of his sleeve to wipe blood from his left eye and peered at the back wall of the apartment. The only route to Sally Hobbs would be through the windows, which taunted him, fifteen feet overhead. Scanning the yard, he located a large trash dumpster and a half-dozen metal garbage cans. He rolled the receptacle under Sally's window and placed a metal trash can on top. The structure gave him about ten feet but wouldn't provide the leverage he needed to break the window and crawl through. He found a plastic milk crate half-buried in mud and grabbed an extra garbage can. He placed the two garbage cans together on top of the dump-ster and set the milk carton on top. A wicked smile creased his face. He climbed up his make-shift scaffolding and stead-ied himself against the wall. He could taste the nearness of his victory and peered through the edge of the window, where the shade stopped short of the window frame. He heard both a radio and a television, which seemed unusual, but trivial. He quietly nudged the window but found it locked. He moved slowly, flicking the thumb release on his holster.

Mara sat on the bed rocking back and forth while crying softly, her favorite Raggedy Ann doll in one hand and pepper spray canister in the other. She couldn't understand why her sister was not yet home and was afraid to consider a possible connection between Rocky's phone call and her sister's uncharacteristic tardiness. She had been under the bed a couple of times already, but decided she couldn't defend herself properly with the spray from that position. Instead, she chose to lock herself in her room, vowing not to come out until she heard Sally's voice from the other side of the door. Her paranoia grew, her skin breaking into hives that had a maddening itch, adding to her misery.

Suddenly, the bedroom window exploded, a long shard of glass ripping through the thin shade before being knocked free by a man crashing through behind it. Outside, falling trash cans echoed against the apartment building. Shrieking, Mara dropped her doll and raised the canister, pulling hard on the trigger. Hommer's battle cry escalated into a wail as the powerful stream slapped hard against his eyes.

The joint pitch of their screams produced a sound that sent chills through the apartments, causing more than one resident to dial 911.

The spray soaked Hommer's eyes and sinuses. His scream abruptly stopped with a direct hit into his gaping mouth. Mara, paralyzed with fear, voided her bladder as she continued to spray. Hommer reeled sidelong across the bed. Pepper spray saturated the lacerations on his face and arms as if he were dipped into a pool of molten lava.

Mara emptied the can on him. As her brain registered the significance of no longer having a weapon, she began screaming again and threw the can, smacking him on the left temple. She turned and ran to the door, away from the sputtering behind her. Utterly panicked, she fumbled with the lock as the man dragged himself to his feet. Finally flinging the door open, she rushed out as he blindly stumbled toward her. In the living room she tripped over an ottoman, landing in a heap. She looked up to see him wildly waving a gun around the room. Realizing he couldn't see, she lay motionless as he thrashed about, knocking down pictures and a lamp from the bookshelf.

The apartment door burst open and Sally entered, a look of horror across her face.

"Sally, help!"

Martin spun and fired, splintering the doorframe next to Sally's head.

"Noooo!" Mara jumped up and charged Hommer, slamming her body into his back, sending him sprawling forward. He crashed into Sally, grabbing her and taking her to the floor. He sat up and raised his gun toward her face, hissing indistinguishably from his throat.

John Truley raced in and grabbed a lamp that was near the door. He ripped it from the wall just as Hommer swung the gun toward him and fired. John dove, rolled once, and popped up with the lamp swinging hard. He connected squarely with the side of the man's head. Hommer crashed into the bookshelf, which toppled as though in slow motion over his motionless body.

Sally rushed to Mara's side. "Are you all right, baby. Are you hurt?"

John took a couple of deep breaths and tried to calm down. He looked at the crumpled security guard and his torn and bloody uniform. "My God, I think this guy's from Blackmore. They must have sent him here to get you. We've gotta get outta here."

Mara unburied her tear-streaked face from her sister's shoulder and looked at John.

Sally gave a weak smile. "Mara, I'd like you to meet Dr. John Truley."

Mara's eyes grew wide as John nodded.

Sally led Mara toward the door, carefully stepping over Hommer's tattered legs. "You're right. We better go."

The sirens made Rocky nervous. When a police car rolled up to the front of the Cambrian Apartments, he slid down low in the driver's seat of the black Continental.

The officer used his radio to inform the dispatcher that he had arrived on the scene and was promptly ordered to wait for backup before entering the premises. When John, Sally and Mara walked out of the front gate he jumped out of his car.

"Hold it right there."

The officer carefully scrutinized the three. "We had a report of unusual noises and gunshots coming from this building. Do you know anything about that?"

Remembering her frightening experience in jail, Mara wanted nothing to do with police, and stared, tight-lipped, at the ground. Sally and John had decided during the drive up from Laguna to avoid the police if possible until they could decide how to best deal with their predicament. John was relieved when Sally spoke first.

"We heard something like that, too. But you know, that's pretty common in this neighborhood."

Another car with lights flashing pulled up, and more officers emerged.

"What've we got?"

"These three were just leaving the premises when I arrived."

"Has anyone been inside yet?"

"No, I was the first one here."

"Let's get names and ID." One of the officers retrieved a pad and pen from the squad car and began writing when a piercing scream echoed from inside the apartment building.

The other two officers reflexively went to their holsters, quickly drawing sidearms. "Holy shit, this thing's in progress!" The two rushed up to the security gate and tried the handle. They looked back at the group. "Hey, do you have a key for this?"

Sally looked at John and he gave a secretive nod. She reached into her pocket and pulled out a key ring.

He took the keys and shoved the pad toward John. "Give me all your names and addresses." He ran over to the gate and opened it. After a quick look back at the three, who appeared to be intently writing down the requested information, he shoved the keys into his pocket, drew his gun and followed the other two officers into the Cambrian Apartments.

Rocky's pulse quickened as he watched Mara leave the apartments with her roommate and another man, and then be questioned by not one but three policemen. After the police went through the gate, he saw the man toss the pad and pen into the patrol car and the three of them dash to a white Ford Explorer. He noticed that Mara had gotten into the back seat. He didn't know who the hell this new guy was, but at least they weren't sitting together. Rocky started the Continental and followed them west on Beach Boulevard. He held his breath as two more police cars, complete with flashing lights, sped by in the direction of Mara's apartment.

After the Explorer was safely traveling south on Interstate 5, John and Sally listened to Mara's story of how Rocky had called and said he was coming for her. She told them how the intruder had broken through her window, forcing her to use the pepper spray.

"I'm sorry, cookie. I tried to call and warn you that I wouldn't be home on time. It wasn't until I was already down in Laguna that I realized someone might try to get me in the apartment. We drove back as fast as we could."

"And it looks like we made it just in the nick of time," John added.

"Ahh, I had it under control." Her face twitched slightly as she smiled. Sally and John laughed at her brave humor.

"Mara, honey, we're still in danger because of what I did at work." Sally went on to describe as best she could the events leading up to their present flight with the famous Dr. John Truley.

"I liked the programs you did. You really showed those two guys who tried to make you look bad." Mara still clutched the Raggedy Ann she'd managed to grab before leaving the apartment. "You do that a lot?"

"Never before, and I was scared to death." John smiled.

"I know the feeling." Mara glanced down at her wet pants. "So how we gonna stop Blackmore from using that drug on people?"

Sally looked surprised. "I think you should fight bad guys more often. It seems to lift your spirits."

"Yeah, I'm not sure how in the hell I did that. I just hope I never have to do it again."

"You did great, kiddo," Sally said approvingly. "I don't think that guy'll be trying that again."

"Or anything else." John shook his head.

They rode in silence for a while and neither sister dared spoil the momentary victory by bringing up Rocky.

"Well, Dr. Truley, my sister asked you a question. How are we gonna stop Blackmore?" Sally looked at her driver. She was amazed at the warm flush his presence triggered. She had dated occasionally in the past and had a couple of friendly relationships, but for the most part she didn't seem to have time for men. Now, she wondered if it was because she had never met the right one. No one had ever made her feel like this before. It both frightened and excited her.

John had been thinking about Blackmore, trying to come up with a plan. He reflected on their predicament and all that had happened. He chuckled and shook his head.

"Something funny?" Sally asked.

"I was just thinking about how I was so dissatisfied with my life a short while ago, and how I'd decided I wanted to make things happen. Now, I'm amazed at how simple things were before that decision. I would have never believed it if someone had told me all I could get myself into if I really tried."

"Yeah, but are you happy?" Mara was stretched out across the back seat, her head resting on Raggedy Ann.

John chuckled at the insightful question. One he really hadn't considered lately. "As a matter of fact, yes, I am, Mara."

"How about you, sis? Are you happy?" Sally asked.

"I'm gettin' there."

For a few moments Mara listened to the purr of the tires and the soft voices in the front seat and then drifted off to sleep.

Chapter 22

Charles Tomine expertly picked the back door lock of McBride Chiropractic. The two men entered, shutting the door behind them. A security light was flashing on a box on the wall and Brock Helton calmly went to work on it. Soon the light turned green and they glanced around the large office.

"Nice place." Brock noted the plush carpet and rich wallpaper.

"Yeah, too bad. Let's get busy."

The men began by pulling patient files from the large steel cabinets that were against the back wall of the reception area. They piled them on the floor, then disconnected the half-dozen computers and stacked them on the pile as well. Searching a large meeting room adjacent to what appeared to be the doctor's private office, they found stacked boxes full of video tapes entitled, *Dr. John Truley and the Power that Heals*, and *Speaker's Training and Media Guide*.

Brock removed the plastic explosive material from his pack. He attached part of it to one of the centrally located boxes, then implanted a radio-controlled detonator to the lump. Using a similar amount he repeated the procedure on one of the CPU's in the stack of computers and patient files.

"Let's take out the X-ray unit too, Brock. We'll shut this McBride fellow down. I'll see if he has back-up data hiding anywhere."

Brock finished his work with the new X-ray equipment and then moved on to the adjustment rooms. Uncertain of how fast the fire department would respond, he decided to ensure maximum damage. Using a razor-sharp knife, he sliced open the leather, powder blue adjusting tables.

Charles returned with a smile, holding up a box of zip drive back-up disks. He nodded approvingly at his partner's handiwork. "This should put a damper on the party. Let's go."

The men returned to their car and drove several blocks before Brock pulled the transmitter out of his pocket.

"Would you like to do the honors?"

Charles pushed the small button and the men nodded as they heard the distant boom.

Their next stop took them to a seaside Del Mar residence.

"I hate this part. I'm not gonna miss this when I call it quits," Brock complained.

"Why are you talking about retirement? You've still got some quality years left in you, pal."

"I don't know. The older my kids get, the more I want out. I don't want to work for Reginald Arfarian the rest of my life."

"I know what you mean, partner, but let's get our game faces on." Charles pulled out the ski masks.

They waited in the dark until they saw the light go on inside the house.

"Looks like somebody gave him the bad news; let's go."

The men approached the house and positioned themselves behind tall bushes in the front yard. Within a couple of minutes, the garage door opened. They waited until they heard the car door. Rushing into the garage, they grabbed Jimmy McBride from behind as he was sliding into the driver's seat. Slamming him back against the wall of the garage, the two men went to work, striking him several times with the retractable three-foot rods which were standard issue for all of Arfarian's men. Jimmy fell forward in a heap. The men stood on opposite sides, kicking his torso and face. They then stood him up and slammed his face into the back window of the Mercedes, leaving a spiderweb of shattered glass. Jimmy slid down the side of the car and crumpled on the garage floor.

Chapter 23

"The subject and two others have entered his residence in a gated condo development called Sand Pointe." Charles Tomine, phone to his ear, waited for instructions.

They were parked six houses away from John Truley's at the end of the cul-de-sac. The doctor and two other subjects had just driven into the garage and shut the door. Lights blinked on in the house and a moment later John Truley emerged and walked across the grass to the house next door.

At the Michaels', John visited briefly with Jeffrey, then asked him to go play with Todd while he spoke with Frank and Mary. He gave them a brief description of his predicament with Sally and Mara, who were temporarily staying in his house. They agreed to watch Jeffrey and put him to bed at their house, if it got too late.

"Be careful," Mary whispered as John said good-bye to Jeffrey.

From inside the black Continental parked just outside the court, Rocky carefully watched the activities, now fully aware that he was not the only one with an interest in the people inside the condo. He occasionally shot a glance at the two mysterious men, noticing that one was talking on the phone and nodding.

The situation was more complicated than Rocky had expected and he cursed himself for not acting sooner. He wondered what kind of trouble Mara was in. Was she involved with big players in the drug trade? It was worth finding out. Suddenly, the garage door opened again. Rocky recognized the man he had seen earlier with Mara and watched as he got into his truck. He appeared to be alone, but Rocky considered the possibility that Mara was already hiding inside the vehicle. The man backed out as the garage door closed. Rocky instinctively slid down in his seat as the Ford rolled past, and noticed that the mystery men did the same. He didn't know whether to follow on the chance that the man might be trying to sneak Mara away, or stay, hopeful that she remained in the house. The two men helped him decide by starting their car and tailing the Ford.

Inside John's house, Sally and Mara tried to make themselves comfortable. Sally had spent months watching her little sister deal with her fears, blaming most of it on paranoia. But now she understood as she experienced an incredible uneasiness of her own in the new surroundings. She felt they were safer here at Dr. Truley's, and thought it unlikely that Blackmore knew anything about him or his recent involvement with the CD4C information. She did her best to put up a show of confidence for her sister, but Mara quickly saw through it as Sally went from room to room, checking under beds and inside closets.

Sally was plagued by images of Officer Hommer coming after them in wet, muddy clothes, blood dripping from cuts all over his face, arms, and legs. She wondered what the police had found when they looked in her apartment. Was the lunatic dead? Though he had terrorized her, she could not bring herself to hope that he was. She knew what they had done was in self-defense, but there was no one else to witness it and the fact that she and Mara fled couldn't look good. Try as she may to remain positive, Sally found their predicament hopeless. Mara was on probation for car theft and drug charges and was not supposed to leave Orange County without notifying her probation officer, while Sally's custody of her was issued on a twelve-month trial basis. Had she jeopardized the sisters' precious and short-lived venture as a family? She tried to clear her mind of questions she could not answer and forced herself instead to focus on their survival and how they were going to stop Blackmore from using CD4C.

Satisfied no one was hiding upstairs, the two girls went down to the kitchen to see if they could find something to eat. Mara stayed close as Sally looked in the refrigerator. Finding a bachelor's supply of groceries – mustard, ketchup, a half-eaten bagel and little else — they decided to split an apple. Mara washed it at the sink while Sally looked through the drawers for a knife.

"Sally, what you're doing is so brave and no matter what happens, I'm proud to be your sister. You're the most awesome thing that's ever happened to me."

Sally stopped her search and looked at Mara. "I love you and I feel the same way." As she hugged her little sister, a voice as chilling as anything she'd ever heard sliced through the warm embrace.

"Well, isn't this cute? You girls lesbos?"

Her sister's hopelessly pathetic expression told Sally in an instant who the voice belonged to. "We're sisters, you asshole!" She lunged for the only drawer she had yet to open. Her fingers quickly found a large butcher knife just as Rocky pounced on her and grabbed her wrist. Sally swung around facing him as he tried to wrestle the weapon from her. Mara screamed and jumped on his back, ripping at his face with her fingernails. He groaned in pain as she found her mark, clawing down across an eye.

"You bitch!" He slammed backwards into a cabinet, causing doors to fly open. Dishes crashed, and Mara fell limply to the floor. Rocky struck Sally with his free hand, sending her sprawling away from him.

He grabbed the butcher knife from the floor. "Now, I'm gonna show you what happens when you come between me and my girl."

A grin creased his face as he raised the knife.

"Hey, you!"

Rocky spun around to the sight of a coiled cobra ready to strike from an enormous biceps and then a fist appeared, shattering his nose and caving in his front teeth.

Slowly, Sally got up and walked cautiously to where Rocky lay on the floor. "Oh my God!"

Only the whites of Rocky's partially open eyes could be seen. Blood streamed from both nostrils, one tooth stuck oddly on the outside of his lip.

Sally looked up at the imposing figure rubbing his knuckles. He sported a sheepish, almost embarrassed look on his face.

"Thanks," she said, nodding at Rocky.

"You looked like you could use a little help."

"I'll say."

He moved over and knelt next to Mara. "I'm John's neighbor, Frank Michael. Who's this?"

Mara moaned and blinked her eyes.

"Oh my God, Mara!" Sally fell to his sister's side, cradling her head. "Are you okay? Can you hear me?"

Mara's eyes opened wide in horror and her body jerked reflexively. "He's here! Rocky's here!"

"No. Mara, no. It's okay. He can't hurt you anymore."

Mara's body relaxed slightly as she stared at her sister. "He can't hurt us? Really, he can't hurt us?"

Sally looked at Frank and then at an unconscious Rocky. "I'm sure, Mara."

"I think you girls would be safer at my house next door. I'll walk you over as soon as I tie up tough guy, here."

Frank and Sally helped Mara up and moved toward the door. They stepped over Rocky and Mara hesitated and gazed down. She looked up at Frank. "Damn!"

Frank left them in the living room and returned to the kitchen. Soon, he came back and led them across the lawn to his house.

"Honey, this is Sally and Mara. They're John's friends. They need ice packs, and maybe something to eat and drink."

Mary took one look at the scrapes and bruises forming on their faces and went into full swing as mother and protector. "Oh, you poor dears. Come into the den and sit down." She led them to a cozy room and pointed toward a well-worn sofa.

"I'll make tea and some sandwiches. Boys, go get our guests a couple of ice packs, will you?"

Sally and Mara eased onto the couch and glanced at their surroundings.

"Now, I can make you turkey and avocado, roast beef with sliced tomatoes, or peanut butter and jelly. Then we can have some apple pie and ice cream. Is tea okay or would you rather have coffee or fresh juice?"

Mara looked at Sally. "I wanna live here."

Sally laughed. "Me, too. Ow, it hurts when I laugh."

The boys returned with several ice packs wrapped in paper towels. "Here, this is what we use when we get hurt."

Jeffrey nodded. "Yeah, and when my dad gets back, you'd better have him check you."

"Ohh, my head." Mara moaned as she pressed the pack on the back of her skull.

Sally eased hers against her jaw. "Mine, too."

The boys entertained them as they rested, telling them stories of their adventures in the neighborhood. Mary appeared with sandwiches and drinks, which she placed in front of them on TV trays. The girls nibbled gingerly, too excited and exhausted to be very hungry.

John frantically raced from room to room. "Sally? Mara? Sally?" He threw open the door to the kitchen. "Oh, my God."

Rocky sat tightly strapped to a dining room chair. His wrists and ankles bound with duct tape, a post-it stuck to his shirt. John squinted at the battered face and opened one eyelid with a thumb. A glassy, bloodshot eye peered back. Blood oozed from his nose and mouth and he listened to the man swallow with difficulty. He read the note aloud. "I'll explain. Frank." John shook his head. "I'm afraid you messed with the wrong guy, my friend."

Jeffrey practically tackled John as he entered the Michaels' and happily received a bear hug from his dad.

"Hi, little buddy!" John glanced up at Frank. "The girls okay?"

"They had a big night, but they're fine. Did you get my package?"

John raised an eyebrow. "Looks like somebody else got it! What happened?"

Frank had a slight gleam in his eye. "The poor slob broke into your house. I heard the girls screaming, so what could

193

I do?"

Sally gave John a hug. "Thank God, you're back. Is everything all right?"

"Yes, and I may have a way to tell the public about CD4C, but it will take a day to make it happen. We'll lay low tonight and wait for a call."

"I don't know if that's an option, John. Get a load of this." Frank pointed at the television. Marlene Johnson and Ralph Manstone were delivering late breaking headlines.

"Police are searching tonight for three suspects wanted for industrial theft involving Blackmore Pharmaceuticals. Sally Hobbs, an employee of the medical drug giant, reportedly broke into a restricted office and stole sensitive proprietary information that is estimated to be worth several million dollars. Earlier this evening, a security guard from Blackmore was found badly beaten in Ms. Hobb's apartment in the La Habra area. He remains in critical condition at Valley Hospital. Police have confirmed that the suspect is traveling with possible accomplices Mara Jones and local chiropractor, John Truley."

Pictures of the three flashed on the screen.

"The suspects are considered to be armed and dangerous. Anyone seeing the three fugitives or having information on their whereabouts should not attempt to apprehend them, but immediately notify authorities."

The announcers reappeared. *"Didn't you recently interview Dr. Truley on one of your segments, Marlene?"*

"Yes, I did. He seemed like a genuinely nice person. I guess you can never tell. We'll keep you updated as the massive manhunt continues through the night."

The den was silent as the broadcast went to a commercial describing a pain reliever.

Frank shook his head. "Boy, you're a celebrity now, John. You'd better get outta here. The cops are gonna be swarming your place any time." He walked over to a drawer and picked up a ring of keys. "Take my truck and go hide in our place in the desert until you decide what to do. Mary and I can share her car and take care of Jeffrey until you get back."

John looked at Jeffrey, who started to cry. "It's okay, son. I just have to take care of some business. Everything will be all right."

The boy wrapped his arms around his father's waist.

"In the meantime, I want you to be good for Mary and Frank."

Jeffrey held tightly. "I will, Dad."

Mary hurried to the kitchen to pack food and drinks. Sally and Mara thanked their hosts and said good-bye to the boys.

Frank pulled John toward a corner of the room. "You want my pistol?"

The seriousness of the situation reached new proportions in John's mind. "No, thanks. I think with the police involved we'd be better off if we didn't fit the armed and dangerous description too closely."

"You might be right. Now, call me if there's anything else I can do."

John looked over at his son. "Frank, you are doing enough already."

Frank gave John's shoulder a squeeze then turned and opened the door that led to the garage. Frank's customized, maroon pickup rested neatly inside. Huge knobby tires elevated the truck off the ground, and shiny chrome bumpers matched a big roll bar that sat on top with large fog lights mounted to it. The truck was Frank's pride and joy and John nodded to let him know he was aware of the magnitude of the gesture. He opened the door for Sally and Mara then turned and gave Jeffrey one last hug before climbing in. The three nervously buckled their seatbelts as the garage door raised behind them. The boys ran after them waving until the truck was out of sight. Jeffrey turned his head, trying to hide his tears as he and Todd returned to the house.

Mary softly brushed back his hair. "Honey, don't you worry. Everything's going to be fine. I'm sure your father will be back soon."

Frank stood awkwardly next to them "That's right, and

in the meantime, you're gonna hang out with us and we're going to have some fun. Let's see if you guys are any good at Monopoly!" He went to find the game as the doorbell rang.

Mary gave her husband a look of concern and he shrugged his shoulders. "It's okay, honey. You guys all stay here. They probably forgot something."

He opened the door to two men wearing ski masks. One fired his Taser gun into Frank's chest, the probes hitting a bull's eye in the center of the Gold's Gym logo. Charles held the device while 75,000 volts discharged down two wires and arced through every muscle in Frank's body. His face went rigid, as they watched his enormous trapezius and pectoral muscles flex into tetany. His body thudded to the floor.

"Frank!" Mary rushed to her husband but a backhand stopped her cold. She landed next to him.

Brock rubbed his hand. "God, I hate doing that."

The boys appeared in the doorway, their faces pale.

"Mom? Dad?" Tears streamed down Todd's face.

"I guess that makes you Jeffrey!" Charles pointed to the other boy.

Todd wailed as he fell on his mother's motionless body. "You killed them! You killed my mom and dad!"

"They're not dead, kid. They'll just wake up with a bad headache in a while. Now, Jeffrey, you need to take a ride with us. We'll go find your dad. Would you like that?"

"No." Jeffrey backed quickly out of the room and then turned to run.

"That's what I thought." Charles raised the recharged Taser and fired into the boy's back.

"Jesus, was that necessary?"

Charles studied his partner for a second. "It was for his own good. I assure you, he'll end up with fewer injuries and he won't be a pain in the ass. You're the one that knocked the lady out." The men stared at each other for a few seconds, then Charles tossed a blindfold to Brock. "Get him into the car and I'll take care of the house."

Charles systematically ripped the phones from the walls,

putting the cords in his pocket. He returned to the entry-way.

"Listen, boy, if I see you leave this house to go to the neighbors for help, I'm gonna come back and cut your mom and dad's heads off. You understand?"

Todd looked up meekly from where he was rubbing his mom's forehead. "Yes."

Charles jumped into the Lexus where Brock waited behind the wheel. "Trunk?"

Brock nodded. "In case we get pulled over. Hey, about what happened inside . . ."

"I know, pal. Don't sweat it. Let's get outta here."

The men drove out of the cul-de-sac and through the little neighborhood. The exit gate for the complex was automatic and they waited as it began its slow roll. A police car suddenly squealed up to the other side.

"Charles?"

"Stay cool, brother." He deftly chambered a round in his Heckler Koch semiautomatic pistol.

The gate was now halfway open.

Charles knew that reaching into one's coat, where holsters are often kept, made policemen very nervous. With a minimum of motion he carefully placed his firearm on his lap under yesterday's newspaper. Brock slowly unsnapped the thumb release on the concealed carry holster under his left arm, then replaced his hands on the steering wheel. One thing he had managed to avoid during his years of service was killing a cop. He thought about how fast this once innocuous-appearing mission had turned ugly. Then he thought about his children and his retirement. The gate completed its course.

For a moment the occupants of both cars regarded one another. The officer on the driver's side nodded and motioned for the Lexus to come out. Brock eased through the gate and was forced to pull alongside the black and white in the narrow passageway to the street. When he stopped to check for oncoming traffic, the officers looked the men over, then quickly accelerated to make it through the exit gate which had begun to close.

Brock let out a sigh as Charles reholstered the HK.

"What the hell was that all about?"

Charles shook his head and grabbed the cellular. "I don't know, but I'm gonna find out if it was more than a coincidence."

Brock sped north on I-5 and had gone only a few miles when Charles slammed the phone with his hand.

"Get off, goddamn it!"

Brock swerved to the Oceanside off-ramp. "What's going on?"

"There's an APB out on Truley. Something about industrial trade secret theft. That means those cops were on their way to his house, and it's only a matter of time before those people or that kid see the cops outside and tell 'em about our unwilling passenger. Damn! I should have capped all three of 'em!"

"Why weren't we warned?" Brock demanded. "The cops could have showed up while we were there!"

"They said they tried to reach us. We must have been inside. You know those cops got a good look at us. We've got to lose this car. This is some sloppy shit."

"What do you think, a grocery store?"

"No, it'll be reported too quickly. No. Wait. You're right. Pull into that lot."

Chapter 24

The two officers grew impatient waiting at John Truley's door. They could see the lights, but it was apparent no one was going to answer.

"Let's go around back."

The back door was slightly ajar as the men approached. "Forcible entry."

Both men drew their pistols and crept into the house. They carefully made their way through the first two rooms. At the stairway, they split up, one man taking the upper level while the other made his way toward the kitchen where the light shone brightly.

Rocky flinched slightly when the officer came through the door.

"Jesus!" The cop kept his gun trained on the battered figure until he saw the tape. He moved on to secure the rest of the house.

Next door, Mary dabbed Frank's face and he came to with a start.

"What? What happened?"

"Thank God, Frank. I was so worried. Todd's okay, but they took Jeffrey!"

"Son of a bitch! Help me up. What happened to your eye?" He leaned slightly on her and stumbled to the front window. "Look, the cops are next door." Frank held his forehead for a moment, trying to clear his brain. "Go tell them about Jeffrey. I'm gonna call John's pager. I've got to let him know what happened."

"Frank, they ripped the phones out and took the cords. I tried to call 911 when you wouldn't wake up."

"Damn! Did you look upstairs?"

She shook her head and watched her husband wobble up the stairway using the railing to pull himself along. "Todd, honey, stay here, I'm going to go get the police from next door."

John's pager sounded, causing Mara to yelp. He flashed the light on the number. "It's Frank. I have to find a phone." He pulled off the freeway at the next exit and drove to a convenience store about a half block down the street. A squad car was parked to the side of the store and an officer leaned at the counter inside, flirting with the female clerk. Sally reminded John that the police were looking for them and knew what he looked like. He knew she was right, but the wait would kill him. He wasn't familiar with this part of town, and in his frenzy, couldn't decide if it would be faster to search for another pay phone. He thought the officer would likely leave within a minute or two and he would be wasting time if he didn't just sit tight and wait for the man to buy his coffee.

The next few moments proved the longest John had ever experienced. He sat motionless, praying that Jeffrey was all right, torn between his natural instinct to race home and protect his son and the reality that it was John, Sally and Mara who were in danger. Who could be better than Frank at protecting Jeffrey anyway? He looked at the sisters next to him in the cramped cab. They were in the greatest peril and were counting on him. It wasn't just the cops that were after them, and who knew just how far Blackmore was willing to go to suppress the information that Sally had? He looked at the long, shiny, auburn hair that fell across her pretty face. A face John had found himself increasingly drawn to. One side was swollen and turning a dark maroon that reminded him of a plum. She looked intelligent and determined, her strong jaw clenched as she watched the policeman laughing at the counter. Mara, nearly as beautiful yet more frail, also watched the store. The resemblance was easy to see at this angle. Both had slim, sculpted faces, each accentuated with an attractive nose turned up ever so slightly. They had experienced their own challenges in life and survived, reuniting as a family after so many years. They didn't deserve to be running like this, fugitives from justice and targets of some drug company cover-up.

John tried to focus on his responsibility to the two passengers with him, but couldn't stop worrying about his son. He had been overly protective since the day he had experienced the cruel mixture of wondrous joy at gaining a son and the life-shattering sorrow of losing his wife. He had never quite recovered from the grief, which in a single moment changed forever the way he viewed life. His soul aged a hundred years that day, replacing his carefree, positive outlook with a large dose of cynicism and an equal helping of resentment that bordered on the need for revenge against the medical establishment that played an undeniable role in the death of his wife. For years he tried to understand the purpose, in the grand scheme of things, for what happened, but found no explanation, no reason, that could provide the peace that was ripped from him the day she died with their son in her arms. God had taken one love and given another – and John would never allow the remaining one to be taken from him, too.

When the patrol car finally rolled out of the parking lot, John ran to the phone and dialed Frank's number. Sally and Mara watched as he talked for a moment, then slammed the receiver down. He sprinted back to the truck and flung the door open.

"They took him!"

"Jeffrey? They took Jeffrey?" Sally stared at him wide-eyed. "Who took him? Blackmore?"

"I don't know who it was, but they're gonna pay! And if they hurt him . . ." John's words choked off as he started the engine. His head shook, eyes thick and moist as he spun the truck around and squealed the tires out of the store's parking lot.

"We're going back." John pounded the steering wheel and raced back toward the freeway, running the stoplight as he stomped the accelerator. In a moment, they were once again on I-5, this time speeding southward. They rode in silence, save for John's seething breath sounds and occasional moans of profanity.

"I'm sorry, John. I got us all into this. It's my fault. Just like it was my fault that Mara was attacked by the security guy. I should've just minded my own business and kept my big mouth shut."

"Look —," John paused for a deep breath. "I'm furious and scared about Jeffrey. He's the only family I've got. But it's not your fault. It's just not that simple. We all create what happens to us either actively or passively and have to take responsibility for it. None of this is an accident. I took certain actions that put me on that radio show, causing you to think I was the right person to help with this CD4C thing. You took actions that put you in a position to know that lots of people are potentially in danger. If we have any faith that our purpose in life is to do what we know is right, then I can't believe Jeffrey will be harmed. If I'm wrong . . . Well, if I'm wrong, it'll be the worst lesson I've ever learned. And I'll spend my last dying breath finding the bastards who took him, to teach them their lesson."

"Poor, baby." Mara whimpered. "I know how scared he is."

The boy came to in the blackness of a trunk. His brain was foggy, making it difficult for him to understand what happened and where he was. His mouth was stuffed with something big and dry and he could only move his hands a few inches from his waist. He knew by feeling the smooth metal pinching his wrists, and the short distance he could move them, that he was handcuffed. The chain was threaded through a belt loop on his pants, keeping him from raising his hands to take the dry thing out of his mouth or to pull off his blind fold. He tried rubbing his head against the floor of the trunk, but a bolt of pain surged through his skull. His mind kept flashing on pictures of little boys on the back of milk cartons, and he remembered the stern admonitions from his father and teachers to never talk to strangers, and to never, ever, get in their car.

Now he was handcuffed, blindfolded and gagged, locked in the trunk of a car driven by strangers who had already hurt people whom he loved. He remembered what they did to him at Todd's house and hoped the men would not shoot him again. He wondered where his Dad was and whether the men had hurt him, too. A dark feeling enveloped, much like a suffocating blanket in a bad nightmare.

The car stopped and started several times like cars do at traffic lights and then he felt the distinct sensation of going backwards. The car stopped again and the engine turned off. He heard the doors open and felt the shocks give as the men got out. The trunk popped open and fresh, cool air washed over his skin. Hands grabbed him, pulling him up into the night air. He kicked and struggled, but the hands were strong. He was carried a few feet and then lifted high for a second before being dropped. The sensation was frightening because he couldn't see or put his hands out to break the fall. He abruptly landed head first into something semi-soft. As he tried to comprehend his situation he heard the doors slam and then the car roar away.

Jeffrey hoped that the men were gone for good, but a thought even more frightening than his own predicament came to him. What if they were going after his dad? He remembered how the big, strong, Frank Michael had looked, lying motionless in the doorway.

The stench of rotting trash brought him back. Kicking his feet against metal and hearing the reverberation made him realize he was in a container. Maybe one of those big trash dumpsters. His body angled down, his head wedged in rubble. He could breathe, but something wet stuck to his face, giving him the creeps. He strained to pull himself upright but couldn't. Frustration at his helplessness, coupled with fear for his father, racked his entire body. Tears ran up into his blindfold.

His legs were the only thing he could move. He began kicking and then thrashing desperately somewhere near the top of the trash pile. He finally stopped, trying to calm himself long enough to think. He kicked his shoes off and with the slight play the short chain afforded him, managed to move his hands enough to reach the buttons on the front of his denim jeans with his fingers. Awkwardly, he unfastened one button after the next. With great concentration, he brought his legs as far forward as possible and began to painstakingly slide his pants down over his upraised butt. Sweat trickled up his chest and then around his ears as his body strained to work his legs through. He kicked furiously, working the trousers down past his knees. He stopped for a moment to rest and catch his breath.

He felt exhilarated as he realized what it would mean to clear his pants past his feet and he was hopeful for the first time since waking up in the trunk. He made one last tremendous heave, pulling his thighs as far toward his chest as possible and flexing his knees to bring his feet in close to his buttocks. The pants slid over his feet. With hands suddenly free from his waist, Jeffrey exploded up and out of the trash. Yanking off the blindfold, he saw the dark insides of the dumpster. He let out a muffled scream as he ripped the duct tape from across his face. He coughed, pulling the dry thing from his mouth. He realized that it was someone's dirty sock and quickly added the contents of his stomach to the trash around him. Using his pants, Jeffrey wiped off his mouth and spit several times.

He climbed to the corner of the bin, where he found a fairly stable area and pulled himself up and out. Turning, he lowered himself onto the pavement. Not bothering to retrieve his shoes, he made his way out from behind the back of the large grocery store in socks, underwear and T-shirt. It was late, the grocery store closed, but Jeffrey quickly saw what he was looking for. His pants were rolled around his hands, and he dug around in the pockets for change only to discover that it must have fallen out when he was upside down, kicking his legs.

A longhaired man slept on a cardboard sign near the phone. Jeffrey wasted no time in approaching him. When he got close, he was startled to find the man's eyes open, peering curiously at him.

"Excuse me, sir? I was kidnapped and I need a quarter to call my dad."

"That's a good line, kid. I'm gonna have to try that one

myself. You forget something?"

Jeffrey looked down at his bare legs. "I'm telling the truth. My pants are stuck here around the handcuffs."

Jeffrey let the pants drop from his hands so they hung by the belt loop through which the chain had been threaded.

"Damn, you're not kiddin' are ya?"

The homeless man rose to his feet with surprising agility and motioned to Jeffrey with a leathery hand. "Come closer."

Jeffrey cautiously approached as the man began to dig in his pocket. He brandished a pocketknife and opened the blade, causing Jeffrey to gasp.

"I'm not going to hurt you, boy. I've got a good kid just like you somewhere." He slid the blade through the loop and cut it, allowing the pants to fall to the sidewalk.

"Now put those on and let's see about getting you some change."

Jeffrey pulled his pants on while the man reached into a paper bag and withdrew a cup half-full with coins.

"Local call?" the man eyed him inquisitively.

"I don't know. Where am I?"

"You're in Oceanside. Where do you live?"

"Me and my dad live in Carlsbad."

"You got it made, kid. You're not far from home." He handed him some change.

Reaching up with both cuffed hands, Jeffrey quickly dialed the number that he had memorized when he was just five years old. The number was like a security blanket for him and with it he could reach his father no matter where he was.

Jeffrey looked at the scruffy man. "Thank you, sir."

"Ah, don't worry about it, kid. While we're waiting, why don't you tell me what happened."

John's pager went off and he grabbed it, hoping it was Frank with good news. His heart sank when he saw a number he didn't recognize. He considered going the rest of the way home, then returning the page, but he began to get a feeling that the call had something to do with Jeffrey. He pulled off the freeway into a gas station with a pay phone. He nervously dialed the number, praying that it would not be dreadful news.

"Dad?"

"Jeffrey!?! Oh my god! Jeffrey! Are you okay!?!"

"I'm all right, Dad. Some men took me from Todd's and they hurt Frank and Mary. Dad, they're coming after you."

"Where are you?"

"I'm in Oceanside at a grocery store." Jeffrey looked over at the store for the first time. "It's Lucky's, Dad."

"Stay there! I'm close by!"

"Hurry, Dad!"

Jeffrey hung up the phone, unable to suppress a smile as he turned back to the man.

"Good job, kid! I see you got hold of your old man."

John returned to the truck smiling broadly. Sally and Mara knew immediately, hugging John and each other. Jeffrey was only one exit away and John knew exactly where the store was. Within a few minutes, the little truck with big wheels pulled up in front, where the handcuffed boy and homeless man waited. Everyone jumped out, ran to Jeffrey, and hugged him.

"Dad, this is the man who helped me." Jeffrey nodded toward the scruffily bearded fellow.

John smiled politely. "Thank you, sir. You have no idea how worried I was about my son."

"He's a good kid who just got in a scrape and needed a hand. No problem."

John noticed the man's cardboard sign and plastic cup. Something struck him as odd. Maybe it was the remarkable twinkle in his eyes.

"Well, I'm indebted to you and I'd like to show my appreciation."

John retrieved a couple of twenties and a business card from his pocket.

"If *you* ever get in a scrape and need a hand, call me, okay?"

He stepped up to hand him the money and got a closer

look into the man's astonishingly crystal clear eyes before turning back toward the group.

"Thanks, Johnny," the man called after him.

John knew that he had just given the man a card with his name on it, but the way the extraordinary character said his nickname made John stop and turn to take another look. He squinted at the figure from whose silhouette radiated the florescent glow of the grocery store's lighting.

Sally and Mara were completely captivated by Jeffrey's description of his wild and frightening adventure.

"Uh, excuse me. I'm going to call Frank and tell him we have Jeffrey. Then we'll go to his place in the desert."

They nodded at John, then Jeffrey quickly took up where he left off.

"Frank, it's John. I found Jeffrey and he's fine."

"Oh, John, thank God! Where are you guys? Wait, never mind, don't tell me. The cops are here. They've already radioed in that Jeffrey was kidnapped."

"Well, let them know he's okay. Frank, they handcuffed him and left him in a dumpster."

"Those sons of bitches. John, I've got bolt cutters and a hacksaw in my toolbox. The key is in the glove compartment."

"Great, Frank. Those'll come in handy. Are you guys okay?"

"Yeah, we are, but if I ever get my hands on those bastards, they won't be. Look, John, so far the cops don't know what you're driving, but I don't know how long it will stay that way. They know you're not in your Ford because they've seen it at your house. They certainly won't get any help from me."

"Thanks, Frank. We'd better get going. Sorry about all this. I'm just glad you and your family are safe."

"John, we've been watching the news. Your friend, Jimmy McBride, had his office bombed. The place burned to the ground. He's in the hospital; it looks like somebody worked him over pretty well. These are bad hombres you're messing with, neighbor."

There was silence as the sickening news sunk in.

"Jimmy? Why? . . ." John was interrupted by his pager. He numbly shut off the beeping. "I've gotta go, Frank."

In stunned disbelief, he rested his forehead with a thud against the pay phone. He pictured his friend lying in the hospital, battered and beaten, a pile of ashes where his once-beautiful office stood. Anger began to well up inside as he started to get the big picture of what was happening. Unconsciously, he slipped the pager from his belt and raised it eye level without moving his head from the phone. The call he had been waiting for had finally come. With renewed determination fueled by white-hot anger, he pounded out the number.

"Dr. Bill here."

"It's John. What have ya got?"

"Damn, Truley, what the hell's going on? Your face is all over the news. Are you guys all right?"

"We're fine. Did you work something out?" John suddenly felt he and his group had been out in the open too long.

"You're gonna love this, Truley. I personally spoke to Marlene Johnson, and she thinks she can get you and Sally Hobbs on live for tomorrow's six o'clock edition. She went nuts when I told her I was your liaison and that I was looking for the best station for a live interview with my fugitive friends. Hell, this might get me in the door with a television station. God knows I need a job, now, thanks to you."

"Funny how things work out, isn't it, Bill? Good job. Tell her we'll be there."

"Just don't spoil our chances and get caught by all the cops out looking for you."

"I'll do my best."

John slammed down the phone. He walked over to the truck, glancing around for the homeless man.

"Where'd that guy go?"

They looked at John and shrugged.

"He just disappeared without saying good-bye."

John looked at his son and nodded. "Yeah, and that's just what we're gonna do."

Chapter 25

Their spirits were high considering the obstacles that stood between them and the possibility of remaining free and safe during the next twenty-four hours. Jeffrey's return helped to bolster their faith in the providence of their mission, something they clung to like a tattered lifeline in a hurricane besieged sea. John was forced to fall back on a philosophy that carried him most his life — truth would prevail. He remembered a quote from B.J. Palmer. "Be sure you're right — then force the fight." If the forces of good were not to triumph in the end then what else did they have going for them? Why not just quit now?

He told the others about the live television interview arranged by Dr. Bill and watched as the good news broke across their faces. He knew the interview provided an important goal for the desperate group to focus on. They weren't just running scared, but to see another day. A day in which they might take the offensive and deliver a blow to the overwhelming foes that thus far had sent them fleeing from their jobs and homes.

Sally was relieved that she would be able to warn the public about CD4C. By helping her accomplish this feat, John would be helping demonstrate to the public that medical drugs were not to be taken without considering the potential consequences. No doubt this was an exceptional circumstance, but he was sure that this would help people think twice about the motives behind the proliferation of pharmaceuticals.

Mara's ambitions were less lofty. She was just thrilled to have the chance to meet her hero, Marlene Johnson. Jeffrey was happy because his father was there and maybe things were going in the right direction.

John did his best to hide the grief he felt for Jimmy and decided not to tell the others until later; they had been through enough for one night.

The ride to the desert near Palm Springs was mostly

uneventful and the blanket of night, coupled with the unre-ported truck belonging to Frank, seemed to protect them from the highway patrol cars that occasionally drove by. The cab of the truck was crowded and the sisters took turns letting Jeffrey sit on their laps. Thankfully, the night was warm, because Jeffrey's stench forced them to drive with the windows down most of the way. Many jokes were made and he good-naturedly played along, adding a few of his own.

At last they reached the dirt road that led to Frank's desert getaway. It wound through rugged terrain littered with large rocks, no doubt the way Frank liked it, to dis-courage traffic. With the truck's four-wheel drive and high clearance, the four had a safe, albeit bumpy, ride.

Frank's place was more a bunker than house, built into the side of a mountain. Upon seeing it, John remembered Frank's description of how he had designed it as a place to dig in and hide if society broke down in the new millennium. With this in mind, Frank had incorporated many survivalist features, and stocked the place with a year's supply of rations and water. John recalled brushing aside as paranoia Frank's ramblings regarding everything from solar power to hidden weapons and found it ironic that he was now the beneficiary of this soldier of fortune mentality.

Jeffrey, who had spent many fun weekends at the house with the Michaels, showed the group where the food was, how to work the butane lanterns, and how to get hot water. He also found some of Todd's clothes and got ready for a much-needed shower. Sally and Mara teamed up in the kitchen and tried to get creative with the canned food and dry goods that were available for dinner.

After helping Jeffrey get situated with his shower, John explored the place more thoroughly. He had never seen any-thing like it. The entire structure was embedded in the side of the small mountain with the exception of the front wall, which ran the width of the house. Four large windows, that would provide good light during the day, were completely secured with heavy gauge steel bars to prohibit entry.

Lanterns were affixed to the ceilings in each of the three main rooms and were connected by a copper line to a butane tank in a closet. Two wood-burning stoves, one at each end, heated the house. The place was comfortably furnished and surprisingly well decorated, creating a cozy and relaxing atmosphere, which, under different circumstances, John could imagine to be quite renewing. In the front room, he found what appeared to be an aerial map of the house and surrounding area. Frank must have drawn it because the bunker was exactly in the center with about a twenty-mile radius of terrain and roads sketched in. The map was mounted on a wall above a desk with a phone, which John had previously not noticed. He picked up the receiver, listened for a dial tone and then decided to make a call.

He heard Janine's familiar voice on the answering machine announcing the office hours and reciting his emergency number.

"Hi, Janine, this is Dr. Truley. As you may have figured out by now, I won't be coming to work. Good luck with the angry mob. Jeffrey and I are fine. We're just lying low until tomorrow night. We will do a live interview with Marlene Johnson at six at the television station, if we can get there safely. If you have any important information relevant to our situation, I want you to call Frank Michael. I think you better erase this tape as soon as you hear it."

John hung up and wondered what would happen to his patients if he never returned to his practice. Then he thought about Jimmy.

Sally entered the room from the kitchen. "Oh, there you are. We're almost ready to eat. Mara is putting the finishing touches on some industrial strength pasta that we found."

"Great, I'm starved." He turned toward the kitchen, glad for the distraction.

"John, wait —," Sally suddenly wrapped her arms around him, surprising herself. She laid her head on his chest feeling his heartbeat, her own racing wildly. She felt so vulnerable as she yielded to her feelings, feelings for a man she had only recently met but felt she had known a lifetime. It started when she first saw him in Laguna Nigel. It was as if she had been unconsciously looking for him and recognized him on sight. The physical attraction overwhelmed her and she knew that she would give herself freely to him, yet it was much more complex than that. She loved him as a protector of her and Mara, as a father to Jeffrey, and as a man with principal who would risk his life for what he believed. She was swept away by all of it. She had never before allowed herself the dangerous luxury of attachment, and it was a frighteningly helpless feeling. Now she was ready to lay bare her soul, knowing that with a few words he could reject her, something she had always been able to build a sturdy wall against during her many years as an orphan hoping to be adopted. She had much to lose. She had opened a door that she may never be able to find again. It didn't matter. It was too late. She was hopelessly carried away and had no alternative but to express how she felt, regardless of the consequences.

"I think I'm in love with you, John."

He looked into her eyes, seeing something he had missed before, which she now revealed. His hands glided across her back until he held her tightly with the full measure of each arm. Her body felt good. He could feel not only her feminine attributes, but also her vibration, the indescribable energy that either attracts or doesn't and has the power to override anything physical. She felt right. She had the magic. He was amazed at the intensity of the attraction and desire. These were feelings that had long been dormant in his life. But at this moment, he was transported from stress, struggle, and enemies to a garden in paradise, two glowing souls uniting in nature.

The bathroom door suddenly rattled and they could hear Jeffrey working to open it. They released one another and smiled sheepishly as he emerged in his towel.

"Hi." He glanced back curiously as he padded down the hall toward Todd's room.

"John, before we go back, I need to tell you something. You know by now that Mara and I have never really had much of a family until we found each other less than a year ago. We're both touched by the way you've cared for us and protected us. It means more than you think, especially under the circumstances. I also want to apologize for getting you and your family and friends into so much danger."

"Sally, listen, I – "

"No, wait. Let me finish. I was so scared when they took Jeffrey. All I could think about was how terrified he must be and how if it wasn't for me he'd be safe at home with you. I want you to know that no matter what happens tomorrow, Mara and I will never forget the kindness and the love you've shown us." She hugged him and kissed him on the cheek.

John gazed into her green eyes and smiled. "I guess you get to know someone pretty quickly when you experience so many things with them in a short amount of time. I have to tell you something, Sally. I'm not sure whether this will make you feel better or worse, but my partner and good friend was beaten tonight and his office was burned."

Sally covered her mouth "Oh, my God. That's terrible."

"They bombed his office instead of mine because it was the headquarters for a group we created. It disseminates information about medical drugs and their potential danger. We had recently become extremely successful, and now I have no doubt that someone is trying to shut us up. I think it's these people who are responsible for my friend's beating and Jeffrey's abduction. There's no way that Blackmore could have known where to find Jeffrey so quickly, let alone who my friends are, and where they work and live."

Sally looked suddenly pale. "Then Blackmore and the police aren't the only ones after us?"

"I'm afraid not. It also means that you're not responsible for much of what has happened."

Sally's eyes welled and John placed his hand against her cheek.

"I don't see any reason to share this news with the others, do you?"

She shook her head and they turned and walked slowly into the kitchen.

Mara stood proudly over her steaming creation of pasta, olives and Parmesan cheese, while Jeffrey sat at the table, beaming, smelling of soap and shampoo. The four seated themselves around the table and paused for a moment, looking at each other.

"Would anyone mind if I offer a blessing?" John prayed occasionally and felt strongly compelled this evening.

Sally nodded.

"Dear God. We're thankful for Your guidance and protection. Bless this food for our bodies and nourish our spirits. May both be equal to the task that's before us. God, if we're right, then give us power over our enemies and courage to follow through on our convictions. Amen."

"Amen."

They ate in silence until Jeffrey accidentally burped, lightening the mood into airy chatter about being at the television station the following evening with Marlene Johnson. Not far beneath the surface, however, lay their sobering reality: how to make it from the bunker to downtown San Diego, with the incredible obstacles that faced them.

After dinner, everyone pitched in and cleaned the kitchen, making it appear once again as if no one was living there. Sally and Mara were encouraged to share the master bedroom for the evening, while John and Jeffrey retired to the bunkbeds in Todd's room.

"Dad, will we be okay tomorrow?" Jeffrey lay in the darkness on the top bunk.

"We'll be fine. I don't know just what'll happen, but if we use our heads and do what's right, it should work out."

"I believe you, Dad."

Soon he heard Jeffrey's regular breathing and knew he was sleeping soundly.

John lay awake staring at the bunk above his head for several hours, wondering how they would ever manage to safely reach their destination.

Chapter 26

"Come out with your hands up and no one will be hurt!" Tear gas canisters banged against the bars of the windows, falling harmlessly to the ground before releasing noxious chemicals.

John cautiously peered through the front window. At least fifty men dressed in combat fatigues crouched behind Army-green jeeps, their rifles trained on the bunker. He ran to the kitchen and found Sally and Mara praying at the table.

"Did you hear that bullhorn!?!"

Mara looked up, her jaw set in determination. "I ain't going back to jail."

Sally nodded. "Let's not surrender, John." She stood and leaned into him. "Remember the children." Her lips grazed his ear, her hot breath sending tingles down his body.

Jeffrey ran into the kitchen and plunked two large M16 automatic rifles on the table. "Here, dad, use these. Frank's got some other cool stuff, too!"

A barrage of gunfire shattered the front windows and some of the bullets bore through the wall into the kitchen, sending pictures flying. John grabbed one of the M16's and belly crawled back into the front room where he could peek out the window. Two tanks were now in position down the hill about 150 yards away. John saw the fire and smoke come from their barrels and turned his head, yelling for everyone to get down. The concussion of the explosions rocked the bunker, but the shells were falling short and hitting the hillside below, sending smoke and dirt flying in through the broken glass. John's mind raced. He knew there was always a way out of every jam. The M16's that Jeffrey found were useless until the foot soldiers moved into range of the front windows. He looked again. The soldiers were suddenly running the other way, taking cover behind the tanks and a few jeeps scattered beyond them. Everything became eerily quiet except for a distant high-pitched sound coming from two specks on horizon. The specks became dots and soon John could make out the F-16's moving in at attack speed.

"Everybody out! Get out now!"

The others were in the room, now, watching in amazement as the fighter jets screamed toward them.

Jeffrey looked up at him. "Where do we go, Dad?"

John's heart felt as if it would explode as he looked at his son, then at Sally and Mara. An intense wave of love began to envelop him, congealing in the air and surrounding the entire group. In slow motion, John looked out the window and saw the rockets detach from the F16's, and drop down into a straight trajectory toward the bunker.

From somewhere deep inside, he commanded, "Don't let us die; get us out of this now!"

John snapped awake with a gasp. He stared at the hatch pattern of Jeffrey's bedsprings, feeling his heart beginning to slow its pounding. Beads of sweat trickled down the sides of his forehead. He gradually became more conscious of his surroundings and it finally registered that the ringing he was hearing was real. He rolled out onto the floor from the low bed and stiffly got to his knees, then raised himself. Jeffrey's bunk was at eye level and he paused to see his son's angelic face, relaxed and sleeping peacefully. He was all there. No signs of shrapnel wounds or napalm burns.

He made his way to the front room toward the ringing phone. The bunker faced west so John could not yet see the sun, but the window provided a surprising amount of light and he looked out to the horizon. He recalled the terrible dream and a shudder moved through his body. He picked up the phone and listened.

"John, it's Frank. The cops were just here grilling me for information. I'm sure they know you've got my truck. They wanted to see both of my vehicles and when I gave them some bullshit about my truck being in the shop they wanted to see a repair invoice and, of course, I didn't have one. I gave them the name of some shop across town, but it'll only take 'em a minute to find out it's not there. They're going to figure out that you may be hiding in the desert. My title to that place is, unfortunately, public record. I swear this goddamn communist society takes away all of our privacy. I'm sorry, Johnny."

"It's all right, Frank. It gave us a good place to stay for the night."

"What's your plan, John?"

"I don't have one. All I know is that I've got to be in downtown San Diego this evening."

"What? You should be getting the hell out of here, not coming back!"

"I've got unfinished business with Marlene Johnson and the six o'clock news. After that, I have no idea what's going to happen."

"You'll never make it, John."

"Thanks for the pep talk, coach. I'd better get going."

"Call me if I can do anything."

"I will, neighbor."

Janine arrived early to work, with no idea what to expect. There was already a large crowd at the front door, including more camera crews than usual, some already filming. She parked in the back lot and walked quickly to the office's rear entrance. A group of reporters spotted her and came running, but she managed to get inside and turn the lock before they could reach her. They brazenly pounded the door, yelling countless reasons why she should open it and talk to them. She left the lights off and moved quickly toward the back office where they kept the answering machine. After entering the small room, she closed the door to the hallway to hide the light from anyone peering through the front window. The answering machine flashed a lime-green, digital 24 and Janine's pulse quickened as she wondered if the caller she was hoping for was among them. Scanning the first few words of each and hitting the save button, she finally heard the familiar voice. Dr. Truley had, in fact, called to let her know what to do. She listened carefully to his message and got a lump in her throat as she thought of the peril he and Jeffrey were in and how she was helpless to do anything about it. Interrupted by the ringing phone, she considered not answering it, fearing it would be reporters or, even worse, the police. She decided that it might be Dr. Truley needing something and quickly picked it up.

"Truley Chiropractic, Janine speaking."

"What's happening, Janine? This is Flash Robinson. I need to reschedule my appointment from this morning to this afternoon. My lady and I are on our way home from a little trip and I don't think I can make it in time."

"Haven't you heard about Dr. Truley? It's been all over the news."

"What? What happened to my man? Is he all right?"

Janine quickly explained what she knew about Dr. Truley's situation.

"Whew! That boy got himself into some big trouble. Where is he?"

"I don't know."

"Janine. Now, how's Flash gonna help him if I don't know where he is?"

"I don't know, but he left a number of someone who knows how to contact him. I just don't know if I'm supposed to give it out."

"Girl, give me that number!"

Before she knew it she was reading Frank's number to Flash Robinson. She knew that he and Dr. Truley had become close and she trusted him. She hung up the phone, encouraged by the initiative that Flash had shown. With sudden inspiration, she brought up the patient telephone list on the computer and began dialing phone numbers.

Frank was beside himself worrying about John. He had thought of several plans, but none could be placed into operation fast enough to be effective. It killed him that with all his experience as a bodyguard he couldn't do a better job of protecting his own friend. The phone rang providing a welcome time-out from his frustration.

"This is Frank."

"Hello, Frank, Flash Robinson here. I understand our man, J.T., is in trouble. Now, you sure no one is listening to this line?"

"Listening?"

"Yeah, bugged. Tapped. You know, like in the movies."

"Oh, that. Ah, I don't know. I suppose it could be."

"To be on the safe side, can you get to another line and call me right back?"

Frank agreed and wrote down Flash's number. He hung up and ran to a neighbor's house. Flash Robinson. He couldn't believe it. He loved the guy. He wondered what he could do to help John. At least he was thinking. Frank kicked himself for not previously considering the security of his phone line. Man, was he slipping. Fortunately, the neighbors were home, and after he explained that he was having trouble with his line, they consented to let him use theirs.

"Mr. Robinson?"

"Just call me Flash, my friend. Now John Truley's a good man and we can't let him go down. Tell me what he needs."

Frank spoke quietly into the phone. "John, his son and two women are hiding out at my place in the desert near Palm Springs. He has to get to a television station in downtown San Diego by six this evening. He has a major transportation problem. I gave him my truck, but the cops were here this morning and figured that one out. It's only a matter of time before they find out I own a place in the desert, if they haven't already, and go search that."

"Shit, is that it? That's all? I just happen to be driving

back from Death Valley, now. You see, my woman's got this thing for motor homes and camping, but never mind that. We're just past San Bernadino and I can be in Palm Springs within an hour. You have a phone out there so I can make arrangements with Doc?"

Frank's heart leaped and he quickly gave Flash the number. "Flash, there's one more thing. The cops aren't the only ones looking for John. There are some other desperate characters after him that have already bombed his friend's office and originally kidnapped Jeffrey after knocking me out with a Taser gun."

Flash could hear the humility in Frank's voice.

"Damn, my man. Sounds like you're knee deep in this shit, too. Hey, aren't you the Frank who lives next to Doc, who spent some time in the pros?"

"Yeah," Frank said in astonishment.

"Well, what do ya say after we finish saving our man, let's have a few beers and swap war stories?"

"Count me in!"

"Woman, get me that map of Palm Springs."

Kitty Robinson came up from the back of the RV and sat down. She folded her arms and looked at her husband sitting in the captain's chair behind the wheel. "I told you about asking nicely."

Flash gave her a big grin. "Oh, you think I'm not nice? Who else would buy you a house on wheels, just so you could go camping?"

"A lot of men!" She smiled mischievously.

Flash gazed at the pouty lips, playful eyes, and the rest of the package that made up his wife of eleven years. "You may be right. All right, pretty please, get out that map of Palm Springs. John Truley needs our help."

"Your chiropractor?" Kitty unfolded the map from the compartment in front of her.

He picked up the phone, dialing the number Frank had given him. "Yeah, he's in trouble."

"Hello!" John shouted over the roar.

"Damn, Doc. What the hell is that, a helicopter?"

"Flash?"

"Look, never mind. I'm coming to get you."

"I think someone's beating you to it, Flash!"

"Is it the cops?"

John looked out the front window and could easily see the chopper hovering about a hundred yards directly out from the bunker.

"Yeah, it sure is, and I don't see how we're gonna get out of here. There's a couple of four-wheel drives making their way up the road now. They'll be here in a few minutes."

"Dad!" Jeffrey was jumping up and down. When his father ignored him and kept talking on the phone, he started tapping his arm and shouting.

"Not now, Jeff! Look Flash, it's too late. I think they've got us."

Jeffrey got right in his father's face and screamed. "I know how we can get out!"

"What'd that boy say?"

"What is it, Jeffrey?" John asked impatiently.

"Frank has a secret tunnel that goes out the back of the mountain!" Jeffrey was jogging in place with excitement.

"Hold on a minute, Flash. Are you sure, Jeffrey?"

"It's an old mine shaft. Todd and I play in it all the time. It goes to a dry creek bed on the other side of the mountain. We look for rocks and arrowheads over there."

John looked at the map above the desk and found the creek bed. He followed it to the East with his finger until it came to a little road. "Paradise Road."

"Paradise Road!" Flash said to Kitty, who had the map open in her lap.

"Flash, we may be able to make it to Paradise Road; do you think you can meet us there?"

Kitty held up the map and pointed at the spot.

"Okay, brother. I'll be there in thirty minutes. I'm

driving Big Bertha."

"What's Big Bertha?"

"You'll see."

"Okay. Gotta go!" John slammed the phone down. The police vehicles were now only a quarter of a mile away.

"Damn!" Kitty said. "You'd better step on it, Sugar Cheeks."

Flash winked flirtatiously and stomped his right foot down onto the accelerator.

John shouted the plan to the other three over the deafening whir of the helicopter. They could see the sheriff's vehicles race into the driveway and four deputies from each jump out. The door exploded with pounding fists. Mara screamed at a face peering between cupped hands on the bars of the front window. When he spotted her, he turned and yelled to the others. They ran to the back of the house, while a bullhorn blared from outside.

"John Truley, this is the sheriff's department. We have you completely surrounded! We know that you and Sally Hobbs are in there, and we don't want anyone to get hurt! Come out of the house with your hands in the air! If you are not out in two minutes, we will enter forcefully!"

Jeffrey led them to the basement where he stopped in front of a six-foot cabinet. It had large doors that extended from its base to approximately halfway up. The upper half was open shelving stacked with canned goods. He lifted a step stool and placed it in front of the right side. Stepping up, he reached over and slid a few cans from the top shelf. "Dad, push against the cabinet." He released a latch that had been hidden behind the cans. Shoving the cans back in place, he quickly jumped off the stool and put it back where he had found it.

"Okay. You can let go now."

The right side of the cabinet began a slow swing outward.

"Wow!" Mara's eyes widened. "Your neighbor is cool!"

"Surrounded, huh? We'll just see about that!" John stared in amazement.

A rectangular hole big enough for a man to crawl through was cut into the wall below the level of the cabinet doors.

"This way, you guys." Jeffrey dashed through the hole.

Mara followed, disappearing into the darkness.

John nodded at Sally. "After you, Ms. Hobbs."

By the time John climbed through the hole, Jeffrey and Mara had already switched on flashlights stored inside the tunnel. Jeffrey shut the entrance by pulling a leather strap fastened to the back of the cabinet. He pulled the cabinet tight against the wall, sealing the hole, then hooked the end of the strap over a steel stake driven into the ground a few feet into the tunnel.

"Now no one can tell there's a tunnel here." Jeffrey grinned.

Sally shook her head. "Amazing. Jeffrey, can you lead us out of here?"

"This way." Jeffrey shined his flashlight into the darkness then scampered down the tunnel.

The Lieutenant peered at his watch and then looked up with a scowl. "Looks like they want to come out the hard way, boys. Kick that damn door down!"

The largest of the men bashed his heavy boot several times near the door handle. He cursed and then rammed the door with his massive shoulder. On the inside of the solid oak, the inch-thick steel bars that secured the door in two places on each side, vibrated lightly with the pounding.

The man rubbed his shoulder and shook his head at the lieutenant. "It didn't budge, sir."

Another deputy approached the men. "The front windows have steel reinforcements, but we may be able to hook one of them to the Jeep wench and rip it clear."

"What are you waiting for? Do it! And you other men, find something to ram this door down." The lieutenant spit tobacco as he surveyed the structure, which provided no roof access and apparently offered no other entrances. It was built like a little fortress. "What kind of psycho would have a place like this?"

A few of the men paused and shrugged.

"Get back to work!"

A narrow path ran along the house under the front windows before the hill sloped steeply away. The men were forced to run the wench cable sideways from the protective bars, over to the driveway. The cable was brought tight and the wench whined loudly against the strain.

"Lock it down and back up that jeep!" barked the lieutenant.

One of the sheriff's deputies nodded and jumped behind the wheel. The jeep's tires were soon spinning, and the vehicle slipped sideways along the length of the cable.

The lieutenant fumed. "Give it some slack and then yank it!"

"But sir . . ."

"Do it, goddamn it!"

The jeep pulled forward a few feet then backed up slowly until the cable tugged.

"Let me do it. We'll be here all day at this rate." The irritated lieutenant shoved the driver out of the way. He pulled the jeep ten feet forward, giving the cable considerable slack. He jammed the gearshift into reverse and popped the clutch, jerking the vehicle quickly backwards. With a deafening pop, the cable flew wickedly through the air toward the jeep, shattering the front windshield and striking the lieutenant's arm. He screamed profanities as the men raced over.

"Are you okay, sir?"

"Get back!"

Slowly he emerged from the jeep shaking glass from his hair. He inspected the injury and wondered if his arm was broken. The area felt hot and hard and blood steadily oozed into his shirtsleeve. Too stubborn to leave, he turned his attention back to the front door, where despite his men's repeated efforts with a ramming device, it stood fully intact. The men sweated profusely in the desert sun and some rubbed their shoulders and necks. All looked questioningly at the lieutenant.

He snatched up his radio with his good arm. "This is Lieutenant Dicks on the ground. Come in chopper."

"Chopper here. What's going on down there? Over."

"This place is like Fort Knox. We need some explosives. Is that SWAT team almost here? Over."

"Affirmative. This is the chopper. Will return shortly with the ordnance. Over." The hovering helicopter banked sharply and roared away.

The tunnel was high enough to allow the adults to walk with their heads and shoulders bent forward, while Jeffrey just cleared the reinforced ceiling when standing fully upright. John, Mara and Sally marveled at the engineering of the old mine shaft.

"Jeffrey, why didn't you ever tell me about this tunnel?"

"Sorry, Dad, its top secret. Frank made Todd and me swear we would never tell anyone, unless it was to save our lives."

John chuckled, wondering if his son, who was growing up so fast, had any other secrets he kept from him. Soon they came to a steel gate that matched the front window bars. The gate was secured by a combination lock, and the steel posts at each end were cemented into the ground. Jeffrey nimbly worked the combination and the lock fell open. They crawled through into a chamber that ended abruptly at a large piece of heavy plywood. Hinges similar to those on the cabinet fastened the left side of the wood to a large redwood post, also cemented in place.

"Jeffrey, let me go out first and see how things look."

"Okay, Dad, just don't let go of the door. Frank does *not* like it if it slams open." Jeffrey finished closing the steel gate behind them and snapped the lock.

Brilliant sunlight flooded the chamber and John held the door partially open for a moment so their eyes could adjust. Jeffrey collected the flashlights, turned them off and placed them behind a rock that sat near the gate. John squinted and peeked out the hole. They were on the side of a rocky slope, approximately thirty yards up from a dry riverbed. He looked as far as he could see in every direction and, finding no sign of people, climbed out of the tunnel. He held open the plywood door as Jeffrey and the sisters crawled out into the beautiful morning air. The outside of the door was painted gray like its surroundings and plastic rocks matching those of the riverbed were affixed to it, so that when closed, it blended perfectly into the terrain.

"The road is this way." Jeffrey pointed to the right.

"Okay, son. Now everyone stay alert. If we see the police or anyone else for that matter, we'll hide behind the bigger rocks."

They slid down into the riverbed and began walking along the firm clean sand. John checked his watch and found that fifteen minutes had passed since he had talked to Flash. He looked back toward the mountain and saw that it blocked their view of the house. Hopefully, it would keep them from being spotted as well.

They walked for a few minutes until they heard the sound of the chopper.

"If that's on the way to the house, it's going to fly right over us!" Sally yelled.

They looked around and found that they had entered a wider and flatter section with no big rocks to hide behind.

"Follow me!" Jeffrey ran swiftly up the riverbed.

The chopper was flying directly toward them. The riverbed suddenly jogged right, and John could see where Jeffrey was leading them. The road was only fifty yards away and, under it, a large drainpipe had been built. As they raced toward the pipe, John was certain the helicopter was going to spot them. Jeffrey was the first in, followed by Sally, then John. Mara stumbled. The helicopter was almost on top of them.

"Stay there, Mara! Don't move!" John squinted up into the noise.

Mara lay motionless, face down in the sand as the helicopter whirled over the group without slowing and continued to the other side of the hill. Mara looked up and John motioned forward. They sat panting, looking at one another, appreciating how close they had been to getting caught.

John checked his watch again. "Come on, Big Bertha! He should be here in another ten minutes."

After seeing how many police cars were racing past them with their lights on, Flash began to worry. He knew the cars were after John, and hoped that his doctor and the rest of the group had somehow made it to the meeting place. He turned off of the main highway where Kitty had instructed and now they were just minutes away. A news bulletin on the radio announced that the police had surrounded and trapped the fugitives wanted in association with the theft from Blackmore Pharmaceuticals and the beating of one of its guards. There were reporters on the scene describing the ordeal for the listeners, many predicting that it would only be a matter of minutes before the criminals were captured.

Flash turned onto Paradise Road and slowed the motor home slightly as he and Kitty began searching for the meeting place. The road was barely wide enough for two cars to pass, but so desolate that seeing another car seemed unlikely. The road was long and straight with no landmarks save a small bridge over an old creekbed about a quarter mile up. Suddenly, John appeared near the guardrails on the bridge and Flash raced to him. The others soon emerged at his side.

"Open the back door, Honey."

From the lounging area in the big vehicle, Kitty flung the door open. The passengers jumped in as the vehicle barely stopped moving. A helicopter suddenly rose above the mountainside and circled overhead.

"Oh, shit, I hope they're not looking at us!" Flash peered up through Big Bertha's enormous windshield.

Just then an explosion rocked the mountain and a cloud of smoke lifted. The nose of the helicopter tilted down as it sped off, disappearing in that direction.

"What the hell was that, John? Did you booby trap the place?" Flash looked back at the four with a mischievous expression.

"I think that was the police trying to get into Frank's house. You'd have to see the place to believe it! By the way, thanks for the lift."

"Well, this *is* exciting, but we're not out of the woods yet." Flash turned Big Bertha around. Kitty had already planned their escape route and knew from the map that Paradise Road dead-ended and would only let them out the way they had come, back toward the main highway where they had seen a disconcerting number of police cars.

"Thanks, Flash." Mara smiled shyly.

"Piece of cake, my people. Piece of cake. But for now, you guys better hide. We'll get to know each other later."

Kitty climbed down from her seat and led Jeffrey to a compartment under the couch, which he thought was cool. Mara climbed up on a bunk above the driver's compartment and hid behind red velvet pillows.

"Now, where we gonna hide two big people?" Kitty shook her head and looked around.

"Woman, you better find something fast or the big people are gonna be in big trouble!"

Up the road about a dozen cars were in line, waiting to pass through a gauntlet of flares, sheriff's cars and deputies.

"Uh, oh. A roadblock." Kitty quickly shoved Sally and John into the tiny shower near the middle of the motor home and slammed the door.

"Get your pretty little butt up here, girl, and get a seat belt around it." Flash looked nervously at all of the policemen. "You have our cargo stashed?"

"Don't you worry, sweet-stuff. I took care of it."

Inside the dark stall, John and Sally faced each other. They were pressed together in the tight space, neither able to move without rubbing against the other. As Flash began braking the RV, the loss of momentum pushed them against the wall, causing Sally to gasp. John could feel her heartbeat against his chest and her breath on his neck. It seemed that Flash was trying to ease the speed down gradually, but as the braking became more forceful, John's body was pressed harder into Sally's, pinning her against the shower wall. He could feel the roundness of her breasts squeezed against him and became aware that their thighs were interlocked. He felt the full fit of their bodies, and was embarrassed when he felt himself quickly respond to the sudden and overwhelming sensation. Sally felt his excitement and her heart quickened. Before she knew it, her arms were around him and her mouth was searching out his in the darkness. The RV at last came to a rest, but neither noticed.

For John Truley, time seemed to stand still as he forgot his surroundings and the desperate circumstances that brought them together. He was suddenly ravenous for her and he felt the rush of feelings that he no longer doubted. The intoxicating combination of animal lust and spiritual connection gave him a surge of power that he felt could blow the walls off the small shower stall.

Their lips abruptly parted as Flash released the brake and moved the vehicle forward. John clutched a handle next to them to keep from slamming back into the wall behind him. He tried to catch his breath and put things into perspective. Then the slow braking began again, pressing their bodies luxuriously together with increasing force until the process climaxed with a last lurch and the motor home once more came to a complete stop.   It remained momentarily motionless, then the brakes released and the acceleration began. John gripped the handle on the wall tightly as Sally's body swayed into his and they kissed without interruption. John heard a loud moan in the darkness.

"Was that you or Flash's brakes?"

Her lips touched his ear. "Me."

Her breath created a sensation that radiated through his head and quickly down to his center. It then moved out through his arms and legs, almost sending him over the edge.

The RV's starting and stopping continued for almost twenty minutes as Flash worked his way up the line of cars. Finally, a sheriff's deputy approached the passenger side of the cab. "Ma'am, we're going to need to take a look in your vehicle."

Kitty looked at Flash and he nodded. She went back to the coach area and opened the door. The man's voice could be heard very close to the shower stall.

"So, where you folks going?" the deputy asked looking first at Kitty and then Flash.

"Me and my lady come to Palm Springs this time every year to, uh...uhh..."

"See the flowers!"

"Yeah, the flowers." Flash took a breath. "We heard on the radio that something was going down, is this part of it?"

The deputy looked curiously at them. "We're looking for some fugitives. Where did you two stay when you were in town? I know there's only a few places to park one of these rigs."

Flash was speechless as he realized he had gotten himself into a corner. Kitty spun her chair around to face the lounge area where the officer stood. Kitty was an attractive, petite woman, with short dark curly hair and a body kept fit by a daily aerobic workout. Her shiny bronze skin was well moisturized with a combination of lotion and oil that gave off a delectable scent. She was proud of her appearance and felt quite comfortable with little clothing, especially when traveling with her husband in the RV. She leaned forward and squeezed her elbows together, resting them on her thighs, effectively making her cleavage strain at the halter-top.

"We stayed at the Camping Bare Resort. It was just wonderful. Hey, didn't I see you there? I almost didn't recognize you with your uniform on."

The deputy's face flushed as he recognized the name of the clothing-optional resort.

"Uh, no ma'am, you must be mistaken." He gulped and then took a closer look at Flash.

"Hey, aren't you Flash Robinson?"

"That's me."

"Wow! We're really big fans. Would it be too much trouble to get your autograph for my son?"

The man handed Flash a small note pad that he signed and handed back with a big smile. The deputy had a look of wonder as he glanced down at the signature, then back up at Flash's smiling face, and finally at Kitty who continued to lean forward. They waited for a moment and Flash finally broke the silence. "Officer? Is there anything else?"

"Oh! Uhh, no! Thank you very much. Thanks for everything."

John and Sally heard the door shut, and in a moment, the motor home lunged forward and then steadily picked up speed. They could hear Flash and Kitty laughing uproariously.

"Good one, Sugar Bowl!" Flash hollered between guffaws. "How on earth did you know about that place?"

"Oh, I've been researching some alternative vacations for us, Honey Buns."

"Is that a fact? Well, you do know how to keep things interesting, now don't ya?"

After a few more minutes, Kitty opened the door to

the shower. She looked at John and Sally with a mischievous twinkle in her eye.

"Did you two do okay in here?"

John felt his ears turn crimson.

"We had a wonderful ride!" Sally assured her, winking at John and making the rest of him match his ears.

John was thankful he had a moment to straighten out his clothes and regain his composure as Kitty went to help Jeffrey and Mara from their hiding places.

"I think we're safe now," Flash said. "We're on the main highway and, unless that poor deputy Kitty was flirting with filed a complaint, we should be clear."

"I don't normally get too many complaints when I flirt with my men."

"You can say that again, woman. It's just not often that I get to hear you talk to police officers as if you've seen them in the buff!"

"And it worked beautifully, Mrs. Robinson!" Sally added.

"Girlfriend, please, call me Kitty. You're gonna make me sound old."

"Okay, Kitty. I'm Sally, and this is my sister, Mara."

"Nice to meet you both. The big teddy bear that's driving is my husband, Flash."

"Everybody knows who Flash Robinson is!" Jeffrey exclaimed.

They laughed and Kitty said, "We know who you are, too! You're that little teddy bear that's in your dad's office all the time."

"That's right!" Jeffrey laughed delightedly.

"I'll tell you what, Jeffrey, why don't you, Sally, Mara, and I go back and see what we can find to eat, and let these big boys talk. I bet you didn't exactly have a leisurely breakfast this morning, did you?"

"Right again!"

"Boy, you're as sharp as a whip, aren't you?" Kitty said, smiling and putting her arm around Jeffrey while leading him in the direction of the refrigerator.

John seated himself in the big passenger chair across from Flash and glanced around the cab. "Nice ride."

Flash eyed him for a moment, smiling at John's calm, given the situation. "This is Big Bertha's maiden voyage, at least in regards to aiding and abetting criminals. What the hell you got yourself into, man?"

"We're totally innocent, Flash. Sally saw some secret information, but it was only after her boss gave her the keys to his office and told her to go in and work with the files. Blackmore, her employer, is trying to be the first one on the block with a new drug, and they're hiding records which demonstrate that the drug is potentially dangerous."

"Are they the ones who kidnapped Jeffrey and bombed your buddy's office?"

"Believe it or not, no. The work my friend Jimmy and I have been doing has attracted its own set of enemies."

"You guys must all be onto something big."

"We're stepping on the toes of a billion dollar industry, Flash. An industry that makes a lot of its money by brainwashing the public into thinking it needs a drug for everything. When people started believing in their own natural power to get well, the industry decided to shut us up. They left my son gagged and handcuffed in a dumpster last night and my friend is lying in a hospital bed. The ashes that were once his office are probably still smoldering. Oh, we're onto something big, all right."

"And tonight at the television station?"

John looked at Flash with an intensity his friend had never seen before.

"Flash, I'll give you a lifetime of care as my thanks if you can get me to that station by six, in one piece."

Chapter 27

It was five-thirty and the crowd at the television station was large but orderly. All who could, pushed into the medium-sized lobby, while an equal number waited patiently outside, kept at bay by the security guards trying to enforce the fire marshall's predesignated maximum occupancy limits. About half of the group were patients of Dr. John Truley, and Janine worked the room, greeting each personally, thanking them for coming. Another large contingent displayed name tags designating their affiliation with the National Vaccine Information Center. Several of these waited with their young ones, many of whom were obviously physically and mentally challenged. A large number of signs were brandished by the group; one woman's read WAKE UP AND SMELL THE DANGEROUS DRUGS, another's HANDS OFF MY DOCTOR OF CHIROPRACTIC. The group was in good spirits and ready to demonstrate to the masses that they were aware of what was going on in the battle for medical drug dollars. They knew about the kidnapping of Dr. Truley's son; they saw pictures of his friend's office in flames and read reports of his beating. They knew he was traveling with a woman who was wanted for theft at a large drug company. And now they prayed for his safe arrival, waiting in great anticipation for the vindicating message that he surely must have.

Big Bertha rolled to a stop in the parking lot of Seaport Village, located on the outskirts of downtown San Diego. Inside, the passengers tensely waited. They were so close and yet the risk of capture was greater now that they were nearer their destination. An older model Honda Accord pulled alongside them and parked.

John cautiously looked out the window. "It's him."

Sally opened the door and Dr. Bill stepped up into the coach, his face radiating excitement as he looked around at each of them.

"Okay. I'm going with you to show you the route I worked out. With a little luck, we'll be in the studio in fifteen minutes." He extended his hand and grinned from ear to ear. "John, I'm proud to say I gave you your start back on 960 AM!"

"Yes, thank you. If it wasn't for you, I wouldn't have every cop in Southern California looking for me right now." John laughed.

"Fame has its price, doesn't it." Dr. Bill enthusiastically shook his hand.

Flash turned from the driver's seat. "Where to, Chief?"

"Flash Robinson!?! Oh, man. This just keeps getting better! Okay, go back out the parking lot, take a right and follow the street around. When we get to the Convention Center, we'll take a left and I'll lead you in from there. We'll be entering through an alley."

The group sat down as the vehicle moved toward the exit. Mara and Jeffrey sat on the couch holding hands while John and Sally sat across the breakfast table from Dr. Bill, who explained what he thought was going to happen.

"Marlene Johnson had to pull a few strings with the program manager to make this work. The management is concerned with the legality of assisting criminals and they are also worried about the content of your message. They decided the risks would be offset by the national publicity they'll receive by having you both on the station, live, while the police are looking all over the state for you. Of course, I didn't mention how our station went belly up after all of our drug advertisers pulled out following your show."

"I meant to apologize for that."

"Yeah, John, I'm sure you're all broken up about it. Now, you understand, I've made no arrangements for your escape and you'll be on your own after the broadcast."

"You've done plenty. We'll take care of ourselves afterwards." John gazed around at the others.

"Yes, we appreciate you making this happen, Dr. Bill." Sally squeezed John's leg.

Dr. Bill looked at her and nodded. He then turned toward Flash. "All right, you need to make a left here and then we'll go a few blocks to the alley which is on the left, just past the big billboard with the Channel 20 news team on it."

Sally cradled her stomach and moaned.

John touched her arm. "You okay?"

"Yes, it's just a bad case of butterflies."

"Remember, it's just you and Marlene when you get in there." Dr. Bill sat forward, looking out the windshield.

John smiled at the familiar advice. His first radio show with Dr. Bill now seemed like an eternity ago.

Flash had turned up the alley. Cars lined one side, spilling out of the studio's lot just ahead.

"I don't see any police cars. Good job, Dr. Bill."

"Are you kidding? I wouldn't mess this up. This could be my meal ticket to the big leagues."

"Well, I hope you all get what you want." Kitty smiled. "We love you and know you'll kick some butt!"

Flash drove slowly through the lot. "I'll get as close as I can."

John grabbed the doorknob and waited for the motor home to stop. "Are you guys ready?"

"Let's do it, John!" Sally's eyes sparkled with excitement.

He nodded and opened the door. "Everybody stay close together!"

John stepped out of the motor home and held the door for the others. The lot, though full, was eerily quiet; somehow John had expected more difficulty getting into the studio. Dr. Bill got out and joined John in leading the way. Sally and Mara held Jeffrey's hands as the five of them moved away from the motor home toward an alcove with double doors.

"Most of the studio's employees have not been informed that this interview is going to take place.

Marlene Johnson personally wrote this pass to make sure we don't have any problems." Dr. Bill held up the paper. "This baby will get us on the set, no questions asked."

John was looking at the pass when it suddenly flew out of Dr. Bill's hand and his shoulder exploded in red. Dazed, John caught Dr. Bill before he hit the ground and looked up in disbelief. Two well-dressed men in a tan Mercedes pointed pistols out the windows. Another bang made Dr. Bill's body jolt as if hit by a baseball bat.

"Run! Go! Go! Go!" John shoved Jeffrey toward the alcove as he dragged Dr. Bill. Mara was screaming and John could hear Jeffrey whimper as he looked back at the Mercedes.

The two men threw open the car doors and were stepping methodically out when Big Bertha lurched across the lot toward them. They scrambled to get back in as the RV crashed broadside into the Mercedes, slamming the doors shut and pinning it against the wall. The driver screamed in agony, his body folded in the middle by the door, like a mouse in a trap.

John dragged Dr. Bill to the studio doors.

Two security officers, firearms drawn, rushed over to them.

"Hold it right there!"

"He's shot! It's Dr. Bill! They did it!" John pointed. "They're parked next to the wall!"

"Don't move." One of the guards ripped a walkie-talkie from his jacket. "We have a shooting! One man is down! We need backup! Over!"

John looked at Jeffrey, Sally, and Mara, relieved they were uninjured. He eased Dr. Bill's limp body onto the pavement, propping his back against the wall. "Call an ambulance!"

Dr. Bill looked up at John. "Don't let them stop you. Finish this."

"It's no good. They won't let us in."

Dr. Bill's voice was barely audible and John leaned down.

"Show them –" He coughed. "Show them the pass."

John looked out into the open parking lot. The white card was sitting like a small island in the sea of blacktop. He looked back at Jeffrey and Mara huddled in the middle of the entryway, then at Sally.

"We can't stay here, John. We're sitting ducks."

"Everybody stay put!" Gunfire erupted from inside the Mercedes, blowing out the front windshield as John ran. Bullets whizzed by his head. He reached down and snatched up the pass, as the shooter slapped a new magazine into the handle of the pistol. His partner remained pinned in the door between the Mercedes and the wall.

"Charles, please — help me —"

John scrambled back toward the alcove, gunfire hitting the parked cars behind him. He knew that at any second one of the bullets could carve an ugly swath through his brain, right in front of his frightened son. From the corner of his eye, he saw a familiar figure rise up in the cab of the motor home and thrust a large shotgun through its shattered front window. The barrel exploded point blank into the Mercedes, then again, silencing both the gunshots and the pitiable moans as John tumbled into the protected doorway. He held up the pass to the security guards.

The guard pulled him up by the arms. "Get in here. The ambulance and police are on their way. Follow me!" He shouted to his partner. "Stop anyone else from entering unless it's the police."

John pulled Dr. Bill into the building and knelt next to him as the guard shut and locked the doors.

"You're a . . . a dangerous guy to hang out with, Doc." He coughed, motioning with his fingers for John to go.

The security guard's call had alerted the local police that there was a shooting at the television station. The guard had given descriptions of the group and when John heard the sirens he knew every cop in town was now on their way to the station. He'd never get on the air if the police got their hands on him first. All the running and hiding, not to mention the danger and personal sacrifice of people like Jimmy, Frank and Dr. Bill, would be wasted if they couldn't make the last 100 feet to where Marlene Johnson would take their interview and tell the world their story.

The security guard led John and his group up a corridor that passed the lobby before turning toward the studio door. John was stunned to see people jammed into every corner and for a moment wondered what they were doing there.

He had just read one of the signs when someone screamed, "There's Dr. Truley! He made it!"

The crowd surged forward, causing the security guard to panic and reach for his gun.

"No, it's okay." He recognized several of his patients. The security guard saw John's big smile and released his grip.

People waiting in front of the building saw the excitement and pushed inside. Soon, the rest of the crowd attempted to follow, surging toward the lobby, impatiently waiting to squeeze through the crowded doorways. John looked over the top of the gathering to the street where a multitude of police cars now screeched to a stop. The officers quickly jumped out and rushed in.

"We have to hurry!" John pleaded.

The guard escorted them into a studio where Marlene Johnson and the rest of the news team were preparing to broadcast. On their heels, the crowd flooded in, too quickly for the other security guards to stop them.

Marlene spotted John and quickly took charge.

"Look, we don't have time to get this crowd out of here, but for God's sake, make them quiet. Dr. Truley and Ms. Hobbs, will you please come up here?"

She motioned them to sit in chairs next to hers. "You really know how to make an entrance!"

A man in a headset stood in front of the group and counted down with his fingers. Two large cameras were in position, looming directly in front of them. The man pointed at Marlene.

"Welcome to the Six O'clock News. In tonight's special edition, we bring you an exclusive interview with Dr. John Truley and Ms. Sally Hobbs, fugitives of an extensive, statewide manhunt during the last forty-eight hours. They are here, live, in the studio and, even as we speak, police are entering the building, preparing for their imminent arrest. Let's quickly have a word with them while we still can.

"Dr. Truley, Ms. Hobbs, why did you come here tonight after successfully eluding the police for the last two days, when you must surely realize that you will be arrested?"

John looked directly at the camera. "We have a message that is more important than our safety, or our freedom, for that matter. First, let me say that we're both innocent and are being pursued by other groups besides the police. These groups are affiliated with the pharmaceutical industry and their mission is to keep us from telling the truth."

"Are you suggesting that these groups are trying to kill you?"

"Yes."

"So what is the truth, Dr. Truley?"

"The pharmaceutical industry is doing whatever it takes to get more drugs into people, especially children. These children are being killed, maimed or brain damaged at an alarmingly increasing rate by federally mandated vaccines. The FDA approves these vaccines with little or no evidence of efficacy or safety. Sometimes the drug manufacturer will provide bogus studies, or what we would call "junk science" performed by people on their own payroll. The FDA, which has a significant percentage of members who are invested in the pharmaceutical industry and stand to gain monetarily from the public's increased usage of drugs, will accept these studies and approve the vaccine. Currently, medical doctors acting as agents of the state, are injecting 37 doses of these dangerous compounds of unknown toxicity into children before they turn two years of age. Many of these vaccines are laden with mercury, aluminum and lead as well as other poisons in levels which can exceed FDA allowances by 40 times. There are currently over 200 new vaccines being developed in hopes of inclusion in this federally mandated list. Computer tracking of children's medical records is being unconstitutionally instituted without parents' knowledge to aid in compliance of this barbaric system and often assists the health department in taking children from their parents under the guise of neglect. Marlene, there is no end in sight. Children are being sacrificed on the altar of the mass vaccination policy of this country and it is threatening the biologic integrity of the human race.

"All drugs, including the over the counter variety, interfere with our body's innate ability to heal itself. This weakens the immune system, setting up a vicious cycle of illness where only the drug manufacturer wins. We need to return to a state where we allow our internal doctor to heal us, to have more faith in our own power. I know there are circumstances where medications save lives and I support that, but an extremely large percentage of drugs on the market today mask the problem, are unnecessary, and are directly responsible for this country's poor health. Two thousand people die each week in the U. S. from medical drug reactions. Think about this, and ignore the billion-dollar-a-year advertising that brainwashes you into believing that you need drugs in order to be well. Learn the facts and your rights. Remember, the industry will stop at nothing to hide the truth."

John looked to Sally who took a big gulp.

"Ms. Hobbs, what is your role in all this?"

"I worked for a large drug manufacturer in Los Angeles and assisted in the research of the new cold vaccine, CD4C. Although the research indicated that the vaccine was not yet safe, the company, Blackmore, discontinued our work and is now distributing the vaccine for use on small children."

"That is quite an accusation. Do you have proof that the company has disregarded the safety of the public?" Marlene asked.

"No. When I went back to gather the information on the specific dog breed that was killed by the vaccine, it was removed and replaced by falsified information." Sally became frustrated at not being more believable and started to get choked up. "Ever since I learned about this, the company has been trying to kill me!"

"Sally, what you're saying is very serious. You've been accused of felony theft of trade secrets and, from what I understand, you were caught on tape during the act. Is it possible that you're making this claim in an attempt to cover up your crime?"

"I went back to the files without authorization because I was afraid that if I didn't do something, people would die." Sally cried uncontrollably. "You would have done the same thing if you saw what happened to the Labradors when they were injected with CD4C!"

Marlene looked sympathetically at the sobbing girl.

"But, Sally, it's their word against yours."

"No!" a voice boomed from the crowd in the studio. A tall, skinny man with spectacles stepped forward. "It's their word against ours."

Shocked by the interruption during the live interview, Marlene looked dumfounded at the man and then back at Sally.

"Dr. Weedleman!" Sally shrieked. "He must come up, he's the scientist who developed CD4C!"

Marlene regained her composure and addressed the cameras. "Ladies and gentleman, this is obviously a unique interview and you must bear with the unusual format. It appears that we may have the developer of the vaccine in question here on the set. Can you come up here, sir?"

While Dr. Weedleman made his way through the cameras toward the platform, John saw that the police were now filing into the studio. Marlene also noticed the police and raised her eyebrows at John to acknowledge the drama of the moment. The tall man stepped up on the platform and, before taking a seat, extended his hand to Sally.

"I found out what you were doing and I couldn't let you carry the whole burden yourself. You're a brave woman and I admire you for it. I called Dr. Truley's office to see if I could help and his secretary directed me here."

"Please sir, can you introduce yourself and explain what you know about CD4C?"

"My name is Dr. Lamont Weedleman, and I know everything about CD4C. You see, I made it."

"What are your feelings about the charges that Ms. Hobbs has made against Blackmore pharmaceuticals?"

"They are entirely correct."

"So you are saying that CD4C presents a danger to the community?"

"I am, indeed."

"Doctor, are you aware that the vaccine has already been used in a trial sampling of one 106 toddlers in Nevada, with no apparent side effects?"

"I wasn't aware of that, but I can tell you that I'm greatly relieved to hear that there were no complications."

"Is it possible that you and Ms. Hobbs are exaggerating the potential dangers of the new vaccine?"

"I certainly hope so, Ms. Johnson. All I know is that I was not allowed to finish my research because this company wanted to beat its competition to the market, which means safety is being set aside in place of profits."

A courier suddenly rushed up to the side of the anchorwoman and whispered in her ear while handing her a slip of paper. There was an awkward silence while she read the paper and then read it again. When she looked up, a tear was running down from her eye and she cleared her throat.

"I have just been handed a note informing me that earlier today a second trial group was administered the new vaccine, CD4C, and there are reports of violent reactions to the drug, including six deaths and eight children in critical condition. All of the injured were of Asian descent." Marlene paused and gracefully cleared the tear from her cheek. "It has been confirmed that there were no children of Asian descent in the first group who received the new vaccine in the Nevada sampling I mentioned earlier in the interview. Let's go to a commercial." Marlene's eyes glazed over as she stared blankly.

The room remained in shocked silence. It registered like a quake, the disaster uniting the large group for a moment. John stood up and the police rushed onto the stage throwing he and Sally face down, snapping handcuffs in place.

John experienced a momentary wave of deja vu as he looked up and saw his patients standing by, watching in shocked disbelief. Janine yelled at the police imploring them to stop and many from the crowd joined in. The emotionally charged supporters pressed toward the stage in anger, confronting the police who reacted by reaching for their batons. More than one of the intimidated officers went to their holsters.

John was being hoisted by his wrists. "No! It's okay, everybody. We'll be all right. Just stay calm."

The dozen or so policemen formed a defensive ring and started to lead the two away from the stage and toward the door.

Someone started clapping, then quickly, others joined in, until John and Sally were showered with thunderous applause as they were escorted out of the studio. In the lobby, the applause continued and the crowd closed in behind them as they were led through the front doors to the police cars. They were pushed into a car by an officer, while a wall of uniformed men blocked the crowd's access.

As the police car pulled away, John and Sally watched Jeffrey and Mara crying and waving from the curb.

Chapter 28

At the police station, John sat impatiently in the interrogation room while two police officers asked him to tell his story for the third time. He wondered how Sally was holding up and where Jeffrey and Mara might be.

"Look, I'm innocent. I have a family to take care of. I have a son who needs me."

"So, you think we should just let you walk right out of here after it took two days to catch you?"

"You didn't catch me. I basically turned myself in after I accomplished what I had to do."

"And what was it that you had to do?"

John shook his head sadly. "Haven't you heard what I'm saying? Didn't you see the news broadcast?"

"I don't watch the news. I'm more of a *Wheel of Fortune* kind of guy." The officer leaned his head back with a cup of water, washing down two antacids followed by a couple of aspirin.

"We'll it's too bad you missed it. You might think twice about poppin' aspirin like they're breath mints. Did you know you lose about a teaspoon of blood from your intestines for every one of those little pills?"

The officer scowled at John. "It's none of your business, pal. Now, let's get back to this. You say a couple of guys were out to get you. So why didn't you go to the cops?"

John sighed and began his explanation yet again. A man escorted Sally into the room. She smiled cheerfully at John.

The men interrogating him looked up in surprise. "Captain?"

"It's okay fellas. I want you to take Dr. Truley's cuffs off. Get these people some refreshments and I'll be right back."

After removing John's handcuffs, the investigating officer and the man, who had been taking notes, began to relax and talk quietly while John and Sally sipped coffee and ate doughnuts.

"I always tell my patients not to eat these things, but I must admit this is the best damn doughnut I've ever had!" John smacked his lips.

One of the officers laughed. "They're special police doughnuts. Watch out — they can be addicting."

The other one nodded his head, while lightly patting his belly sagging over his belt line.

The police captain came back into the room.

"I have bad and good news for you two. Bill Bordello was dead on arrival at Mercy Hospital. Apparently, a bullet penetrated a big vessel near his heart. Was he a friend of yours?"

John stopped chewing and suddenly felt the doughnut lodge in his throat. "Yes, as a matter of fact, he was."

"Sorry about that."

John just nodded, trying to understand why Dr. Bill's life would be cut short like that. He thought with admiration of the man's courage and zest for life. Sally wiped her eyes with the back of her hand.

"The good news is that Blackmore has dropped all charges. I think they have enough to deal with at the moment. Now, if you people will answer a few questions, you might be on your way shortly."

John and Sally nodded.

"Orange County PD thinks that the security officer found in Ms. Hobb's apartment broke in and someone maced him before ringing his bell with a lamp."

"That's right." Sally glanced at John. "He followed me that day and then broke in when my little sister was home alone."

"Well, it looks like she was quite a handful for him!" The captain chuckled. "You know, they found pieces of that guy's clothing and skin all over the bushes and fence behind your apartment. He must have been hell-bent to get to you. I wouldn't worry though; he'll be facing several charges when he gets out of the hospital, including attempted murder. It seems he shot a juvenile who belonged to a local gang up there. Now, tell me this, how does a man who was videotaped robbing, shooting and killing a convenience store clerk, wind up with his face smashed in, tied to a chair in your kitchen, all in one night, Dr. Truley? I believe his name was Rocky Lelucci."

"Sally should answer that one, too. I didn't have much to do with it."

"Let me guess, your sister?"

"Not quite. He was my sister's boyfriend from another time in her life. He stalked her and we reported it to the Orange County Police, but they couldn't do anything about it. When Mara and I were at John's, he broke in and tried to take her. We fought him and he was going to kill me with a kitchen knife when Frank, John's neighbor, showed up."

"I see. That would be a Mr. Frank Michael, I presume?"

"That's him."

"He was arrested today for aiding and abetting criminals."

"He saved us. He didn't do anything wrong."

"We'll be the judge of that, Dr. Truley. Technically, the man has committed a felony. Next topic of discussion is the messy little scene in the back lot of the television station, where Mr. Bordello was killed. The report says a man in a large motor home got a little shotgun happy and blew away some boys in a Mercedes."

"That's my patient, Flash Robinson."

"*The* Flash Robinson?"

"Yes, that's right."

"Well, he's been charged with murder, among other things."

"But, he saved our lives, too."

The captain looked calmly at John. "You seem to have some pretty good friends, Dr. Truley."

"Yeah, people either really like me or really want to kill me. Who were those guys in the Mercedes?"

"We're investigating that now. Both had fake identification, but they matched the physical description given by a couple of our boys who saw them leaving your neighborhood last night. Just a little while ago, we found a Taser gun in their car. It matched the one used on your neighbor, Mr. Michael. It seems they were the same men. They appear to have been quite professional. You're lucky to still have a son."

John solemnly nodded.

"All right, we're not finished with you two yet, but you can go for now. Don't even think about leaving town. We'll have more questions as this investigation progresses."

John and Sally gathered their things from the clerk at the booking desk and walked out of the police station into the warm night.

Sally breathed in the humid ocean air and let out a big sigh.

John shook his head. "I can't believe we're free and Frank and Flash are in jail."

"John, the police'll get it worked out. They just need a little more information."

"I hope you're right."

"Oh, man, I could use a hot shower and about ten hours of sleep."

John nodded in agreement and hailed a cab that was driving up the street. "I have to go somewhere first." He motioned for Sally to get in. "Good Samaritan Hospital, please."

When they arrived at the hospital, John used a pay phone and called Janine to ask if she knew where Jeffrey and Mara were.

"They're right here, and we just finished dinner!"

"I had a feeling you would take charge for me. Thank you very much. The police let us go and we're at Good Samaritan. Can you bring them over?"

"We can be there in ten minutes."

John and Sally walked over to the information desk to

inquire about Jimmy McBride. Without looking, the woman told them the floor and room number where they would find him. On the elevator they remarked how curious it was that the receptionist knew his location without looking it up, but as soon as the elevator opened, they knew the reason. It was a circus. Nearly fifty people were standing in the hallway and crowding into a room down the hall.

John looked at Sally and smiled. "Jimmy!"

The crowd saw them and opened a pathway. John could hear people whispering his name as he walked to the room.

"Johnny!?!" Jimmy sat up in bed. "You son of a gun, you did it! I saw the news!"

His face was puffy and bruised. Several stitches held together a large laceration over one eye. Over a dozen people surrounded him, including several of the hospital nurses.

"It looks like you're okay, friend." John grasped his hand.

"Just five broken ribs and a few bruises is all."

"I'm sorry about your office."

"Don't you worry, Johnny. I had it well insured and besides, I couldn't have paid for this much publicity!" He looked at Sally then back at his friend. "Well, aren't you going to introduce me?"

"Jimmy, I'd like you to meet my friend, Sally Hobbs."

Jimmy shook her hand and flashed a mischievous smile.

"Friend, huh? Okay, whatever you say, John!"

They talked a while, describing their adventures, then Jeffrey, Mara and Janine showed up.

"Daddy!" Jeffrey ran to his arms.

Sally embraced Mara, then hugged Jeffrey.

After things calmed down, Jimmy grew serious. "It was tragic what happened to those kids with the vaccine reaction, but the attention you've caused should raise the public awareness and make these companies accountable. You may have saved hundreds of men, women and children."

Sally looked at John. "You okay?"

"Yes, I'm fine. Say, do you think you could excuse me for a bit? I need to see someone else while I'm here."

"Sure, John. Jeffrey can stay with us."

Up on the seventh floor, John entered the familiar hallway, walking past the nursing station without hesitation. A young doctor stepped from a room and looked up from his chart. A flash of recognition registered in the man's eyes.

"Hey, I know you. Dr. Truley, isn't it?"

"That's right." John remembered the unpleasant exchange the first time they met.

The MD held out his hand. "I want to apologize for what I said before."

"That's okay. Emotions were running high that day."

"No, let me finish. I heard about what you did, and I think you're a credit to your profession. I also think that our professions could learn a lot from each other."

"Thank you very much for saying so. I always thought it would be ideal if medicine and chiropractic could cooperate to do what's best for the patient."

"I agree. Maybe someday it will be that way."

Their eyes remained locked and then the young doctor walked a short distance down the corridor, grabbed a chart from the wall and ducked into another room.

Connie Prespo sat on her daughter's hospital bed. An encouraging clarity was returning to Katie's eyes. Every day the little girl was able to do a bit more. She had started chewing and swallowing food and could now signal to her mother when she needed to go to the bathroom. Connie was reaching into her bag for the homemade lunch that she had packed for her daughter, when a voice she had not heard in a long time instantly brought tears to her eyes.

"Mommy?"

Connie looked up, an involuntary sob issuing from her. "Yes, honey. I – I'm here."

"Mommy, I almost left."

Connie covered her mouth, not knowing whether she could handle her daughter's words. "What do you mean, baby? When?"

"I was going to leave. Then I saw you crying in the hallway next to the room where the doctors were helping me. You were so sad. I stayed."

Katie's eyes welled, tears forming at their corners. Connie dropped the lunch bag and wrapped her arms around her daughter. "Thank you, honey. Thank you. I love you so much. Thank you for staying with me."

John went the remaining few feet to Katie Prespo's room and knocked lightly.

"Uh, maybe I can come back later?" John felt the intensity in the room.

Connie Prespo's face broke into a smile.

"Hi, Katie, it's good to see you. And I'm glad to also find you here, Connie."

"I stopped by on the way home from your big show at the station."

"I thought I saw you there, but how . . ."

"Your secretary called and told me what was going on. So I called my N.V.I.C. group and nearly all of them showed up at the studio."

"Well, thanks for being there. Without the crowd it may have never worked out. Boy, you two look great!"

"We're doing better. The doctors say she can go home next week. The neurologists think that within a couple of years Katie's brain should be able to make new nerve connections and be as good as new, almost."

"That's great! I'm so happy for you."

There was a silence and Connie looked intently at John. "Dr. Truley?"

"Yes."

"I think what you did was incredibly brave and both my husband and I want to thank you for making something good from this tragedy." Connie looked peaceful for the first time since they'd met.

"Thank you, Connie, but you, your husband and Katie are the brave ones for handling this and coming out on top."

"Yes, thank you. We'll be fine. Oh, you might also appreciate knowing that the three doctors who saved Katie that day told me recently that they're certain her injuries were caused by the vaccine. Through the grapevine I've learned the doctors broke ranks with the hospital management and took quite a bit of heat for it."

"Well, thank God for that. It's a good place to start the healing and perhaps someday prevent things like this. Now if you'll both excuse me, I have some tired people to take home. Good bye, Connie. Good bye, Katie."

"Dr. Truley?" Connie called, as he was stepping out the door.

"Yes?"

"Do you think it'd be possible to bring Jeffrey here for a visit with Katie tomorrow?"

John smiled.

"Would you like that, Katie?"

The girl nodded slowly, making a lump appear in his throat.

"Then we'll be here!"

John walked into the hallway where he paused for a moment to wipe his eyes and take a couple of breaths.

Rejoining the party in Jimmy McBride's room, John found Jeffrey playing happily with Mara, while Jimmy entertained Sally with his stories.

"John, I had no idea you were such a wild man!" Sally winked as he walked into the room.

"Don't believe a word that guy says!" John laughed and shook his head. "Well, Jimmy, it looks like you have enough company to keep you from getting lonely. I think we'll get going. We've had kind of a long day."

Jimmy smiled and grabbed John's shirt to bring him down close. He nodded toward Sally. "Is she a keeper?"

John just shook his head at his friend and looked around the room. "You're bigger than life, Jimbo."

Jimmy stuck his hand out to shake John's. "No, that's not true, but as a team, we sure are!"

John smiled. "Maybe so."

After good-byes, they walked down the corridor toward the elevator. Mara and Jeffrey ran ahead, playing hopscotch on the hospital's white tiles.

John looked mischievously at Sally. "You're welcome to have that hot shower you were talking about at my place."

Sally eyed him coyly. "Oh, I don't know. Does your shower have handles like Flash's did?"

John laughed, putting his arm around her shoulders. "We'll think of something."

THE END

About The Author

John Adams graduated from Palmer College of Chiropractic-West in 1987 and practiced in San Diego for ten years. As a Californian native, he grew up in the bay area, Los Angeles and San Diego. Currently he divides his time between a busy practice in Colorado, his family and writing. He is presently working on his next novel.

For ordering information and volume discounts for *The Power* :

Website: www.john-adams.net
E-mail: Healthydr@aol.com
Voice: (970) 255-8840

For more information regarding vaccination:

www.909shot.com

For more information regarding chiropractic:

www.worldchiropracticalliance.org